THE SOUND OF SIRENS

THE SOUND OF SIRENS

You Want Me To Move To a 55+
Community. No Way!

MITCHELL G. KUHN

ISBN-13: 978-0-578-47199-0
Library of Congress Control Number:2019915159

DEDICATION

To the wonderful friends I have made, especially for their tolerance and what seems to be their acceptance of my charming personality.

ALSO BY MITCHELL G. KUHN

Chaos reigns during Presidential Election

I

"MIKE, ARE YOU planning on taking me dancing this week-end?" my wife Helen said with her Cheshire cat smile.

That's my wife, circumspect as ever. Okay, I wondered, *what's really on her mind? Go dancing; that's pretty funny. We haven't intentionally gone dancing once in forty-three years of marriage.*

Truthfully, I couldn't remember her actually asking me a question she really wanted an answer to. Evasion and subterfuge were her *modus operandi*—she was a real creature of habit.

"Absolutely," I replied. "And not only are we going to disco until our feet cry out for mercy, but we're going for dinner before that to the Four Seasons. And I think we should stay overnight at the Ritz Carlton Hotel on Park Avenue. Pretty awesome idea, huh?"

Her face now glowing with excitement, she asked, "Are you serious?"

"Oh sure, and I'll ask Prince Charles, who's visiting New York, to join us for drinks afterwards," I added with a smirk.

She gave me a delayed double take and then groaned. "Can you be serious for a moment? I want to know what you have planned for us to do tomorrow aside from sitting here watching curling on TV."

"So, why didn't you ask me that in the first place? In any case, what's wrong with watching all those healthy young Wisconsin girls curl that stone and sweep up after themselves?"

"Give me a break, Mike; you know I don't want to go dancing."

"Then stop playing games," I said a little impatiently.

"Well," she said taking a deep breath, "I want us to go see La Palazzo."

"What the hell is a La Palazzo and what does it have to do with dancing? Is it the new must be seen New Jersey version of New York City's old Roseland?"

"No, wise ass! It has nothing to do with dancing. It's an active adult residential community in South Jersey."

I felt like my best friend had taken a bowie knife and plunged it deep into my heart.

"Why don't we just take two shovels from the garage, go to Fairlawn Cemetery and dig ourselves two graves and then jump in? It would be quicker and more humane for us than waiting for the next ambulance to stop at our home as it works its way up and down the streets of the 'fossil farm' retirement community you want me to move into," I said as my voice increased in volume, betraying my agitated state of mind.

"Take a deep breath, Mike. All I'm asking you to do is to just look at some fifty-five plus communities. We have to seriously plan for the next phase of our lives. Staying in this house is not realistic. It's too big for us. The taxes are too high. All our friends have left the area, and our social life has dwindled to saying good morning to our millennial neighbors. We're the surviving dinosaurs of Montvale."

2

THE BULLDOG JUST wouldn't let go. For months she'd been nagging me to get a hobby, to volunteer, to do anything but sit in front of the TV or play games on the computer.

"You've been watching the boob tube since you retired months ago. Get a life. Get another job. Volunteer somewhere. Do anything that's fruitful. It's driving me nuts seeing you so unproductive," she'd said, raising her voice as her pent-up frustration came to the surface.

And I of course, more often than not, replied that I had worked my ass off for forty-five years and now I could do whatever the hell I wanted. I'd earned the right to veg-out forever.

Today I was hoping to drown my sorrows in anticipation of my impending doom by watching the New York Jets lose their fifth game in a row by downing a six-pack of Bud. But Helen, my wife of forty-three years, pointed out in a grating, guilt-edged voice that the snow was piling up on the front walk. I guess she wanted me to feel I was remiss in fulfilling my masculine responsibilities.

"Mike, please turn off that stupid game and shovel the steps so I don't break my neck tomorrow."

"I'm too drunk and too old to risk wrenching my back or getting a heart attack. I won't shovel snow any more, and I refuse to weed or mow the lawn. We can either wait until the snow melts, or break down and hire some needy soul to do what you want."

I guess she expected that reaction from me but hoped I'd surprise her and change my uncooperative behavior. She just stared at me through squinting eyes, not saying a word. It seemed an eternity went by. Neither of us wanted to break the ice, but of course I gave in first.

Why ruin the entire weekend totally ignoring her? I reasoned.

She'd get her way—she always did—and I was resigned to my fate, sacrificing my football games to waste a full day looking for my final resting place in the waste lands of southern NJ—mecca for track housing, endless views of a boring flat landscape, and of course, a shopping center located around every turn of the road. I couldn't be happier at the prospect of living in a place like that!

The next morning, we got into my newest toy, my pride and joy, my symbol of achievement—a luxurious Lexus 450—and drove for two hours to Nirvana. We barely exchanged a word of conversation. Instead, we listened to some light jazz on the radio while Helen looked out the window at the stunning array of gas storage tanks and the one-story semi-trailer truck facilities that dotted the landscape for miles on end. I knew Helen couldn't wait until we got to the place where she would spend the rest of our days in utter bliss, turning mahjong tiles, melding, and going to an endless parade of luncheons, while I once again sat in front of the TV or my computer dreaming of days gone by.

No way, no how was I going to live with all those old wheelchair-bound, farting, drooling, *Ensure*®-drinking, toothless, close-to-death, *Depend®* -wearing, boring people. These are the folks, no doubt, who take the Greyhound buses to Atlantic City's casinos so they can have a free lunch and play the slots with the free roll of quarters they give all passengers.

As a last resort, I'd threaten divorce; I would, if I had a real pair, but I don't! It didn't matter—we'd been together for so long, having raised three wonderful children together. I felt trapped by a situation I had very little control over.

3

FINALLY, AFTER THREE cups of coffee, four pee stops, and two mind-numbing hours of listening to Helen harangue me over the uselessness of my current life, we arrived. Thank God!

Ah, what a beautiful sight greeted us: the requisite high stone-walls, gigantic steel gates, keeping the inmates in, a guardhouse, and of course a waterfall surrounded by New Jersey palm trees. The term grotesque popped into my mind. I wonder why? Doesn't everyone appreciate gaudy?

The thought of Royal Palm Trees growing in Jersey was just too much—they had to be plastic. Why else would the sun's rays glisten off the bright green stiff, unmoving palm leaves? Trees in full bloom with baby green coconuts...IN THE MIDDLE OF FRIGID FEBRUARY! My head was pounding; my sensibilities were offended beyond my ability to ignore.

We stopped at the...not very welcoming, gatehouse. The uniformed gentleman, who looked like a recently escaped convict from NJ's Rahway State Penitentiary, opened the sliding glass door protecting him from possibly getting frostbite, and asked me whom I was there to see.

I replied, "The Undertaker."

I was imagining that Saint Peter might actually be waiting for me on the other side of the gate, even though it wasn't really big and pearly!

The guard showed no reaction. Not even a slight smirk. He just stood there with a blank vacant expression on his face. I could tell Helen was furious with me by the way her eyes glazed over and from the pleading expression on her face for me to cool it.

So what's new?

"Can I ask you a question, sir?"

"Sure."

"Why is there an ambulance parked on the street over there?"

"It's parked there every day waiting for a call from 911 to say that it's needed."

"Needed by whom?"

"A resident is always calling for one—usually on a daily basis."

"Great! Sounds like such a reassuring place to live a healthy lifestyle."

Helen reached her arm across me, pushing me back against my seat. Then, leaning over me as far over as her seat belt would allow, she said to the guard, "Sir, we're here to see the models."

"Oh, okay," he replied. "I misunderstood your husband. I thought he said he wanted to see the undertaker or something or other."

"I did, and judging by the frequency the ambulance is called, I'm not far off. Anyway, I'm not her husband," I replied. "I'm just chauffeuring her around."

"Oh, excuse me; my mistake, sir," the gatekeeper replied shaking his head in confusion.

Was this guy for real?

"No sir, I'm pulling your leg. I'm her indentured servant."

Helen punched me in my arm…hard. "Stop being rude, Mike!"

Turning toward her, I said in a barely audible tone, "Okay, Helen, I'm sorry. It's my mistake; it won't happen again; forgive me, I lost my head."

That got me a slight reprieve from the warden. But for sure I'd pay later for my transgressions.

The guard handed me a paper pass—instructing me to put it in on the dashboard—and a map with directions to the sales office.

Off we went in search of our future.

HELP ME! What did I do to deserve this?

During the short ride to *Nirvana's* sales office, I was amazed we hadn't passed one single person in a motorized wheelchair. For that matter, no one was walking, jogging, or riding a bike in the street. Not a single person was outside. It was a ghost town. No, I reconsidered; this place was more like Pleasantville: that spooky, desolate community of prim and proper conformists.

All the houses were lined up in a row, one after the other. They were identical: the same plants, trees, windows, roofs, siding color. Even the mailboxes were placed exactly in the same location on the street in front of each house. I thought back to the old jokes about Levitttown, LI, when the husband went into the wrong house, the wrong bedroom, and the wrong bed, in which to his delight, was his neighbor's wife in a shear nightgown lying seductively on her mattress beckoning him to join her.

I should be sooo lucky! Hey, might not be too bad…One point for death's waiting room. I couldn't help it, my face brightened, and I felt a tingling sensation in my loins, forcing me to involuntarily smile.

"What are you smiling for?" Helen asked, a quizzical look on her face at my sudden change in mood.

"Just remembered something that happened at the office last year."

"And what was that?"

"Nothing really; you had to be there to appreciate it."

Helen straightened her back and took a deep breath. I knew what was coming. She was about to begin her waterboarding interrogation of me. I didn't want a confrontation now during which I'd say something I'd later regret, so I forcefully announced we'd arrived at the sales office.

4

***

ONCE INSIDE, A voluptuous twentyish-year-old receptionist with flowing blond shoulder-length hair, striking aqua blue eyes, and a figure the envy of a Playboy centerfold, greeted us as if we were her long-lost grandparents.

"It's so good to meet you. I hope your trip here was a pleasant one?"

Her prattle went on and on, until finally I asked her if I could use the facilities. "Sir, unfortunately the pool is closed for repairs," she said, obviously not having the slightest idea what I had asked.

My eyelids started to twitch and my head involuntarily shook from side to side.

"Miss, I think you misunderstood me. I was asking where the men's room is?"

"Oh, that's what you want."

"Yup, you got it!" I said.

Definitely graduated Princeton Summa Cum Laude; you can spot those Ivy League girls a mile away.

Upon my return from the pool, our post-doctoral student asked us to sign the visitor's registry, and told us Ms. Linda De Marco, the Managing Sales Associate for New Community Members would be with us shortly. In the meantime, she suggested we help ourselves to the smorgasbord of epicurean delights, which consisted solely of caffeinated and decaffeinated coffee and tea, and an unappetizing assortment of chocolate chip cookies. I was anticipating platters of lobster and shrimp and goblets of Mimosas. What did I know? I expected so much more considering the palace-like decorations and furniture adorning the reception area.

Within five minutes, Linda De Marco pranced out of her office as if she were a movie starlet. The way her arms reached out and her dress billowed in the air reminded me of Loretta Young making her grand entrance as she descended a huge spiral staircase to greet her adoring guests.

Linda however was no Loretta, not even close.

Instead of extending her hand in greeting, Ms. De Marco, and I'm not making this up, hugged each of us!

Yuck! I was shocked Linda encroached on my personal space; Helen, on the other hand, smiled and eagerly embraced Linda in return. Men and women are so different. Then again, if the receptionist had welcomed me that way, I would have been more receptive.

"Welcome to La Palazzo; your new home, Mr. and Mrs. Chandler," said our new best hugging buddy. You're just going to love it here. We have everything you could ever want."

I bit my tongue to stop myself from asking whether that included a bordello open twenty-four seven. I was so proud of my self-restraint. There was no way I was going to be able to hold back from making some wise ass retort during the rest of the visit though —it's part of my DNA makeup.

"Tell me Linda, how long have you lived here?" I asked, hoping my facial expression didn't give away my inward laughter. I knew there was an age restriction and Linda definitely looked younger than fifty-five. She was obviously offended by the question. Why, I couldn't possibly imagine! *C'est la vie.*

"No, I wish I could, but I'm not old enough," she responded in a voice laced with arsenic, her eyes throwing daggers at my chest.

Dropping the subject, Linda again picked up the registration form we had just filled out and said, "I see you've indicated you're now living in Montvale, NJ. That's a beautiful area. How long have you been there?"

"Thirty-four years," replied Helen.

Are you living in a private home or an apartment?"

"We live in a beautiful seventy-year-old colonial."

"And, uh, how many bedrooms do you have?"

"Four, plus a master suite, and a maid's quarters."

"That sounds grand," said Linda. "Before I show you the models, can you briefly tell me what you're looking for?"

"What do you mean?" asked Helen.

"For instance, how many bedrooms do you want? Are you interested in a house with a loft? Must you have an eat-in kitchen and separate dining room? Does the master bedroom have to be on the first floor?"

"We're not committed to any particular details as of yet. I'd like to see every model and floor plan you have, so we're in a better position to make decisions," Helen answered.

"Hold on a minute. Just how many models are there?" I wanted to know.

"We have fifteen different primary designs, with the option to modify any of them within certain parameters," Linda replied.

As if it were an involuntary reflex reaction, I smacked the side of my head in disbelief.

"Is it possible to see all of them in just an hour?" I asked, knowing I'd go bonkers after traipsing through the first two or three models.

"Not exactly. Realistically we'll need two to three hours to see all the models. That includes seeing the clubhouse and all the recreation facilities on the property. But don't hold me to that, since the speed in which we can see everything depends upon both of you, not me.

"Then when we finish, we can come back here to my office and review what you liked and didn't like, and I can answer any of your questions," Linda said.

Linda had no idea what was in store for her, between Helen's oohs and ahs, her incessant questions, and my less than pleasant demeanor. Linda's chance of selling me a house in La Palazzo was as likely as me winning the Mega Lotto Jackpot two times in a row. I wanted to tell her to save her time, energy, breath, and chocolate chip cookies, and send us on our merry way, but the devil on my shoulder said, *"Drive her nuts."* If she didn't drink heavily before, she would after dealing with me for three hours; you can be sure of that.

Off we went to see the first model: "The Milano". It was a large closet. Its two bedrooms and one and a half baths, Linda described as charming and cozy; a place to enjoy a tranquil retirement.

Right on. For the last forty years I've dreamed of nothing more than returning to the luxurious abode I lived in Manhattan right after graduation from college; a three-story walk-up studio apartment, with a trundle bed that had more space than the broom closet the "Milano" offered.

Helen even commented that it was just a tad too small for her needs. What a diplomat! That didn't stop her, though, from spending a full thirty minutes opening every cabinet door, touching every single window treatment fabric, examining every lighting fixture, inspecting every appliance, and topping it all off by asking the most inane questions, such as, "Can I have a lime green refrigerator instead of this stainless steel one?"

Normally, I would have been the one to start a debate over color selection, just to irritate Helen. But this time it was too much fun listening to Helen and Linda discuss the merits and drawbacks of cleaning finger smudges from stainless steel, as opposed to the ease of cleaning a lime green vinyl facing, and how retro design was the newest craze in home décor. Truly, you couldn't make things like this up.

Finally, we were off to the second model: the understated "Venetian". A house decorated in "early Jersey" motif popularized by the *House Wives of New Jersey* television show. We entered an obscenely large foyer with white marble floors and walls, dominated by the largest "fake" crystal chandelier I'd ever seen.

"Doesn't this take your breath away?" Linda asked me, her face beaming with pride, daring me to disagree.

I'm the wrong guy to ask that question, I thought. *Do I, or don't I respond?*

That fellow on my shoulder screamed, *"Do it! You know you want to."*

I couldn't hold back. She'd teed it up for me to smack it three hundred yards down the fairway. *I only wish!*

"That's not exactly how I would put it, Linda. It does leave me gasping for air though. Let's just say, if I had to entertain Tony

Soprano and his Capos, owning this house would be a must. But, since we're in witness protection now, we must keep a low profile, and as much as I want to, I'm not into that lifestyle any more. I don't think my family, friends, or even pets would be able to catch their breath from the stunning beauty and majesty of the foyer and that crystal edifice."

Linda's head looked as if it were pivoting on its axis. Her face was frozen like a deer caught in the high beams of an oncoming car. Helen turned toward her, shrugged her shoulders and extended her hands, palms up. No doubt pantomiming, *"What can I say? He's my burden."*

"Oh, I didn't realize you weren't into Mediterranean décor," Linda said.

Hopefully, Linda had just learned a valuable lesson. Namely, avoid at all costs, asking my opinion about anything, or be prepared to accept the consequences.

"I think what Mike was trying to say, Linda, was…No, what Mike should have said was that this style of decorating was not his cup of tea."

Linda and Helen exchanged looks of understanding and pity. They bonded. They became sisters in an unholy alliance against me. I was a piranha to be avoided at all cost.

I kept a lid on offering my two cents until we entered the Roman bathroom. It was a replica of Julius Caesar's palace bath from the set of Cleopatra. It defied belief. I ignored its immense four hundred square foot size. The walls and floors were tiled in the same glaring white marble that bedecked the entrance foyer. The fixtures and faucets were faux gilded gold. And to put the cherry on the cake, it had every man's dream—a bidet! What pushed me over the ledge–something I could not ignore—was a raised Olympic-sized Jacuzzi tub adorned with ostrich plumes and burning incense sticks. The only things missing were the toga-clad slave women feeding grapes and cheese to bathers.

I blurted out, "Linda, why don't you suggest to the developer they rename this model 'The Donald?' It's more fitting. It's so understated."

I lost it...My self-control flew out the window. I followed that comment up with another doozey:

"Linda, I have to ask you this perplexing question."

Linda's fixed saleslady smile vanished, replaced by tension lines, as she awaited my onslaught with obvious trepidation. The women once again exchanged knowing looks. Helen's face tightened. Her eyes bore into me, daring me to be myself. Nevertheless, throwing caution to the wind, I took the plunge after Linda gave me encouragement to continue.

"Yes, Mike, what would you like to know?"

"If I lost my mind, either as a result of a frontal lobotomy, or early onset of dementia, and actually bought this house, could I eliminate the Jacuzzi tub, the plumes, and the incense? And while we're at it, get rid of that hideous chandelier?"

She was perplexed. "Why would you want to do that? Everybody else here loves them. In fact, most of the residents have put identical tubs in their finished basements."

Shoot me now! The idea that possible neighbors to the left and right of me had design taste in their derrieres was cause to immediately veto La Palazzo. It's not that good people cannot have different tastes in home decorations; it's more a matter of my sensitive eyes being exposed to such high intensity lumens emanating from the front of their homes.

"Well, let me put it this way." Sarcasm oozed with every syllable I uttered. "If I'm fortunate to live into my eighties, chances are Helen or I will have some mobility issues. In that likelihood, how the hell are we going to get into and out of that tub? It's wasted, unnecessary, impractical, and an added expense. What were the designers thinking?"

She was dumbfounded.

I can't have been the only one to raise these objections.

"We...uh, do not offer any alternative for the Jacuzzi," Linda stammered.

"Oh, I'm sorry, that's too bad. I guess a lot of people here are forced to bathe outside under a water hose," I said, pantomiming holding a hose over my head.

Linda and Helen totally ignored that comment.

Hoping to placate me, Linda said, "Just for my own edification, Mike, would you be interested in the 'Venetian' if somehow we could convince the builder to make the changes you suggest?"

"Honestly...no...not really," I said. "You'd have to also remove the bidet, the chandeliers from the hall, dining room, living room, kitchen, bedroom, and guest bathroom; take out the Roman columns in the dining room, the red velour drapes in every room, the nude cherubs atop the faucets; then add a towel warmer, and install heated floor tiles. If you did all that, and I survived another frontal lobotomy, I would definitely buy the 'Venetian'. Should I go on?"

"No, please don't. I get the idea. I really do," Linda said, looking at Helen with pleading eyes for her to intervene.

"For goodness sakes, Mike, that's uncalled for. There's no reason to be so offensive."

The remainder of the tour, which took another two hours, was excruciating, both for Linda's patience and my sanity. Helen loved every mind-blowing minute.

We returned to the reception center where Linda gave Helen an armful of brochures, thanked her for coming and expressed the hope she would soon see her again; emphasizing the word HER. Of course, they said their goodbyes and then the women hugged. Thank goodness their lips never met. To no one's surprise, I was a *persona non-grata*, to both of them. No Hugs For Me!

5

IT'S AMAZING WE arrived home safely without getting a speeding ticket, or physically accosting one another. Helen was livid
the entire trip, steam literally radiating off her face. I stayed mute,
fearing I'd say something else I'd regret and have to pay penance for
the remainder of my natural life. Surely, if I believed in an afterlife,
she'd be there to haunt me for eternity.

Later that evening, during dinner, Helen broke the ice. She
reached across the dinner table and patted my hand as she apolo-
gized, after a fashion, for the way she'd sprung the idea of moving.
She promised not to bring up the subject of a retirement community until she'd done some additional research on her own. I
just looked at her without making a comment, which gave her no
opportunity to open the topic to further discussion.

A unilateral truce had been declared. Amazingly, the tranquility in our household lasted one month.

Unfortunately, the subject matter reared its ugly head sooner
than either one of us expected, as a result of our former neighbors
and good friends, Gwen and George Gould, calling from Florida to
invite us down for a visit. On the face of it, their invitation seemed

Kosher, but everything is not always what it seems, especially when it concerns Helen. We hadn't seen Gwen and George since they relocated a little over two years before. They knew from our phone conversations and watching the weather channel how bitterly cold the temperatures had been in Montvale these past few years; it might have been reasonable for them to invite us to their home long before this to escape the cold weather. I had a nagging feeling there was more to the offer.

Why did they wait two years? I wondered.

We froze our behinds off last year during a historic frigid winter while they basked in the warm rays of the Florida sun. My money was on Helen orchestrating this charade. I was sure it was part of her master plan to have us move to one of Florida's geriatric communities with a fancy panache sounding Italian name. It didn't matter that most of the residents weren't even Italian. It sounded Continental and that was enough for the want-to-be retirees.

How do I play this? Do I stubbornly refuse to go, and make up some lame excuse, or do I confront, in a rational way, the decision to move or not? Is it possible to have a non-emotional factual conversation with Helen? If history is any judge, she'll likely turn it into World War III.

Mike, I said to myself, *practically speaking you have only two options; the first is to accept your fate, surrender without too much sparring, or being overly obnoxious, but making sure not to jeopardize your ability to maintain a modicum of leverage when it comes to the final selection of my pre-hospice abode; or as a second alternative, revisit the idea of divorce.*

This was a notion I had seriously contemplated acting upon many times over the past several years. Though an unrealistic option, it was a choice nevertheless. Could I really go through with divorcing Helen even though she has been my life partner for close to a half a century? She was, and is, a good mother and grand-mother. I still had feelings for her, but through the years that burning love had ebbed, dissolving into a coexisting semi-comfortable companionship…in which too often we'd argue and go through periods of verbal confrontation. Sexual contact was non-existent… She didn't feel the need.

If I did go down the path of separation, especially only to avoid moving, I'd most likely incur the enmity of both my children; lose at least half my assets; lose any relationship with any blood relative of Helen's; and spend a small fortune on attorney fees. Then I'd still have to move, because the house I was living in was way too big for one person. I would also lose the relationship of any male friend I had who was married to a friend of Helen's, since those guys would be prohibited from seeing or dealing with me, or risk losing their intimacy rights with their spouses. Not only that, but there would be no chance of me being invited to their homes, whether I was alone or with a future female friend. Perish the thought!

Accepting the lesser of two evils and the ultimate outcome of my current situation, I dragged myself into my den and begrudgingly put pen to paper.

Possible Burial Plot Locations:
Southern States—Florida, North Carolina, South Carolina, Virginia
Mid-Atlantic States—Delaware, Maryland, South Jersey
West Coast—Arizona, California, Nevada, New Mexico, Texas

North East—Connecticut, New Hampshire, New York, Vermont

- New or resale, purchase price, real estate taxes, monthly maintenance fees, income taxes,
- Number of bedrooms, bathrooms: two, three, master, guest, walk-in shower, den/office.
- Basement: finished, unfinished, great room.
- Distance from: food shopping, other shopping, golf, hospitals, physicians, dentists, urgent care, movies, theater, hair salons, nail salon, restaurants, **children, grandchildren**, airports, friends.
- Amenities: clubhouse, indoor pool, outdoor pool, health club, golf, bocce, tennis, card room, billiards.
- How many homes are in the community? Are there any Key Clubs? What's the rate of STDs per hundred residents? And what's the percentage of single women?

That's a good starting point, I reasoned.

I knew there were many more variables and permutations to consider. Fine tuning the options would come later.

During lunch later in the day, Helen brought up the subject again of visiting the Goulds.

"Mike, I'd like to accept Gwen's offer as soon as we can. It's been far too long since we've seen them. It's a good time. We're not doing anything the next few weeks. The weather is supposed to be lousy. The kids don't have any recitals that I know of, or soccer games to watch, so why don't we just go? It'll be fun, and you can play golf and go fishing with George."

An opening to rebut; go for it.

"Since when do I fish? I wouldn't even know what end to put a hook on. For that matter, why would I want to spend hours waiting for some mindless creature to impale itself on a sharp metal prong, and then jab myself in the hand trying to remove the hook from its mouth? If that wasn't enough, I'd have to throw the fish back in the water so I wouldn't offend the sensitivities of my grandchildren, if heaven forbid, they ever found out I caught a fish and then ate it. Can you imagine the horror on their little faces?"

"Mike, stop it! Don't make a federal case out of it. I was only trying to say you and George can have some man time together."

"Alright, I suppose it would be fun to spend a couple of days with George."

Practically jumping out of her seat, beaming from ear to ear, Helen said, "Wonderful, I'll call Gwen and make the arrangements."

"You do that little thing. Just let me know the dates and I'll make the plane reservations."

"Wait a second, Mike. Before you do that, maybe we should consider driving to Florida. We've never done that before. That way we can take our time and see parts of the country we haven't been to. What do you think?"

She paused.

Here it comes.

"I'd love to see Asheville and Charlotte in North Carolina, and Rehoboth Beach in Delaware, and the Bluffton-Hilton Head area in South Carolina," she said reciting the names in rapid succession.

"Wow, right off the top of your head you were able to identify three places whose names you've never once mentioned in all the years I've known you. Why is that Helen?"

Wait for it. Here comes the deflection.

"Well, if you must know, it just so happens I learned about them while I was doing my research on the most popular active adult communities. And if Gwen hadn't called, I wouldn't even have suggested we go see them, at least not right away. Now is the perfect time to see them. The opportunity has arisen and we should take advantage of it."

"Funny isn't it, how things just work out that way? Like a bolt of lightning out of the blue, Gwen invites you to Florida, and you can visit two or three, maybe even ten communities with that same punch-drunk husband of yours. It's a wonderful thing."

"You don't think I arranged this whole thing with Gwen, do you?"

"The thought never crossed my mind."

6

I HURRIEDLY LEFT THE kitchen table, went to my den and retrieved, from my desk drawer, two copies of the list I had prepared. It took me less than five minutes to write down my preferences on one of the copies.

"Are you still in the kitchen?" I called out.

"I'm in the kitchen; where do you think I'd be?"

Ignoring her charming "call to arms" I walked back into the kitchen, but made sure the center isle separated us.

You never can be too safe, I reasoned.

I reached over the sink portion of the counter top, attempting to hand her the other copy of my questionnaire, and at the same time asked her to read through the options and jot down her choices. Helen made no effort to take what I was offering, claiming dinner was almost ready. She continued to mince some carrots for the soup she was preparing, refusing to either look at me or the papers I held out to her. I sensed she felt I was trying to control the search process, usurping her role.

"I'm preparing dinner now. I don't have time for this," she said.

I didn't lose my cool.

I remained calm.

In a low voice, I pointed to the clock on the wall behind her and said, "It's only five o'clock. We still have over an hour before we normally eat dinner, and if need be, we could reheat the meal in the microwave."

Helen nodded, took the papers from my outstretched hand, retrieved a pencil from the utility draw next to the refrigerator, and went into the living room.

Nearly an hour later, she joined me in my den…We still hadn't eaten. Why it took her so long is beyond me, but once she appeared, I said, "Don your jousting armor, my dear, and meet me in the living room atop your steed."

Helen actually laughed. She knew she'd won the battle, but the outcome of the war was still in doubt.

"I suggest we start by deciding what negative elements we can agree upon which will immediately rule out a particular geographic area."

"What are you talking about, Mike?"

"Well, do you want to spend a significant part of the year living in an area which experiences a deep freeze, or one prone to drought conditions, fires and earthquakes, or one which experiences unbearable heat and sand storms, or one with long periods of rain and heat, or alternatively one which feels like a steam sauna?"

"Are you going to make me guess what you mean?"

"Okay, if we live in either Connecticut, New Hampshire, New Jersey, or Vermont, we'll have to continue to put up with freezing temperatures and snow a good portion of the year. In California, we'll have drought, fires, earthquakes, and the occasional mudslides.

In Arizona or New Mexico, we'll enjoy one hundred and ten-degree temperatures. North and South Carolina offer sweltering humidity for at least four months of the year. And even though Florida offers 'early bird specials', you must also accept extremely hot summers lasting three to four months at a time, and the joy of hurricane season every year. Delaware and Maryland have decent weather, most of the time, but way too many cornfields.

"So, pick your poison, my dear."

"It can't be as bad in all those places as you make it out to be. Why would all those people live in an area if it's so horrible?"

"If you can only afford one home, your choices are limited. So you select the least offensive location, and stay in one place. Alternatively, if you have enough money, you buy two homes and split the time between two or more locations. And when I use the term 'you', I mean someone else," I said.

"That sounds like a good idea. We should think about that," she said.

Here we go——controversy in the making.

"Hold on, Helen, we haven't come to any agreement that we're even going to move, no less buy two homes. Can we first take some time to discuss why you feel we have to move, and if so, why it must be to a geriatric fossil farm?"

"I've given this a lot of thought. Mike. Are you really open to hearing what I have to say?"

"Can't wait…Shoot."

"Our house is too big for us. We're only two people living in a forty-five hundred square foot home, with five bedrooms. Our property taxes are over thirty-five thousand dollars a year.

The oldest neighbors we have are fifty years old, and Art and Sue Kaufman, the last of our 'neighborhood' friends, are moving to an adult community in Huntington, Long Island. I don't know about you, but I certainly will be very unhappy if I'm alone with no friends and nothing to do but watch young women pushing their newborns in strollers up and down the street. Can you understand that?"

"Young mothers? That's a pretty persuasive argument for staying right where we are. Don't you think?" I said in a weak attempt at trying to lighten the mood.

"Predictable, Mike. You're so predictable."

Damn it, she's made some pretty convincing points. What can I come up with to counter them? Not much, except the ultimate; the Plutonium Bomb: **THE GRANDCHILDREN**! *If all else fails, I'll drop it. But it has to be at the right moment for maximum impact.*

Thinking about being away from them wasn't even a possibility in my mind. I love my grandchildren. I mean I *really* love them! Not because they're mine, but because they ARE mine. We have an unbelievably close relationship, a special bond, so much so that my wife is outwardly jealous when the kids are with me.

"What's going on, Mike? Why are you crying?"

I'm going to blow it. Here comes the bomb.

"It's the kids," I said.

"What about them?"

"When will we ever see them?" I said in a tear-choked voice.

Hell, I was morose.

Helen made no attempt to console me.

"Why did you have to ask me that? It's hard enough for me to contemplate leaving our home, no less moving away from the kids. If we move, we're moving away from them. You can't escape it."

"I know, I know, and as much as it hurts me to say it, we have our own lives to live. I love them all with every fiber of my being. Nothing will change that," she said. "But everything should no longer revolve around the kids. We've been down that road. We were good parents. We cared for them, watched over them, educated them, paid for their weddings, and helped them financially. They were our first priority, now we have to be selfish and look out for what's best for us, in the twilight of our years."

She's serious. This change of lifestyle is not just about me. Helen is also contemplating this change in large measure for herself.

"Okay, let's put the kids aside for the moment. The reasons you've mentioned for moving have a modicum of validity, so let's talk about what area of the country suits your fancy."

Shockingly, by dinner time we had mutually agreed, without so much as a raised voice, to eliminate the West Coast, Vermont, New Hampshire, Arizona, and New Mexico, Nevada, and Texas. I must claim sole credit for vetoing New Jersey. It was bad enough I agreed to move here shortly after we married and incur the constant slings and arrows from my New York City family and friends. Hell, everyone from outside New Jersey has a negative impression of the state. Most of it is deserved; especially when you consider the quality of its elected leaders, and the vast amount of condemned and polluted property occupying much of the land. There was no way I was going to move onto a former pig farm, miraculously converted into a grandiose Tuscan Village Villa, abutting the New Jersey Turnpike, regardless of how enamored Helen was with thirty-five-foot Doric columns guarding the front entrance of the homes. To me they were downright nauseating. I would be mortified living in such a pretentious looking community.

"Helen, we've narrowed the possible areas we'd consider down to Connecticut, Delaware, Florida, Maryland, North and South Carolina. Now, are you seriously suggesting we visit all of them on the way down to see George?"

"Leaving aside Connecticut, which we can drive to at any time, I don't see why we couldn't," she replied.

"Just for kicks and giggles, Helen, how many of these fifty-five plus active adult communities are in each of these states? Can you tell me?"

"I wasn't planning on visiting all of them," she said.

"Ah, what a relief! But just how many were you planning on visiting?" I persisted.

"That's not fair of you, Mike. You know I couldn't have...uh..."

"Okay, let me make this a bit easier for us. If we can agree on some of those other things, I'm sure we can narrow down the number of places you want to see. What's the minimum number of houses you want in a community? Fifty, one hundred, four hundred, a thousand? Give me a number. What's the maximum? Do you want either an indoor or outdoor pool, or both?"

"Mike, I already answered those questions. Look here. I wrote them down," Helen said, holding up the paper, pointing to her answers.

"So you did. Now why don't you take both our responses, and compare them. See where we agree, and where we don't. Then tomorrow morning we'll go over it?"

"It's a deal," Helen said. "Tomorrow, 9:00 a.m., same place, same table, and the same old people."

Before I had a chance to escape to my den to watch the ball game, Helen held up her hand, signifying that I should stay put.

"Mike, one last thing. Were you serious about including STDs on the list of things we should consider? Are they that important?" she asked with a mischievous little twinkle in her eyes.

Helen was obviously pleased with how un-confrontational we were being, and I was flabbergasted by my lack of outward hostility.

Time will tell if I can continue to be so amenable.

7

WE RECONVENED AT the kitchen table, referred to in our household as the 38th Parallel, and continued our negotiations. No mediators were present, just the protagonists left to their own war plans.

"So Helen, what have you come up with?"

"We seem to have quite a few areas of disagreement."

"We do? That couldn't be. Nothing like that has ever happened before...I'm shocked...Like what? Don't keep me in suspense," I said, trying my best not to smirk.

"Are you starting up with me again?"

"Not me. That couldn't be further from the truth," I replied, tongue in cheek.

"Sounds to me like you got up on the wrong side of the bed," Helen said, tired of my continuous teasing.

"Well, it wasn't on your side of the bed. That's for sure."

"Is there something on your mind, Mike?"

"Do you really want me to answer that?"

"Yes, I do."

"You know, I would ordinarily jump at the chance to vent, but we don't have the time, and I don't have the patience or inclination to rehash the elephant in the room again right now. So, for both our sakes I'm going to table that discussion and get back to talking about what you came up with. If that's okay with you?"

I guess Helen didn't have the stamina to withstand another assault on her lack of sexual desire, because without missing a beat, she said, "I think we need a minimum of four bedrooms. You want only two."

I waited before replying, hoping my tone did not portray a sour note revealing the negative thoughts I was feeling. Unfortunately, my best intentions were betrayed. A hint of sarcasm crept into my voice. "I don't see why you possibly need four bedrooms."

"We have two married children and nine grandchildren. Where are they going to sleep when they come to visit?"

Here I go.

"What makes you think they'll want to visit us?"

"Please Mike, they always come to us for the holidays."

"Is that so? Hypothetically, let's say three years from now we're living in Asheville, North Carolina. Our two eldest granddaughters are in college somewhere, two are close to graduating high school, and the rest of them are in junior high or beginning high school. Do you really think they're going to want to spend their vacations with us?"

Now for the real zinger

"Also, remember most of their other grandparents live less than an hour's car ride from the grandkids we have in common."

Bingo! That comment hit home.

Helen's face blanched white. She tried to hide the depression that took over her inner thoughts by turning away and pretending to be interested in some poor imitation of a Picasso we had hanging on the far wall. It took a couple of moments for her to pull herself together, but she managed it.

In a quiet, pensive voice, she said, "But when they do come, they'll each need a bedroom."

"You're not being practical, Helen. If they did come to visit, probably, hopefully, all of them won't come at the same time. And if by some miracle they did, we'd have to get them all hotel rooms to stay in. Assuming, of course, there are any decent hotels nearby.

"Nine grandchildren and six adults is a small army...

"Look, we're talking about exceptions, rare occasions when we'll ever need more than one extra bedroom for guests. You have to agree, it would be infinitely less expensive to pay for a hotel room, than pay the difference in cost between buying a two, or a four-bedroom house."

"I'm still not convinced."

"Here's a thought. What if we look for a two-bedroom home with an office/den that we can put a convertible sofa bed into? Then when we need it for a guest it could be used as a bedroom. How about that?"

"I suppose we could do that, but I'm not sure...I don't want to split up the family."

"Alright, leave that aside for now. What other things don't we agree upon?" I asked.

"I want a minimum of four hundred homes in the community, you want fifty, and no more than one hundred."

"I don't see a problem," I said. "...Fifty it is."

"Michael!"

Danger alert! She only uses my formal name when she's about to implode.

"Yes, dearest?" I said, hoping to tamp down the growing embers of Helen's temper.

"Don't dearest me," she practically yelled, her eyes rolling back in her head. "You can't yes dear me, or dictate to me what we're going to buy or not buy. This thing is a joint decision."

"Of course," I said. "I wouldn't have it any other way."

"Michael! Don't start up."

Oh, she's mad.

"How much time do you want to be away from home during this trip?" I asked, eager to change the subject.

It worked…I think.

"Probably three weeks at a minimum. I'd like to plan on spending at least a week with Gwen and George. So if we took our time driving, I'd say we should plan on spending at least three additional days driving each way. The rest of the time we can spend looking at some of the communities," she replied.

Now I was nervous.

"You mean to tell me you expect me to waste over a week just looking at those nursing homes?"

"Stop saying they're nursing homes; they're active adult retirement communities, where your days can be spent doing countless things with someone other than yourself."

Wow, she didn't challenge me saying it was a waste of my time; probably an oversight on her part.

"Are you implying I play with myself all day?" I said, pointing my finger at my pants' zipper feigning anger.

"You really are a pig, you know that!"

"I do what I have to do, Helen," I said, unsmiling, my facial expression portraying no sign of humor.

It took her a couple of seconds to process whether I was serious or not. Literally, you could see her brain cells working in overdrive.

I was…She knew it…And most upsetting of all, she didn't care.

She changed the subject. "Can I call Gwen to firm up a date for us to visit them?"

"I suppose so," I said, very deliberately making no attempt to hide my irritation, while debating with myself whether I wanted to be aggravated by continuing down that rabbit hole again…I chose not to. "Once I know the dates, I can plan the trip accordingly. It'll take me a few days, so be patient."

The ball was in my court. How, I wondered, could I prevent the impending weeks of isolation alone with Helen from turning into a full-blown, out of control venting, on my part, of her aversion to a physical…no, our non-existent sexual relationship? It bothered me greatly…It was front and center in my psyche. Years would go by without any meaningful intimacy occurring between us. It was hard for me because I'm the type of person who craves physical affection. Moving away from my safety net of warmth, love, and outward displays of affection from my children and grandchildren just might be the feather that sank the boat.

The reality was that I, and countless others experiencing similar situations, had no easy solution. I was trapped by circumstance and by my own lack of courage. I was forced to focus on the where, when, and how to balance Helen's desire to relocate with my own needs. I was convinced Helen was blind to my needs. I assumed she loved me in her own way, but cared less about me than her own desires for an active social existence.

8

TWO DAYS LATER during dinner, I unveiled my plan.

"So Helen, here's what I suggest...We can spend a day in Delaware, a day in North Carolina, a day in South Carolina, and two days in Florida. All I need you to do is select the communities you want to visit in each location. I'll make the necessary hotel reservations. What do you think?"

"You're kidding, right? What you're suggesting can't work."

"Why not?"

"I can't see how we can possibly go through all the communities I want to in such a short amount of time. We'd need at least another day in each of the Carolinas, and two more days in Florida," she said.

Holy shit! She's lost it. I can't do it. I can't even spend an hour in a department store with her without the need for alcohol. How am I going to survive this?

"You don't mean that, do you?" I said in a doleful voice. "How many of these things are on your list?"

Wait for it.

"Twenty-three."

"Seriously, Helen? Are you crazy?"

Unfazed by my reaction, she plowed ahead. "I've eliminated over thirty others. It's not easy. They all have so much to offer."

"Like what? Basket and hair weaving?" I said. "Do they also offer pool acrobats, *Depend®* changing instructions, and denture cleaning instructions?"

"Mike, now you're just being silly. Wait until you hear all the wonderful things you'll be able to do. Look over some of the brochures, Mr. Know-it-all."

"No need. I'll wait and be surprised."

9

I MADE RESERVATIONS AT Courtyards by Marriott wherever I could,
so we could use or earn Marriott Rewards points. I figured we
wouldn't need a hotel in Florida since we could use George's place
as home base. I also planned to encourage Helen to have Gwen go
with her to tour the communities in South Florida. I'd volunteer to
go back with Helen to those places she truly liked. That way I could
spend time with George on the golf course, and then scope out the
neighborhood bars and strip clubs.

We left New Jersey around 9:00 a.m....Definitely a mistake!
Traffic on the Jersey Turnpike was flowing at its usual snail's pace,
coupled with frequent rubbernecking whenever a car was on the
side of the road, resulting in a constant parade of stop and go driving. If the windows were open, we would have been asphyxiated
by the exhaust fumes hanging like dark, low-hanging clouds. All in
all, including rest stops for coffee, nature release, and a gas fill-up,
it took almost four hours to get to Rehoboth Beach. It wasn't a total
loss though. I passed the exit for La Palazzo at Mach1 speed. Hands
down, it was the highlight of the first day's trip! Helen didn't notice
the huge billboard advertising their community since she had fallen
asleep.

Rehoboth Beach, Delaware, the first stop on our deathwatch search, is a summer destination for tens of thousands of families searching for sun and surf; discount shopping at its grandest, and seafood restaurants by the dozens. But this was mid-February, and instead of bronzed young bodies walking the streets in their skimpy bikinis, we occasionally spotted a hearty seventyish soul walking, braving the chilly winds coming off the Chesapeake. A sightless person couldn't ignore the desolation and eerie silence.

We checked into our motel, unpacked and then drove two miles to the real estate agent's office. Helen had arranged with the agent to take us on a tour of four developments she felt would be of interest. I won't disclose their names for fear I could be sued for slander and libel, but I can share with you what they all had in common.

Each had a beautiful view of cornfields as far as the eye could see. If I weren't the one who had driven there, I would have guessed we were in Iowa. One community had the added benefit of over-looking an expansive marsh, replete with actual wildlife. They were lovely, but as one of the residents I happened to speak with in the men's room of their clubhouse mentioned to me; "The view might be beautiful now, but during the summer months you need a shotgun to kill the mosquitos, they're so big."

All the communities were within a thirty-minute car ride of the beach, restaurants, and shopping. But in the areas separating these communities and Rehoboth Beach were BORING cornfields, chicken, and horse farms. To the city dweller in me, it wasn't pal-atable. The stretches of uninhabited land were on the one hand depressing and the other hand, *down right* depressing!

One person's utopia is another's hell. Viva la difference!

Unfortunately, local planning boards felt the need to punish their native-born residents and transplanted retirees by quadrupling the vehicle population on their roads during the summer months. I've been told by a reliable source that the traffic actually rivals that of New York City's clogged streets. They have mercilessly destroyed tens of thousands of acres of cornfield and farmland in order to make way for old farts from the North East to find cheap housing, extremely low taxes, and a plethora of discount shopping malls.

I must admit, the houses themselves were quite well built, and the floor plans very welcoming to the aged and infirmed. *Not me, but those other people.* Unfortunately, the one community I gave a second thought to, had sold only eighty homes out of a possible seven hundred they planned to build. There was a significant financial risk to us if we bought at that time. Should the builder not be able to sell an appreciable additional number of homes, the onerous burden of paying for the maintenance and upkeep of the golf course, clubhouse, and communal lands would most likely become the responsibility of the small number of actual homeowners. I was not going to take that chance. I imagined living in the middle of a sprawling development of seven hundred staked out vacant properties with only a fraction of the houses built and occupied. No neighbors, no card games, no nuten!

Helen loved the house in this particular community, the brochures they gave her, the little model display showing what the completed community would look like, and the chocolate cookies. When I explained why it would not be a prudent investment, my lovely wife brushed aside my objection saying, "You'll find an excuse to reject anything I want."

"Hey, you know that's not true. I'm simply pointing out that buying here now, might not be the wisest thing we could do with our limited funds."

Carol Wilmont, our real estate agent and tour guide, who had been attached to Helen's hip for the past four hours, I'm sure heard my comment, but pretended otherwise as she busied herself, pretending to read some brochure.

"Carol, what do you think?" I asked.

Unconvincingly, she jerked her head up as if I had woken her from a sound sleep. "Oh, I'm sorry Mike, were you talking to me?"

"Yes, I was."

"I didn't hear what you were saying. I was lost in my own thoughts. Please repeat what you said."

"Sure I will…Considering only a little more than ten percent of the planned homes have been sold in the past two years, what's going to happen to the builder if this trend continues?"

"What do you mean, what will happen?"

She's now on the defensive.

"These builders finance their projects with loans. Their cash flow has to be suffering. At some point, the plug is going to be pulled; they can't go on paying off their loans with basically no sales. Something has to give, and I think it'll be them pulling up stakes to cut their losses. So, when they do, where does it leave those people who already live here? How can seventy homeowners possibly cover the costs of maintaining all community facilities and land, if the builder is no longer in the picture?"

"I can't imagine that happening. Especially since so many couples are clamoring to visit us. We've gone to contract on four homes since Christmas," Carol said as if selling four homes was a momentous achievement.

"That's great," I said. "That means that if this trend continues, it'll take another twelve years to be sold out. I'm sorry, but I just don't want to hear the sound of construction trucks and hammering for that long...Maybe because the other homeowners are already deaf and suffering from macular degeneration, they won't mind the construction of another six hundred and twenty homes, they can't see or hear, but I sure can!"

"You're really painting a very unrealistic picture, Mike. Mark my words, this community will be sold out within two years."

"And if it isn't? Will you guarantee I receive a full refund?" I asked Carol, knowing full- well how unrealistic my request was.

"I don't believe I'd be able to convince the builder to agree to that condition of sale."

"If I were the builder, I wouldn't either."

"But Mike, if what you're saying is a real possibility, how come all these other people have purchased homes?" Helen asked, probably thinking I was just making up an excuse not to move there.

"Beats the hell out of me," I replied.

At that point, Helen asked Carol if she would give us a few moments alone.

Here it comes.

"Mike, are you going to manufacture a reason to object to every place we visit?"

"No I'm not, and I am hurt by you even inferring I would stoop so low. I really believe it's a major risk buying here, on two grounds. First and most importantly is what I've already mentioned: we would stand to lose a significant amount of money if this place goes into bankruptcy after we buy. The second reason primarily affects you."

"And what would that be?"

"The fact that it will take us between two to three hours driving from Rehoboth to reach the closest airport. Can you imagine driving all that distance every time we want to fly somewhere? We fly so frequently, we'd be spending more time driving than flying."

"How do you know how far away the airports are? I didn't hear you ask Carol that question."

"Ask her if you don't believe me."

"I will."

I waved to Carol (who was leaning against her car) to come through and rejoin us.

"Carol, how far is the closest airport from here?" Helen asked.

"Baltimore's BWI and Philadelphia are both about a two hours' drive."

"That's if you drive in the middle of the night," I said. "What about during rush hour? Come to think of it, the Jersey Turnpike is always busy."

My relationship with Carol went rapidly downhill. Even though Helen insisted on going through the remainder of the models, it was obvious she had accepted the reality that I was not inclined to move to Rehoboth Beach.

I reiterated to Helen several times once Carol was out of earshot, how much she loved to travel overseas, and the horrific inconvenience it would be driving two to three hours each way to catch a plane. I'm sure by my saying that, I lessened the verbal tongue-lashing I would have been the target of once we were alone in the car.

FYI, years later we learned that the builder did go belly-up. All construction ceased for more than three years. We lucked out.

IO

IT WAS AFTER six o'clock when we finally left Carol and drove back to our motel. I hoped if I got Helen talking about what I wanted to discuss I could avoid being chastised again for not being positive about any of the communities we had just visited...It worked.

As Helen was putting the brochures we had been given away in one of her tote bags, I said, "I have to admit it Helen, I was impressed by the houses. I thought the floor plans were great; the rooms were large and airy, and the sunlight just poured in everywhere, and the flow from room to room was even better than what we have in Montvale."

"You sure didn't behave as if you liked it," Helen said with a definite sharpness to her voice.

"Wait a minute. My only negative comment to Carol was about the small number of home sales. I didn't tell her I thought the decorations in them reminded me of sale items displayed at a Home Depot Tent Sale event, and I didn't point out the measly plantings the builder was providing. Did I?!"

"I suppose not."

"So, can we concentrate on finding a restaurant and getting some good stiff drinks and a four-pound lobster?"

"But what am I going to eat? Helen jokingly asked.

"I suppose you can taste some of mine."

"Generous, aren't you?"

We ate on the second floor of a seafood restaurant at a window seat overlooking the Chesapeake. Even though my lobster was only two and a half pounds and not the four-pounder I threatened to order, it was moist and perfectly broiled. Helen accused me of being gluttonous. I didn't argue the point. I felt I was owed the meal as a reward for not being obnoxious toward Carol.

Our conversation, unfortunately, was dominated by a point-by-point recitation of what we had seen that day. I guess that was to be expected. Thankfully, Helen accepted my negative evaluation of Rehoboth Beach without further recriminations. Surprisingly, she came to accept the possible adverse implications of buying a home in a community during the initial stages of development. She even offered some additional downsides I hadn't even considered. She did, however, bemoan the fact we would not be able to take advantage of the plethora of seafood restaurants and discount shopping Rehoboth Beach had to offer. Helen did love eating out!

I actually survived touring eighteen model homes in four communities without having to be rushed to the hospital with an anxiety attack. And—as an extra-added bonus—we made no home purchase.

Next stop was to be Asheville, North Carolina. But when I explained to Helen it would take at least ten hours to drive there, not including stopping for food or bladder relief, she graciously acquiesced and crossed Asheville off our must-see list.

I was thrilled when I heard her say under her breath, "My children will never drive this far to see me."

It's finally sinking in to her conscious thought. The kids. The kids. At last, light at the end of the tunnel.

II

I LUCKED OUT NOT having to drive all the way to Asheville. It would have been a waste of time anyway, since I would have eventually torpedoed moving there for reasons akin to why I refuse to go camping, sleeping in a tent, and fishing for my food. But I really did miss out on seeing the beauty of the Smoky Mountains, experiencing the fabled hospitality of its residents, and visiting the world-famous Biltmore Estate. Realistically, even though it did have an airport just on the outskirts of town, Ashville was just too far removed from the hub of our family. Everybody I've spoken to who's been there raves about the place, though. As a matter of fact, two of my former colleagues did move there. There must be something to it...But not for me.

Rather than drive straight through to the Bluffton/Hilton Head area of South Carolina, for the next round of "welcome to death's entryway", we opted to make a couple of stops along the way. Well, it really wasn't the proverbial "we" I'm ashamed to say, because I was the one who dangled the forbidden fruit of shopping in front of Helen!

My vast experience coping with the shopping gene inherited by my daughter, granddaughters, and by osmosis, my daughters-in-law, has convinced me that no woman can say no to the chance of buying something, whether they need it or not...It's a metaphysical impossibility. There is a chance I could be wrong...If so, those women who don't like shopping are few and far between.

Helen bit hard into the apple, pits, core and all, and swallowed.

No, I wasn't crazy offering to let her shop...Of course, I had an ulterior motive. Buying something, no matter how frivolous, would temporarily take her mind off moving and hopefully redirect her conversation to the wonderful things she purchased.

This was not an easy decision for me, since I had wanted to take a side trip to visit the newly opened Peter Hasbrook Gubernatorial Memorial Library in Columbia, South Carolina's state capital. Now, for those of you who don't recognize Governor Hasbrook's name, shake the cobwebs out of your head and focus back a few years to the time the Republican Party almost imploded after Governor Hasbrook, the Republican Party's presidential candidate's tragic accident only days after being nominated. If you still don't remember, I suggest you read the book, *Chaos Reigns During the Presidential Election*. If I must say so it's a true masterpiece of political intrigue.

"Helen, did you know that Ralph Lauren's bedding and linens are sold at deep discount at the WestPoint Pepperell outlet in Lumberton, NC?"

"Where is that?"

"We'll pass it on the way down to Bluffton?"

She almost exploded with joy. She physically transformed into a kid whose nose was pressed up against a candy store window. Thank goodness her seat belt was fastened, for if it hadn't been, she'd have flown through the windshield.

Excitedly she said, "How do you know about WestPoint Pepperell?"

"I'm full of surprises."

"No seriously, how do you know?"

"I did some research. I'm always trying to please you. That's my mission in life."

Ordinarily, Helen would have gamely challenged my self-serving response into a mini-disagreement, but the prospect of buying Ralph Lauren sheets was just too much for her to cope with.

Unable to contain her excitement, she blurted out, "When will we get there?"

"In a few hours. Patience, my dear."

Helen was like the child in the back of the car incessantly whining, "When will we be there? When will we be there?" We arrived none too soon. Then, while Helen was meticulously examining the glut of treasures being offered ON SALE, I sat transfixed for nearly two hours, at the front of the store, staring out the window counting cars as they passed by on US 95 just across from the shopping center. No doubt I wasn't the only male who sought refuge from the shopping addicts as evidenced by the large number of seats and couches provided for the male gender...Give the guy a modicum of comfort to ease the eventual pain in his wallet.

What I do for a few hours of peace and quiet.

No matter what anyone says, I got off cheap shelling out only five hundred dollars for three sets of one thousand thread, pure Egyptian cotton sheets. My body will thank me for many years to come.

I was back in the car again, thank goodness! We'd driven south on US 95 for another three hours. The road was straighter than my twelve-inch ruler...Boring! There was nothing to see but vast expanses of vacant land, except of course for the endless array of signs advertising Cracker Barrel and Waffle House restaurants, JR Cigars, and *South of the Border* motel/amusement park.

"It's almost three o'clock now. Do you have any idea where are we going to sleep tonight?" Helen asked.

"Well, I know we won't be staying at 'South of the Border', that's for sure."

"Why not? It's been there forever, and I heard it's perfect; everybody talks about it."

"Yeah, maybe it's paradise for ten year olds, but not us. I've seen pictures of the place. It looks like Disneyland on LSD; designed by a punch-drunk architect strung out on peyote. I'll call Marriott's customer service; they'll find a place for us to spend the night."

An hour and a half later, we passed South of the Border. As we did, I took a quick peak to confirm my description was correct.

"Oh, look at all those beautiful colored lights," Helen said pointing in the direction of the motel/amusement park.

Mexico is now in the Carolinas! How quaint. Maybe they'd paid for the construction of this monstrosity instead of paying for the "WALL"!

From the time we left Ralph Lauren and his sheets, until the time we pulled into the Marriott Courtyard we'd made reservations at, Helen was at peace with the world; all was good. It turned out that her purchase of linen bought me an extra-added bonus. Helen didn't mention adult communities until we were on the road the next morning driving to Hilton Head. That was twelve hours of peaceful bliss.

If I had to spend five hundred dollars for every twelve hours of silence with Helen, I'd be broke in a very short period of time.

12

"MIKE, WE'RE ALMOST at Bluffton. Look at those beautiful trees. Is that moss hanging from the branches? Look at them. They're absolutely stunning, aren't they? They look so soft and fluffy."

"Yes, they're quite impressive and probably very soft, but don't get any ideas about stuffing our pillows or comforters with it."

"What does that mean? Are they hard? Do they have prickles?"

"No, I just said I thought they were soft, but they're rampant with bugs. Don't you remember being told that in Colonial days the settlers used the moss in their bedding? What they got was soft all right, and massive bug bites and insect infestation throughout their entire homes. So why don't we agree to admire them from a distance, okay?"

"You can turn anything from good to bad. Why do you continually do that?"

"I only meant to pepper the conversation with some interesting tidbits of local information. Shoot me for trying to broaden your knowledge and protect you from unsightly bug sores."

"I'm sorry, I was instinctively reacting to your comments, which you have to admit are usually sarcastic, to say the least."

"Apology accepted."

Before I could continue with my trivia lecture, Helen, whose nose was pinned to the side window taking in the natural beauty of the local flora, suddenly became mesmerized by the pristine lawns and flower gardens abutting both sides of the road for at least a quarter of a mile.

"How can they afford to maintain those gardens? It must cost them a small fortune!" she asked.

"With chain gangs, I presume."

"Prisoners? They can't still be using forced labor; its 2018."

"I was only guessing, Helen. We can ask the sales rep. when we get to Bluffton Estates. If they don't use prisoners, I bet there's an army of migrant laborers who come to this area and work for minimum wages."

"That sounds like a more reasonable explanation, Mike." *That's me: Mr. Reasonable.*

A huge sign on the side of the road, which had to be forty feet wide and was crafted out of red brick and cement, read, "Welcome to Bluffton Estates an Active Adult Community—your future home." Alongside it was an equally large printed banner surrounded by dozens of American Flags proclaiming, "We have **twenty-eight** model homes for you to choose from."

I couldn't contain my joy. This was what I'd been waiting for; what every married man yearned for—schlepping through twenty-eight different model homes! You heard me: twenty-eight dissimilar homes, and yet all practically the same. Helen would lose it, ogle over the decorations and the sheer assortment of choices to be made. She'd glow and be giddy at the prospect of buying all new furniture, silverware, glasses, and artwork. In other words, shop for everything, from soup to nuts. Hopefully, the utter magnitude of choice might in and of itself spell victory for me. How could she make a decision given so many choices?...Overload...I should be so fortunate!

I turned into Bluffton Estate's entrance and stopped our car at their guardhouse gate. I told the attendant, a gracious gentleman who was old enough to be my grandfather, that we had an appointment to see the models. He smiled, revealing a mouth devoid of teeth, nodded his head in understanding and then placed a visitor's pass on my windshield and pointed to the sign directing us to the "Welcome Center".

"Pretty shabby," I said, noticing that there was no waterfall or a statue of Venus de Mila.

"Make up your mind, Mike. What do you like? You were so critical of La Palazzo's beautiful gate and plantings because you said they were outrageous, and now you're bad- mouthing this place because it's too plain. You're just being obstreperous."

I didn't respond. I was too stunned by what I saw ahead of me. Though the sign said, "Welcome Center," it would have been more appropriate if it had read, "Welcome to Pitti Palace of the South."

A toga-clad hostess sitting behind a massive Italian Marble desk greeted us. She asked us to complete the requisite registry/questionnaire, handing us a pen and clipboard on which to write.

"Please follow me. You'll be more comfortable here, I'm sure. Henry, our manager, will join you shortly." She led us into their waiting room.

"This is a waiting room?" I asked.

Believe it or not, I was at a loss for words, convinced I'd seen this place on *Lifestyles of the Rich and Famous*. There was an abundance of overstuffed couches, fountains adorned with sculptures of nude nymphs, urns of coffee and iced tea, and you guessed it, platters of chocolate chip cookies.

Within a few minutes, Henry, today's guide, appeared from behind huge brass doors. He was a man in his early fifties, with a huge potbelly, no doubt cultivated over the years by having consumed large quantities of grits for breakfast, and barrels of ale from the local brewery for lunch and dinner. He was pleasant enough, but after all he was a salesman whose income was dependent upon his ability to be friendly, persuasive, and lie without us knowing it. *Caveat emptor*—buyer beware. Let the battle begin!

At this point, Helen asked to use the powder room and left me alone with Henry. Big mistake! She'll never learn.

"I'm so glad you made it here, but I wasn't expecting you for another two days. What happened?" Henry asked.

"It took us over an hour, but we saw everything there was to see in North Carolina...Man, there are so many communities to see, I don't know why it took so long?" I said, trying to get the measure of the man.

"I know you're kidding me, right?"

"Caught me!" I said, trying not to smile. "It really took us an hour and a half."

"No way, that's not possible," Henry said.

"You're right again, Henry. The real reason is a little embarrassing."

"How so?"

"They threw us out. They claimed I was wasting their time... That I was rude and argumentative. Can you believe the nerve of those people?" I said with a straight face.

Henry was dumbfounded. He didn't know whether to pursue his line of questioning, ask me to leave the property, or move on to the job of selling us a home in Bluffton Estates. I made the decision for him.

"So Henry, forget about those people. Can we get started on our tour now? It's 10:30 and we have to be in Savannah by lunchtime."

Inwardly, I laughed knowing Savannah was a thirty to forty-minute drive away, and if I wanted to be there by one o'clock the latest, Helen and me would only be able to spend about an hour and a half with Henry.

Stammering a little, Henry said, "We have twenty-eight models, three golf courses, a woodworking shop. There's also a model train building, thirty card rooms, and a seven hundred- seat performing arts theater.

"Is that all?" I asked.

He had to know I was yanking his chain.

"No, there are three indoor pools, forty tennis courts, and seven outdoor pools."

"Impressive!"

"Mr. Chandler."

"Call me Mike, please."

"Will do. So, Mike...how can you possibly see it all in such a short amount of time? I thought you'd be with me for the entire day, and maybe even tomorrow."

"Well, if you put it that way, I think we can manage an extra thirty minutes," I said with as much indifference in my voice as I could express.

It was bad timing on my part, because Helen rejoined us just as I was saying "an extra thirty minutes".

"What do you mean thirty minutes? We have to wait thirty minutes before we can start the tour?"

"No dear, Henry was just telling me of all the wonderful activities and facilities they have here, and I said I was mystified it would only take us an hour to see it all."

Henry's bottom jaw fell open. He stared uncomprehending at me, not having the slightest idea what to make of me.

"I suggest we don't waste any more time here eating cookies. There's so much to see, right Henry?"

"Yes there is, but can you stay for more than an hour?"

"Of course," I said, "What gave you the impression we were rushed for time. We'll be with you for as long as it takes."

13

LUCKY FOR HENRY, he didn't continue to question the veracity of my luncheon appointment, for if he had havoc would have rained down on him for the rest of the day.

"How many homes have already been sold?" Helen asked.

"We've sold thirty-six hundred homes, and currently we're building another nine hundred," Henry replied.

"You mean to tell me seven thousand people already live here?"

"Yup, that's the approximate number, give or take a few."

"Where are the homeowners from originally?" Helen asked.

"They came from all over the United States and a good number from Canada," Henry replied.

"Anyone from Utah or North Dakota?" I asked, not caring in the least what the answer would be.

"Could be," Henry replied, with a questioning look.

"So tell me, Henry, how can all the residents fit into the theater at one time? Wouldn't that be a fire hazard? Come to think of it, the liability insurance premium must be astronomical," I said.

Henry finally realized not to throw me a lob ball, or dangle the bait in front of me. He now understood: I'm an agitator of the first order.

"The residents here are small, so they usually share seats in the theater," he replied with a broad, knowing smile.

Well done, Henry! Fortunately for you, you didn't say "gotcha", because if you had the game would never end.

"Gentlemen, are you finished now? Because I'd like to see the models before the sun sets, if you don't mind."

The model homes were located on the street adjacent to the "Welcome Center". We walked to them—no need to take a car. And by lunchtime, we'd seen only half the models. Helen suggested we take Henry out to lunch so we could review all we'd seen. Being the big spender I am, I thought the salesman should pay, not the client, but I didn't object. However, if I was paying for this guy's lunch and he would benefit by earning a commission for selling us a home, I'd be damned if we were white table clothing it; assuming this area had restaurants with table cloths. Cheap fast food it would be. Fortunately, I knew from my research there was a McDonald's on the property.

"Henry, what do you say we take you out for lunch at Mickey D's?"

"That's very generous of you, but not necessary."

"I insist. It's our pleasure."

"Well never let it be said I turned down a free meal."

As we walked into McDonald's, I said to Henry, "Please order whatever you want; price is no object."

We each consumed a sumptuous meal comprised of Big Macs, fries, and coffee. Afterwards, we drove back to the Welcome Center (Pitti Palace) where Helen woofed down another three chocolate chip cookies. Her mouth was still full of cookie when I suggested to Henry that we forgo seeing the remaining models out of concern for Helen's feet.

What a caring husband I am.

Cookie flew out of her mouth as she voiced an immediate objection.

I think she said, though I wouldn't bet on it, "I didn't travel all this distance to let you cut this trip short, Mike!"

I took out my handkerchief, cleaned some chocolate chip residue from my face, then moistened a clean area of the handkerchief with some of my saliva and attempted to wipe some off Helen's lips and cheeks.

"Take that away from me. Stop doing that; you're not my mother," she protested, grabbing my hand and flinging it away from her face.

"I was just trying to help," I said.

"You'll help, if you stop trying to control me," she said, emphasizing the word "control".

"That's not my intention at all. I was only concerned you didn't know there were crumbs on your cheek."

She didn't believe me for one second. Was I that transparent?

Henry lowered his head, his eyes closed and his chin sank to his chest. I assume he was either embarrassed or pretended to be disinterested. Which one I couldn't tell. In any case, I quickly recovered from my premature charade of an excuse to escape the house tours and declared, "Henry, I'd like very much to see the model train building you mentioned. I'm thinking that could be a great hobby for me to consider learning about. I remember as a kid playing with my Lionel trains for hours on end. I imagine it really could be a lot of fun."

Helen wasn't fooled for a second. She knew I was blowing smoke up Henry's a…Her face portrayed her disbelief at my unashamed ploy, but her words never hinted that I was blatantly lying.

"Mike," she said. "Let's save the best for last and wait to see the train shop until after we've gone through the remaining models and other facilities. How's that for a plan?"

Wisely, Henry didn't put his two cents into the discussion; he waited to see how I would react to Helen's suggestion.

With a slight trace of optimism in my voice I said, "That works for me so long as we leave enough time for me to not rush through the shop."

Taking his clue from my perceived surrender, Henry resumed his quest to convince Helen that the Bluffton Estates fulfilled her every wish. As they walked through each of the homes, each of the rooms, and each of the massive walk-in closets, I followed behind… Not like a puppy dog trailing its master, but rather as a tiger waiting for the proper time to snare its prey.

It was a game of survival for me. To be most effective, I knew Helen had to think I was a beaten man being led to his slaughter. How and when I would be able to go on the offensive, I didn't know, but I was certain an opportunity would present itself, and I would—make no mistake—take full advantage of it.

"Mike, look at the size of this master closet; it's immense!" Helen screamed without realizing she had done so.

"It sure is, but it's barely big enough to accommodate all your black pants and shoes. Where are you going to hang the rest of your clothes? I mean, I can give up my portion of the closet and put my pair of jeans and sneakers in the laundry room, but what are you going to do?"

"This closet is larger than both of our walk-ins back in New Jersey," she replied.

"I suppose you're right."

"And Mike, I haven't even taken into account the fact that we won't be needing most of our winter clothes."

"Yeah that's true, providing you don't double up on warm weather outfits."

"Well now that you mention it, I might have to shop for some new ensembles."

"I'm sure you have more than enough clothes now to never have to wear the same ensemble more than once every two or three years. And that's a conservative estimate. Practically speaking, dear, we'd have to purchase a second home just to store your handbags, scarves and summer whites. Anyway, if an emergency situation did arise, we could visit the outlets in Savannah; they're only a short car ride away."

"Please don't get me going, Mike. I'm very careful not to buy anything I don't absolutely need."

"Oh yeah, you really needed those three new pairs of shoes because there's an infinitesimal recognizable difference between them in the shade of blue. I defy anyone to discern the difference… They're identical!"

I noticed that Henry clicked the top of the pen he held in his hand most every time Helen and I had one of our little tiffs. He must have been getting a bit antsy listening to our constant dribble and that was his way of not getting involved. His patience finally wore out because he tried to change the topic from closets and clothes to other features in the model he felt were positive selling points. He pointed with great pride to a small-hinged twelve by twelve-inch pass-thru doorway in the wall of the master closet.

"What the hell is that for?" I asked, really inquisitive as to what purpose it could possibly serve.

"On the other side of the pass-thru is the laundry room. If you disrobe in the closet, you can drop your clothes directly into a basket in the laundry room. No need to walk nude all the way around into the laundry room," Henry said with a smile like a father whose child just scored a soccer goal.

"For your information, Henry, when we're in the house we're nude all the time."

"Oh, Michael! What's wrong with you? Please ignore him, Henry…He gets this way after too much coffee."

"Come on, you two, put a little humor in your life."

I waited a few seconds for Helen to calm down and Henry to accept the fact that I was not a nudist.

"Henry, in all seriousness, this is the best, most exciting thing I've seen this entire trip. I mean it; I really do," I said.

Truthfully, this little door was amazing. I was impressed. And if nothing else came of this month-long exploration into the levels of Hades, I definitely planned to hire a carpenter to put one of those into any home I eventually bought.

"I haven't seen you this animated since you scored a hole in one fifteen years ago," Helen said.

"You're right about that, my dear."

Even Henry was taken aback by my positive reaction. He probably wondered whether he had broken through my defenses and would now be able to further entice me. If that was what he was thinking, I made short shrift of that when I asked him about the weather.

"Just how unbearable is the weather here in July?"

"Depends," he said.

"On what? The wind, the humidity, the heat? Or whether the air conditioning is working? Please Henry, I'm a big boy. Give it to me straight."

"Mike, do we have to do this now? We'll have time later to ask these questions," Helen said.

"Helen, the weather has a direct bearing on the number of times we'll have to change our clothes…and the laundry door might not be big enough to accommodate the sheer number of underpants and shirts we'll go through in a day."

"Henry, he's just joking with you again. Let's go on, shall we? I can't wait to see the 'Pines' model. I've heard so much about it from my friends who saw it when they were here last year."

"No, no, no, no, no. I'm really concerned with what the weather will be like. You know how uncomfortable we both get in warm, sticky, humid weather."

"Yes, I do Mike, but this is not the time to discuss it. I promise we'll talk about it later."

"Cross your heart; swear not to buy another pair of shoes for at least one month?"

"I do, I won't. I swear on the health of our grandchildren."

"Good!

"So Henry, where to next?"

"We can skip seeing the 'Moss' and 'Hilton' models and go directly to the 'Pines'," Henry said.

"Why would you do that, Henry?" I asked.

"Neither of those models has a laundry pass-thru," Henry replied with the biggest smile he could muster.

"Another point for your side Henry," I said, returning his smile with one of my own.

If you can believe it, the "Venetian" at La Palazzo was a shack compared to the "Pines". Architecturally the "Pines" was a replica of a pre-civil war Southern Plantation decorated to the nines in Ethan Alan traditional style furniture and fixtures. I envisioned Rhett Butler standing under the columns of Tara, holding Scarlett O'Hara in his arms and gazing deeply into her eyes.

I hadn't asked Henry once what the price was for any of the models he took us through, but I had to know what this elephant cost.

"Henry, what's the price for this baby?"

"Without any upgrades, it's three hundred and ninety-eight thousand dollars. If we include the deluxe package, you get granite kitchen countertops, a mosaic tile backsplash, and foundation planting. We also give you Wolf and Sub-Zero appliances; a marble walk-in master shower with spa showerheads on two opposing walls; heated towel racks and flooring in the master bathroom; plus nine-foot ceilings with eight-inch crown molding, and recessed lighting throughout the entire house. You get all that and probably some other things I left out, for only an additional seventy thousand dollars. Add another forty thousand if you want to be on one of the golf courses."

"Does the price include his and her bidets?"

"Yes Mike, it does," he said, waving his hand in a dismissive manner. "And if you buy today the builder will include a one-year golf club membership and waive all closing fees."

"Will the builder give us a Confederate flag to hang out on Robert E. Lee's birthday?" I asked.

"Most certainly. I'll even come over and put it up for you," Henry responded in a tone I thought was just a trifle too agreeable.

Maybe this guys a Rebel yearning for the South to rise again? I sure hope I misinterpreted his eager response.

Helen had had enough, from her exaggerated deep breaths to her head shaking sideways, her displeasure and impatience were quite apparent.

"Gentlemen," she said cutting off Henry in mid-sentence, her hands on her hips, her posture defiant. "If it's not too much of a bother, can we dispense with the jokes so Henry can show us through the rest of this beautiful house?"

"Before going any further, I've got just two more questions we really need answers to."

Helen took a deep breath. "Okay Mike, what are your questions? Ask them now, please."

"What are the yearly taxes, and what's the square footage of this baby?"

Helen was surprised by the substantive essence of my questions . . . Truth be told, so was I.

"Your taxes will be approximately twenty-five hundred dollars per year. That includes state and local real estate taxes, and school taxes. Also, when you calculate your costs, consider South Carolina's personal income tax rate is one of the lowest in the entire country."

"Can't be," I said.

"That's what it is. And that's just one of the reasons Bluffton Estates is such an attractive draw for retirees from high tax states such as New Jersey. Mike, your money goes a lot farther.

"And the answer to your second question is, that the 'Pines' is four thousand nine hundred square feet of one floor living space."

"Wow. All kidding aside, Henry, why would a couple of retirees like us, living alone need or want such a large home? This place has three and one half full bathrooms, a kitchen larger than most restaurants have, and a three-car garage with space for a golf cart. The people who buy the 'Pines' must spend their time eating and defecating twenty-four seven. When can they play golf, or re-lay model train tracks?" I asked with a deadpan expression on my face, portraying no hint of humor.

Henry must be a politician when he's not selling homes, because he deflected most of my barbs and zeroed in on Helen's weak underbelly: the kids.

"It's really not that big when you consider it has only three bedrooms. You'll need that many when your children and grand-children come to visit," Henry said.

"Henry's right, Mike; we'll need those rooms for the family when they come down for vacation."

"Hold on. That could be true if they came to visit on a regular basis. But considering how long it takes to get here, the cost of airfare; then factor in their school schedules, it's unlikely those bedrooms will be used more than once or twice a year. Anyhow, you're making quite an assumption when you think our children will want to vacation with us. If I were them, I'd go out west to ski in the winter, or fly to Hawaii and bathe in the surf of the Pacific. Hawaii's more exotic and more exciting than Florida. We'll be lucky if they came here at all," I said.

"What about during the summer?" Helen protested.

"What about the summer, Henry? What's the average temperature here in July and August? And what about the humidity level? From what I've heard from friends who live here, they can't even go outside during the summer it's so unbearably hot and humid. And Helen, don't forget the kids go to camp for most of the summer. They'll never have time to visit."

"Mike, please don't start with that again. It's getting late and I want to see the rest of the Estates.

"I still want an answer about the weather here during the summer months," I protested.

For whatever reason, Helen wasn't interested in hearing Henry's response…I could have insisted, but I didn't. I decided to defer pushing the subject until a more opportune time presented itself. In any case, Helen took Henry by the arm and said, "Henry, can you take us to see the club rooms and the other facilities now?"

"Sure," he replied. "Why don't we walk back to the Welcome Center and pick up my car and then I can drive you around?"

14

W E WALKED TO Henry's car. I debated whether or not I should drive or follow Henry in my car. If I took my car I reasoned, I could, in the event I chose to bail out and leave, do so without being dependent upon Henry to drive us back to our own car. Once again, I weighed Helen's expected negative reaction to my suggestion against the inevitable spat that would ensue...Henry's car it would be. On the positive side, I could sit in the back seat and easily place a rope around Henry's neck and choke him to death; or I could voice my opinions without fear of Helen physically ramming her elbow into my side.

"Okay Henry, the gas expense is on you. Just make sure you have enough Freon in the air conditioner. We wouldn't want Helen suffering from heat prostration, would we?"

They both ignored me...again.

Our first stop was the seven hundred-seat auditorium/theater. In all honesty it was very impressive. From the lobby to the professional computerized lighting board. They didn't miss a trick. It was first class all the way. I counted no less than thirty gray heads busily constructing, painting, or assembling sets for their upcoming production of *Hair*.

"The theater group has close to two hundred members," Henry said smugly as if he were a member of the troupe.

"That's a pretty big cast even for a major Broadway production," I said.

"No, no. The whole group doesn't act; some construct the sets, others do props, lighting, marketing, or ticket sales. They have volunteers for every job that has to be done. It's a big deal putting on one of their productions," he replied.

"I can't wait to see their version of *Hair*. Do you think they'll actually do the nude scene? Man alive, wouldn't that be something to tell the grandkids about? Better still, can you imagine them or our grown children seeing eighty-year-old bodies in all their glory?"

I couldn't shake the image of nude seventy/eighty year olds strutting their sagging stuff on stage. The thought of it was quite disturbing to my delicate mind. Talk about a horror show. Frightening!

"Mike, put a lid on it! Comments like that are childish and unwanted," Helen, her face close to mine, pleaded in a low but stern voice hoping Henry couldn't hear.

"All kidding aside, Henry, this place is beautiful. I'm impressed," I said, anxious to move on. Where to next?"

"Your choice," he said. "Do you want to see the woodshop first or the model trains?"

"No pun intended, but we're somewhat off track. Are you trying to derail me from talking about the weather?"

"That would be the furthest thing from my mind," Henry said. "No kidding, Mike...kudos on your comedic use of the English language. I'm really enjoying your attempt at humor."

"ATTEMPT! You've got some nerve. Well, so be it then," I said. "Off to the woodshop."

We drove at least three-quarters of a mile to get to the wood-shop. The building was huge. It looked like one of those factories you see in industrial parks throughout the country. The place had to be at least fifteen thousand square feet. Inside there were four rows of six large worktables. On top of each of these workbenches were drills, electric radial saws, handsaws hack saws, files of every size, screwdrivers, vices, you name the tool…they had it. I'd never seen anything like it in my entire life. The cherry on top of the cake was the exhaust vacuum tubing system designed to remove any sawdust from the air hanging over every table. On one end of the building was a massive locked gated area overflowing with abundant quantities of an equally large assortment of different types of woods, including Brazilian, Mahogany, and Teak. They had a storage room the envy of Home Depot, stocked with every conceivable hand or electric woodworking tool a person might conceivably need. I counted at least forty men and women either actively working on projects, helping one another carry equipment, or just socializing.

"Tell me Henry, why do they need such a large building and so much high-tech equipment to make salad bowls? It seems a trifle over the top, don't you think?"

"Actually, it doesn't cost that much to operate considering what the builder initially contributed. Couple that with the small annual dues shop members pay, and money these folks make on custom orders, it equates to a very manageable expense budget."

"Custom orders? Are there that many deaths in Bluffton Estates?" I asked.

"What does that have to do with anything?" Helen replied.

"It means the life expectancy for those living in Bluffton Estates is not too good because this shop is obviously making custom caskets for all the residents that die here. That's the only way they could make enough money to cover the overhead of maintaining this place."

Even Henry laughed at my comment. Hell, I was impressed by my quick wit.

"Ignore him, Henry. The Big Mac must have disagreed with him."

"Mike, for your information residents throughout Beaufort County contract with the shop for custom built furniture, as well as for a significant amount of furniture restoration. And for your information…those wooden serving bowls sell like hot cakes at the weekly flea market on Hilton Head Island."

"Well tar my feathers, I'll be darned," I replied in my most affected southern twang drawl.

"Henry, can we just take a quick look at the card rooms and social halls?" Helen asked.

Down the road apiece was a one-story red brick building, with large ceiling to floor windows dominating the entire front of the facility. One could easily mistake the place for a small strip mall. It housed a combination of endless card tables filled with literally hundreds of women playing canasta, mahjong, bridge, and a game sounding much like a disease. Off to the side, in a secluded area, were the poker and pinochle rooms filled to overflowing with men obviously too old for golf or tennis. Actually, these guys would have a hard time playing bocce or shuffleboard, two of the most exhausting strenuous physical exercises south of the Mason Dixon Line.

Truth be told, I too would enjoy an afternoon out of the sun and away from the little women, playing cards with the "boys".

"Snap out of it Mike," my little shoulder pal said. *"You're falling into a trap."*

"Mrs. Chandler, do you play any of these games?" Henry asked.

"All of them except that foot game, but I'm sure if they showed me, I could learn very quickly."

"I think it's a simpler version of canasta, and I believe it's called 'Hand 'n' Foot'," Henry volunteered.

Not wanting to be left out of the conversation I offered my two cents. "I thought it was called 'Hoof and Mouth'."

"Well, since I already know how to play canasta, it should be easy enough for me to learn," she said.

"Sounds like a lot of fun to me, Helen," I offered with as much sincerity in my voice as I could muster.

She just rolled her eyes. "You really are such a child."

I didn't wait for her to ask to see the glass and jewelry workshops, or for Henry to suggest we look at each of the outdoor swimming pools. I quickly jumped into the void.

"What do you say, Henry? Take us to the train on time? TOOT, TOOT!" I said as I mimicked pulling an imaginary cord for a train's horn.

"I assume you're ready to see the train house now, Mike?"

"You betcha Henry. Lead on McDuff."

After another short car ride through one of the many sub-division communities within Bluffton Estates, we parked in front of a modest Low Country style brick building that housed the train club.

Three grown men wearing engineer caps, overalls, and work boots greeted us at the entrance under an imposing sign that read,

"Bluffton Train Depot." Each of these guys wore an ID badge stating their name and rank within the club.

John, whose badge was prominently displayed on his left breast pocket and which identified him as Chief Engineer extended his hand to Helen. "I'm John. Welcome to our depot. I'm going to be your personal tour guide today. Did you buy your tickets yet? The train's leaving in three minutes."

"We didn't realize tickets were required," I said. "Do you have to punch them?"

"No, I'm only kidding. We don't charge visitors."

"Thank goodness for that; we left our money back at the hotel."

John must have appreciated my humor because he fake-punched me in the gut. I returned the favor, doubling over, grabbing my stomach with both hands and moaning in pain. Helen, who was looking at the train display case at the time, and did not see what was going on, reacted to the sound of distress. "Mike what's wrong?"

"Nothing that a visit to the hospital won't cure."

"They're only playing. Mike's not hurt," Henry told Helen.

"I'm fine Helen...really."

"Don't do that again. You had me worried."

"Promise. I'll keep John at arm's length."

John belly laughed. He was a bundle of joy. I liked him.

"Follow me. But just one word of caution: don't touch the third rail."

John led the way, giddy at the prospect of showing us his domain.

Once inside the main showroom it was obvious these men were serious about what they were doing. Beyond the massive rows of glass-enclosed display cabinets housing thousands of antique train cars, were literally hundreds of miles of miniature track laid over hand-made constructed representations of towns, mountain passes, cities, trees, animals, buildings, etc. Situated in the middle of each unit was a control panel where a member of the club stood, of course in uniform, running the trains. Their faces looked as if they were in a trance, hypnotized by the memory of their youth, a dream come true. They were now the "engineers" they'd always wanted to be, averting a terrible crash, or challenging a sharp S-turn on a mountain pass. For me, it was solely a fond memory of playing with my Lionel Trains in my living room. It had been fun then for a few hours at the most, but I couldn't fathom how these men could spend hours on end, day-in, day-out, "playing". It was beyond me.

As much as I could have wise-cracked and made repugnant comments, I didn't. No, I wasn't getting soft or surrendering to my fate. Nothing, I reasoned, would be gained by insulting these men. They were serious collectors as witnessed by the hundreds of classic model trains they displayed behind locked glass cabinets lining the full length of the thirty-foot-long walls surrounding the entrance lobby. Hell, these guys were shrewd investors; their trains were worth a bloody fortune.

After twenty minutes observing and listening to those guys express their passion for their hobby, we thanked John and his crew for their time and courtesy and bid our fond *adieus*.

"Guess that's it, Henry. Can you take us back to our car so we can make it to Savannah before the New Year?"

"Mike, I thought we could go back to the sales center for a little bit before you took off, so I can go over what we saw, and allow me to show how little it will take to get you to buy here."

"Get me to buy here! To get me to buy here, Henry, would take a neurosurgeon administering shock therapy on me while I was awake. Nothing personal, but after all my comments, can you seriously think Bluffton Estates is for me?"

"Mike, I'd like to see what Henry wants to show us. Please temper your humorless retorts," Helen said in a tone lacking any trace of humor.

"How long do you think this'll take, Henry?" she asked.

"Less than an hour," he replied.

Frustrated by what I'd have to endure, I threw my arms up in the air, signifying surrender, and said, "Good, let's get it over with."

Once back in his office, the first thing Henry did was to offer us more cookies and coffee, which thankfully this time Helen declined. Then without missing a beat he got down to brass tacks.

"Which model most interests you, Helen?" he asked.

"'The Low Country'," she said without hesitating.

"Good choice. It's probably the most popular style we have," Henry added.

"Are you thinking about any upgrades or simply the base offering?"

Hoping to derail the freight train before it picked up steam, I interjected. "I want to go first class all the way; from every top of the line appliance to the custom bathroom; of course without the Jacuzzi and bidet. Don't forget to include the premium tree and plant package. And if the right view is available, I'd also want to be on the golf course."

Henry's eyes almost popped out of his head when he heard my request. No doubt he was calculating what his commission would be. But I couldn't imagine he had any idea I was maneuvering him into quoting me a price well above what Helen wanted to spend. Helen was caught off guard. Her face was a mask of confusion. The lines on her forehead deepened, her lips puckered, the look in her eyes was disbelieving. She wasn't sure what I was up to.

"Give me a couple of minutes to add it all up," Henry said.

"Make sure you include the closing costs, and what the estimated local, state, and school taxes will be."

"I'll list them separately, if that's alright?"

He probably wanted to do that so that if the price was higher than we were willing to pay, Helen could eliminate specific items without the need to redo the entire worksheet and still keep us in the ballgame.

"Sure thing," I said. "Oh, while you're at it, Henry, please calculate how long it will take to build the house."

Henry left us sitting in the waiting room. He walked through the huge brass doors into his office with the biggest shit-eating grin you could imagine. Once there, he opened his laptop, pulled up the canned sales cost program, entered some data and made some notes on a spreadsheet. It took him about fifteen minutes to complete his entries and generate a report. He came back to us carrying three professionally bound four-color reports, replete with pie charts and graphs. He gave each of us a copy.

"Pretty impressive," I said, not even opening my copy yet.

"Why don't we go over it together?" Henry suggested.

"Take it away Henry," I said.

"On page..." Henry started to say before I interrupted him.

Without the slightest trace of irony in my voice, I said, "Excuse me Henry, before you start can you please print out from Google or wherever, a chart of the yearly weather for this area? You know: temperature, rainfall, humidity, hurricanes, etc., things like that."

Thought I forgot about it didn't you?

Hesitating, he said, "Oookay, yes, uh, definitely."

Back into his office and back on the computer he went. This time there was no smile on his face.

"Why don't you take us through the reports now, Henry. Start wherever you want."

Decision time for Henry…Take the bullet now and discuss the oppressive five months of hot humid weather and risk scuttling the deal right away, or first try to reel us in with enticing low costs and hope that economics outweigh a senior's dependency for survival on twenty-four seven air conditioning.

His choice was obvious.

"Please open the report to the diagram on page two," he said.

It took us a good thirty minutes to go over the report. Damn it, Henry answered every single question I asked no matter how insignificant or ridiculous.

"As much as it pains me to do so I must say the cost of buying 'The Low Country' together with the unbelievably low income and property taxes is well worth the investment. I don't know how the builder or the State of South Carolina can afford to do the things they do for so little money."

Helen nearly collapsed. I mean it. Her body was literally teetering to such an extent she almost fell off her seat. She was flabbergasted by my comment. Her mouth opened wide…Her lips moved, but no sound came out.

"Are you okay? You look like you're seeing a ghost," I said, reaching out to hold her arm.

"I think I'm okay, but that depends on if you're being honest, or just trying to be cute. If you're serious, I most definitely want to buy a house right now."

"I meant every word I said, Helen. But, and a big but it is Henry..."

"But what?" both Helen and Henry asked simultaneously.

"The weather," I said. "Henry, please show us the report you downloaded from the US Weather Bureau."

The look on Henry's face was enough to tell me he saw his huge commission going down the drain. Unfortunately for him, he wasn't wrong.

Helen and I both read the statistics. To put it mildly, they were harsh. Four to five months of eighty-seven plus-degree days with humidity indexes close to eighty percent. Add to that, that annually, Hilton Head coastal communities of South Carolina experience several hurricanes or hurricane-like weather systems.

Helen was not a fan of extreme weather, whether hot or cold. Daily, she had a hard enough time coping with her own hormonal cycles that affected her comfort levels. Putting on a sweater...taking off a sweater... taking off a shirt...dabbing her face with tissues...re-applying her makeup. It drove her crazy.

"Henry, give us a few minutes alone, please," I asked.

Once he left, I explained to Helen why I was so anxious to get the weather issue out of the way upfront. She agreed with me, even admitting that if we had done so we could have saved a lot of time and disappointment.

"Mike, you were right, I should have listened to you and not assumed you were just being your typical troublemaker self."

"Thank you for your honesty, my dear."

"In the future, can you give me a heads-up when you're bullshitting by scratching your nose first?"

"What if it really itches?"

"Don't scratch it then…So what do we tell Henry?" she asked.

"The truth: that neither of us can physically handle the weather here. I'm sure he'll be disappointed, but he'll understand. Besides, we can't be the first couple to reject Bluffton Estates because of the climate."

"I suppose you're right."

"Of course, I'm right. I always am. How can you ever question my wisdom?" I said, my tongue bulging out the side of my cheek.

Small miracles do happen. Helen actually kissed my cheek and thanked me again. And for my part, being the magnanimous person I am, I said, "Coming here was very valuable for us. We saw how one of these retirement communities should be organized, and how many activities there are for us to partake in. Now we even know what design options are available for us to think about if we're ever forced to buy one of these units and have to furnish it. And, my dear, that's all because you dragged me through all twenty-eight models. How can I ever thank you?"

"Seriously?"

"Of course. I'm not scratching my nose, am I?...You name it. Sky's the limit."

"Well then, you can buy me a good old-fashioned southern dinner when we get to Savannah."

"Deal."

We thanked Henry for his time, information, and chocolate chip cookies. Then we said our goodbyes to the rest of the staff.

For the record, Henry should get an Oscar. He must have been disappointed after spending so much time with us and not closing a sale, but he didn't show it. No sour grapes. No dismissive attitude. He only expressed words of understanding for our objection to the weather, and his thanks for visiting their community. He even smiled when I asked him to reimburse me for his Big Mac and fries.

15

I T TOOK US forty-five minutes to drive from Bluffton Estates to our hotel overlooking the Savannah River, in Savannah Georgia. We decided to forgo showering; instead we unpacked and then immediately left the room to take a short tour along the popular River Walk.

Just my luck, standing outside the first store we passed was a very charismatic sales associate handing out samples of Savannah's world-famous pralines. These three-inch diameter pancake shaped gifts from the Gods packed a whopping four hundred and fifty calories each. Their combination of molasses, heavy cream, and pecans was too much for a man with no willpower to ignore. I ingested two more of those epicurean treasures while waiting in line to pay for a box of twenty-four, just in case I experienced some hunger pains on the car ride to Florida.

Who the hell wants to eat grits and fried chicken when I could pig out on pralines?

By the time we got back to the room, we were dripping wet with sweat from walking along the waterfront. The humidity level had to be over ninety. We had only twenty minutes to get to the restaurant on time to make our reservation so we quickly showered and dressed. No cabs were available outside the hotel, and no air-conditioned buses went anywhere near the restaurant we had to get to. So, lucky us, we could again enjoy the experience of walking the streets of Savannah and avail ourselves of Georgia's temperate climate. Our leisure walk felt more like we were trapped pacing back and forth in a steam bath, but without the availability of a cold towel to reduce our body heat to a bearable level. For the life of me I couldn't imagine how people could function in such an unwelcoming climate. Consider the economics of having to pay the water bill for the countless number of showers we would need to survive, and the cost of replacing all the perspiration-stained clothes we would have to throw out. The cost would require me to go back to work to pay for it all...So much for retirement!

Yup, this place is definitely for me.

Helen however, who tries to see some redeeming quality in everything and everybody, said, "This climate is wonderful for my skin."

Ying/ yang...I say black, she says white. I say sex, she ignores.

Our dinner reservations were for 9:00 p.m. at the Captain's Table, a tourist trap of the first order a few blocks off the Savannah River. The service was average, the décor looked like the set from a grade C film, and the greasy food screamed out "Beware the calories and fat!"

Just as we were finishing, the waitress realized she hadn't asked if we were enjoying our meal. And when she finally did, I replied, "It's difficult for me to say because the food was constantly slipping off the plate so I didn't have a chance to sample the fried pig feet, pork, ribs, or okra."

"Are you joking?" she asked.

Being the gentleman I am, I said, "Truthfully, my stomach hasn't been itself lately. I only tasted the soup."

"I'm so sorry," the waitress said. "Can I get you anything else?"

"No need, I wasn't hungry anyway. Just let us have the check please."

When she came back with the bill, I asked her to ask the receptionist to call us a cab to take us back to the hotel.

"I must say, Mike, I was impressed by the way you spoke to the waitress. Not even an insult. Are you feeling alright?"

"Yes, dear, I am. Now what do you say we get out of here, go back to the hotel, take off our clothes, turn up the air conditioning, turn off the lights and uh…then get a good night's sleep?"

That's exactly what we did. Helen showered and by the time I finished my shower and got into bed, she was sound asleep.

I was actually hallucinating Helen was waiting for me!

16

WE CHECKED-OUT OF our hotel right after consuming a healthy breakfast of grits, corn bread smothered in chipped creamed beef sauce (SOS), bacon, sausage, egg omelets, and three cups of high test.

If we had spent another few days in Georgia, I'd have had to check myself into a hospital for an arterial ream job.

"There it is," Helen said, "US 95!"

"So which way do you want me to go? North or south?"

"You know very well we're going south. Don't get off on the wrong foot today, wise guy."

"How dare you! I'm confused. I guess the heat's finally gotten to me."

"Yeah, sure it has."

"No, really it has. I haven't felt this light headed since, oh... right before our marriage ceremony."

"What did you say?"

"I'm kidding; I'm only kidding."

Quiet...Keep quiet...Don't respond.

Several hours of driving later we stopped in Jacksonville for lunch. Why, I have no idea! Especially since the "lowlands cuisine" we ate refused to be fully digested and sat like a festering caldron of gaseous debris of unrest in both our guts. Hence, during the car ride to Ocala, the car windows were open longer than they were closed.

"Excuse me dear, you might want to open the window," was the refrain alternately from each of us. Eating dinner that night was definitely out of the question.

It took us a little more than five and one half hours to reach Ocala, or as native Floridians refer to it, "The Villages—death's geriatric tanning parlor." The Villages by no one's definition could, in a real sense, fit the description of a village. How could it when over one hundred thousand senior citizens are slowly, and in some cases rapidly, decaying both mentally and physically within the confines of a modern day "company owned town"?

This southern magnet has attracted a significant number of America's senior citizens who yearn for a fountain of youth; who desperately desire to spend the twilight of their years actively (I'm really stretching the meaning of the word active), playing golf (in a cart and rarely walking), competing in contact bocce, pushing the mahjong tiles, laying down the dummy in contract bridge, lifting the cards in canasta, or pretending to exert themselves in pool aerobics. It's exhausting. You get the point. Don't get me wrong though: there are many who do play baseball, tennis, pickleball, bike, hike, and participate in other aerobic exercises. I suspect for those hearty folks, it's just an escape to get away from the house for a couple of hours.

By and far the most popular past time, however, is eating. You know what happens…During breakfast the conversation is where are we going to have lunch? And at lunch the discussion centers on making reservations for dinner. Then the real debate ensues. What kind of food are we going to eat and where? Will it be seafood, ethnic, or ribs? Enough said.

The Villages promises a fulfilling social life, free of stress, and worry; a cultural enrichment...a vacation for the rest of your life. That is, of course, if you have time in between the daily visits to the vast array of medical specialists you have to see. Not only do you visit these doctors for your own needs, but also you must accompany your spouse whenever they have an appointment. Yes, this is the life we've been searching for. We've made it!

Ah, please forgive me. I've neglected to explain the requirements for seeing The Villages. First of all, understand if you want to get the full picture and immerse yourself in the swing of things, you must stay (rent) a "prospective buyer's home" for four nights. With that, you're given a golf cart for your personal use during your stay, an escorted tour guide, and freebees up the wazoo. Of course, you can stay in a hotel outside The Villages and spend less time exploring, BUT no golf cart for you!

How do I know this, you ask? Well, when I called The Villages asking for information, I was greeted on the phone by Austin saying, "It's a beautiful day here at The Villages."

I knew immediately the bullshit was about to fly. How could I make such a rash assumption? Easy: The Weather Channel was at that very moment describing the torrential rains devastating Central Florida for the past week.

I explained to Austin we were thinking of purchasing a retirement home in Florida and wanted to consider whether The Villages was the place for us. I told him we were willing to spend two or three days at the most at The Villages. He told me we'd have to stay four nights in order to take full advantage of their get acquainted program and benefit from their give-a-ways. I reiterated our desire to limit the visit to no more than three days. Austin was equally insistent we extend the time…an impasse. I thanked him and told him if we were interested in accepting his offer, I'd get back to him.

We opted to forgo the golf cart, free golf, a few meals on the house, and sleeping in one of their houses. Instead, we chose to rent a hotel room less than a mile away for two nights. This way we could make our own determination as to what to do and see and schedule our own time, and not be handicapped or obligated by what time frames the guide might impose upon us.

17

WE CHECKED INTO our typical non-descript hotel room, unpacked, got into bed and turned on the TV. We were exhausted by the long drive from Savannah. For some reason, for as long as I can remember, the melodious sounds of the TV always put me to sleep. Helen usually reads long after I fall asleep and is the one who turns off the "telly".

The alarm woke us just before 8:00 the next morning. We showered and dressed in our finest vacation ensembles. Helen went nuts when she saw I had put on a pair of white loafers.

"What are you wearing?" she said.

"What do you mean, what am I wearing?"

"You can't wear white shoes; it's after Labor Day. Honestly, don't you know anything?"

"You're not being serious, are you?"

"I most certainly am. I refuse to be embarrassed by your lack of common dress sense." "Don't take this the wrong way, but if the fashion police ticket me, will you bail me out of jail?"

"Just take them off and put on a pair of sneakers."

"Are white sneakers acceptable?"

"Yes."

"Then, what's the difference between white sneakers and white loafers?" I demanded to know.

"Please just do what I'm asking."

Sorry for repeating myself so often, but you can't make this stuff up.

Swallowing hard, I took off the white loafers…put on a pair of black loafers, changed into Bermuda shorts, and put on high black knee socks folded over at the top. I only wished I also had a plastic pen holder to put in my chest pocket, and a pair of masking tape-wrapped glasses to wear.

"I'm not leaving this room until you take off that hideous outfit," Helen whined.

"What's wrong, darling? Am I not suitably dressed to be seen walking in The Villages?"

"Mike, I'm going down for breakfast. If you want to join me, you'll reconsider your choice of dress. If not…"

Once again, I yielded. There's no way I can ever win, but I'll keep trying because I love the game.

We finished an unappetizing meal of powdered eggs, cold stale bacon, frozen and then lightly heated rolls, and heavily diluted watered-down coffee. A guest who had just come into the dining area looked at my screwed-up facial expression as I forced the food into my mouth. He came over to me and asked if the food was as bad as I was making it out to be.

I pointed to the door and said, "Save yourself!"

As we were leaving the hotel's restaurant, I put my hand down the back of Helen's blouse and pulled out the label so that it was readily visible to anyone seeing her from behind. Then I looked to see what shoes she had on, and by some stroke of luck she was already wearing a pair of gold sandals.

Helen pulled back abruptly then whirled around to face me. "And just what do you think you're doing?"

I smiled broadly and said, "Just making sure your label is showing and that you're wearing gold shoes."

"Mike, are you completely out of your mind? Stop this nonsense and put the label back where it belongs."

"Are you sure that's what you want?" I asked.

"Definitely! And why in God's name did you pull it out in the first place?"

"Come on, you know why I did it…Stop playing the innocent little girl."

"Either you tell me what the hell's going on or I'm taking you to the hospital emergency room, stat! You've lost it. You're scaring me, Mike; you really are."

"Helen, you honestly don't know about the 'I'm available' signal they use at The Villages?"

"I'm available? For what?"

"For SEX. Take me now; I'm ready, willing and able. It's their code for, you know…mufkie-pufkie. Be truthful…you hadn't heard about it before?"

"Mike!"

"I'm deadly serious. That's what goes on down here. Why do you think The Villages has the highest incidence of STDs of any community in the country?"

"What are STDs again?"

"They're sexually transmitted diseases," I said, not willing to accept Helen's isolation from the real world.

How could she forget the meaning of STDs? Are men and women that different, or is it just my wife? Amazing.

"Do you really expect me to believe men and women of our age are so sex crazed that they behave so childishly?"

"First of all, it's not childish and secondly I'm not making it up. I'm only repeating what I've heard a hundred times about this place. In fact, I read about the STD phenomena in *The New York Times*. It's possible, but I can't be certain, I might have seen a segment devoted to the subject on *60 Minutes*.

"If that's the case, don't you think you should have told me about this before now? If I'd known about this, I wouldn't have even considered coming here."

"I did tell you, but you obviously chose to ignore my pleadings."

"If memory serves me correctly, you only indicated that STDs are common in retirement communities. You never specified The Villages."

"What difference does it make? No one's forcing anybody to participate in the mating ritual. Let people do whatever they want so long as it doesn't interfere with our lives. Personally, I think it's rather refreshing. It demonstrates to me that at least some of the residents here are enjoying themselves. By the way, I'm hoping The Villages also have one of those 'Key Clubs'."

Helen gave me her classic deep breathed, squinted eyed look of disgust. I'd reached another low point in her opinion.

"We're here, we've paid for the hotel, so let's make the best of it. Remember you're the one who insisted on seeing The Villages. Keep an open mind, Helen. I know I always do."

"You're some character. You never cease to surprise me, Michael."

She called me Michael? This isn't good.

18

I COULDN'T HAVE BEEN more depressed. The Villages was not what I expected or hoped to find. Aside from the location in the middle of nowhere—and I mean nowhere—it was as close to the perfect retirement destination as I could imagine. The choice of housing was infinite as were the prices. They had everything a man could think of, want, or need; from limitless free golf, a multitude of softball fields and pickleball courts, to countless shuffle board and tennis courts. If you wanted to learn karate, they also had classes for that too. Restaurants were everywhere. They had furniture stores, grocery stores, and golf cart customization shops. There would never be a need to leave The Villages. Your every wish and then some would be catered to. They even provided thirty-five daily scheduled bus trips to Orlando Airport. And to top that off, they operated a state-of-the art, three hundred bed hospital with free concierge medicine provided for the entire population of one hundred and thirty thousand residents.

And with all those glorious benefits I was still reluctant to move there. Once again, I was plagued by the thought of enduring oppressive humidity and frequent one hundred-degree temperatures four months a year. Add to that the forced separation from MY GRANDCHILDREN. No matter how wonderful it would be for me to spend the rest of my life enjoying The Villages, I simply could not conceive of being so far removed from my family. End of discussion, no debate necessary!

We had been out all day: we went on an organized bus tour of The Villages, sampled the food at so many restaurants I don't want to even remember how many, and walked for hours on end. Once back in our hotel room, I stripped out of my geek outfit, including the white sneakers, and flopped down on the bed. Helen was giddy, beaming from cheek to cheek, and practically running in place as if she'd won a free one-day shopping spree in Neiman Marcus.

"Mike, isn't this place just...just awesome? I can't get over how many women's activities they have. Did you see the monthly Activity Newspaper they publish? It has over six hundred clubs listed. If I wanted to, I'd be able to play mahjong from morning till night three hundred and sixty-five days per year. You'll never see me except for meals."

Wow, never thought of that! That alone could be reason enough to seriously consider moving here. That is unless there is some dramatic change in her appetite for intimacy.

"I'll be so tired after playing golf all day followed by downing a few brewskies at the clubhouse; then taking a quick dip in the pool, that against all odds, I probably could come to grips with not being with you as much as I would want."

"Come to grips with. And what's that supposed to imply?"

"I meant to say, you wouldn't realize we weren't spending so much quality time together since we were otherwise so busy enjoying ourselves. On the bright side, we'd still be able to occasionally enjoy cozy breakfasts together, providing of course...I don't have an early tee time."

Shocking...Helen totally ignored me...again.

"Let's setup an appointment for tomorrow morning to see some of the models. I'm really serious about moving here...aren't you?"

Silence. I just stared at her, not blinking. What I couldn't control was the sudden involuntary contraction of my cheek muscles. My face must have looked like a demented killer about to explode, or heaven forbid, as though I were displaying signs of the onset of Bell's Palsy.

"Mike...snap out of it. Are you with me? Wouldn't that be grand?"

Summoning all my tactful husbandly skills, honed over years of marriage, I replied, "Yes darling, let's do just that. Whatever your little heart desires."

"That really pleases me, Mike, it does."

We spent the following day chaperoned by our personal "corporate" sales agent, Sally Finnegan, touring the three main communities (towns) comprising The Villages. Each town had its own multitude of restaurants, stores, and a Planet Fitness type gym. Nightly concerts were presented in the central squares of all three "towns". They had cinemas offering first run movies every day, and big-name entertainers performed weekly in three separate eight hundred-seat theaters.

The Villages occupy a vast geographic expanse of land. It took us thirty-five minutes to drive end to end...It's BIG...It dwarfs anything we had seen or could imagine. We visited at least thirty home styles, explored each of their three massive recreation centers, and three "private" Golf Clubs.

No community we had seen could compare. The variety of styles and options offered fulfilled every need one could conceive. For instance, if I wanted a mansion with five bedrooms, Ionic pillars around the front door, an Olympic size pool, and a five hundred square foot lanai, they would build it…I'd have to pay for it, but they would build it. Or on the other end of the spectrum, I could opt for an attached villa with one or two bedrooms. The choices were mine to make.

I won't bore you with the finite details, but take my word for it…You want it…they have it…plus more than you could imagine.

Sally was particularly proud of their ambulance service, citing statistics reflecting a response time of less than six minutes per call.

"That's unbelievable, Sally. How can they be so efficient?" I asked.

"We have four fully equipped facilities strategically situated around The Villages," she said.

"How many times a day are they called?"

"I don't know the daily usage, but I've been told the annual figure is over ten thousand."

"Ten thousand! If that's the case, how does anyone get any sleep with the sirens blaring all the time?"

"To the best of my knowledge, no one has complained."

"Maybe that's because they take their hearing aids out at night."

"Can we end this discussion, Mike? Personally, I'm grateful for their thoughtfulness in having such a valuable service for the residents," Helen said.

I shrugged my shoulders, again realizing I was getting nowhere. "I guess you're right, Sally. What else is on your mind?"

Not once did Sally try to pressure us into a decision. She knew they had the gold standard product; no need for her to force the issue. After all, they were selling over four hundred homes per month without us. Astounding! The ball was in our court.

Sally gave us her business card and said that if we decided to buy at The Villages while we were here, she was available the next day to effectuate the sale. Otherwise she would await hearing from us if and when we chose to move forward.

We both thanked her. I told her we would seriously consider buying, but that in all likelihood the final decision would not be made for several weeks, if not months. Helen promised to keep in touch.

While I was walking and Helen was floating back to our car, I said, "Let's put off any decision until we've seen what the rest of Florida has to offer. We're only on chapter eighteen, I want to read all fifty chapters before making such a monumental decision."

Helen had no self-restraint. If she had had a facelift, the pressure of smiling would have ruptured the taut skin masking the sagging underbelly of gravity. She was beaming from ear to ear. Then, in a tone similar to a toddler begging for a toy, she said, "Do we have to wait? I'm ready to move here tomorrow."

"As much as I want to say yes, I promised myself I'd give every community we visit a fair shake before making a final decision... It's only right."

I

A S WE BID a fond *adieu* to downtown
governmental designation for The V
upcoming three hours alone again in the car w
full well she would spend the entire time repe
of every home and every amenity available in each
had seen during the past two weeks. Avoiding the *bl*
enthusiasm and insistence that I participate and offer op
not likely. I could affect a headache and ask her to drive
tended to sleep prostrate on the back seat, or develop an ins
neous case of amnesia and insist we postpone the discussion u
my memory returned. Practically, neither of those excuses wou
work, but then lightning struck.

Before Helen had an opportunity to start a conversation I said,
"Helen, I have an idea. I don't think it's necessary to talk now about
anything we saw until we are with Gwen and George. We can save
repeating ourselves and at the same time benefit from their input."

"But I want us to talk about it first."

"I know you do, and I know where you're coming from, but
nevertheless I want to wait. I want to go over everything in my

er than shoot from my hip and say something not
ut. You can appreciate that, can't you? Just give me
d space before we talk."

ust have been some Valium in the water Helen drank
e Villages, because totally out of character she replied,
ery good idea, Mike."

flabbergasted. I actually smiled. Taking her hand in mine,
d her.

the remainder of the drive to Palm Beach, we were
ssed in an audio CD of the book, *Chaos Reigns During the
ential Election.*

20

I WAS SO ENGROSSED listening to "*Chaos*", that when we arrived at Tuscany Villas' entrance gate, at close to 2:00 in the afternoon, I suggested we drive around the community, or park somewhere for another couple of hours until we'd finished listening to the book before going to Gwen's house. But that wasn't to be. Although, surprisingly, Helen, who never had any interest in politics, was equally absorbed in the story. On the bright side, putting off hearing the balance of the story until the ride back north would help us pass the time, without the need to talk about buying a new home...Win/ Win. The reality was we were tired, hungry, and needed a refreshing shower.

I slowly drove up to the gate designated for visitors. An armed, uniformed Pinkerton guard exited his beautiful brick fortress, which housed a mass of computers and a huge bank of security cameras monitoring the entire community. He cautiously approached our car.

"Can I help you, sir?" he asked politely.

"We're visiting the Goulds," I said.

"Can I see some identification, please?"

"Will my driver's license do?"

"That'll be just fine. How long are you planning to be here?"

"We're not sure. It could be a week or more."

"Okay."

The guard took my license, went inside the guardhouse, and called the Goulds to verify they were expecting us. When he returned to our car a few moments later, he gave me my license back and a visitor's pass, instructing me to put it on the dashboard. Additionally, he cautioned me not to park on the street during the evening. I thanked him and asked for instructions to reach George's house.

"They're printed on the back of the pass."

"Very impressive," I said, thanking him again.

In less than six minutes, we pulled into Gwen's driveway. No sooner had I turned off the engine than their front door flung open. Gwen came running full speed to our car, almost crashing into Helen's side door just as she was opening it.

"That was a close call. You almost killed yourself, Gwen," Helen said in Gwen's ear as they hugged each other in a death-grip."

"Oh, I'm so happy you're finally here. It's been far too long. Stand back, let me look at you; I've almost forgotten how gorgeous you are," Gwen said.

"Stop it; you're the good looking one. Florida sure agrees with you," Helen responded.

Neither of these ladies are beauties. Nor on the other hand are they in need of plastic surgery. They are very pleasant to look at, but gorgeous? What can you expect? That's how women talk to one another? A man might be tempted to say, "The crow's feet around your eyes are a little more pronounced than they were two years ago, and your backside has doubled in size. Is everything okay?"

I waited until the referee separated the women before I stepped in to give Gwen a firm but tender hug. I feigned pushing her away.

"What am I chopped liver? Come on…give me big wet one, Gwenie."

She did. In fact, I was somewhat embarrassed by the intensity of the kiss. Thank goodness no tongue was involved…at least if Helen was watching.

"I missed you too, I said. It's so good to see you. If I might ask, where's the old grump?"

Just as I was saying it, George meandered out of the house, beer in hand, beckoning me to join him. Did he hear me?

"Hey pal, put the damn beer down, say hello to Helen, and then help me unload our luggage."

"If you insist…Get over here, Helen, and plant one on me. You know, the way we used to say hello when Mike was working late."

"George, how many beers have you had?" Gwen said uncomfortably.

"Don't be a prude, Gwen; I've only had two or three—the usual."

"Well then there's no excuse for that kind of talk, especially to our friends."

"Well, excuse me. I didn't hear you object when Mike just asked you for a big wet one, did I?"

Not about to admit he was slightly under the weather, George continued on the offensive, asking, "Anyway, when did you join the nunnery?"

"Okay, okay, enough of this," Gwen replied.

"I'm not offended. Actually, I'm happy he feels so at ease with us that he can proposition my wife in front of me. Turnabout is fair play though. What do you say, Gwen? Like old times?"

"I'll consider it and get back to you. All's good."

Hmm. Have I missed something all these years? Could George's friendliness explain Helen's lack of intimacy with me? Surely, it's not my masculinity...Halitosis?...I'm going to give this some serious thought...No, I'm not! I don't know of another married couple like George and Gwen who can't keep their hands off each other. I wouldn't be surprised if they had sex seven days a week, every week.

21

WITH GEORGE'S ASSISTANCE, we unloaded the car and carried into their guest room our four overstuffed giant travel bags and an assortment of rolling carry-ons plus Helen's garment bag.

"Mike, where's your golf bag?" George asked me.

"You're kidding, right? Did you see the luggage we just dragged in? Where did you expect me to put it? On the roof of the car? I'm lucky the front seats weren't filled with her shoes and makeup essentials. She packed as if we were going away for a year. In any case, I'll rent clubs when and if we play."

"That won't be necessary. I'll ask one of my pals to let you use his."

"Great. At least that'll save me some money."

I paused a second, put my hand on his shoulder and told him he was a sight for sore eyes, an oasis in the midst of my manly trauma.

"George lead me to the libations; it's a medical emergency."

"Don't you want the personal guided tour of the house first?"

"No offense George, but can I decline your generous offer until we polish off your liquor supply? I'm house toured out. Do you have any idea what I've been through these past two weeks? Non-stop house touring has put me in a somewhat unpleasant frame of mind. Can't we suspend the inspection until tomorrow after I've decompressed?"

"I hear you, pal…and I empathize completely. I went through the same thing three years ago…pure torture. Tomorrow it is. Now inebriation is on the agenda."

We barely had time to consume our first drink when the women attacked with both mouths blazing.

"Helen said you'd fill us in on everything you saw. Well, I'm waiting," Gwen said, sitting herself down on a couch opposite me, pulling Helen's arm to sit next to her.

"Hold on there: George and I are in the middle of making plans to visit some of the communities around here. Can't this wait until after dinner?"

"Give me a break, Mike. Don't make me laugh. You boys were comparing single malt Glenlivich to Johnny Walker Double Black. We heard you."

"So, that distinction is important to know," I said.

"Oh, I agree. Very important," the good Miss Helen chimed in.

"Helen, there's no place for mockery when discussing Scotch," George countered.

"Then slip into your kilts, put on your Tam O' Shanter and sip the malt while we let Gwen and George know what we've been up to…You promised me."

"Okay. No problem, just so long as I can nurse my drink while we're going over your notes in the three loose-leaf books you've compiled during the trip."

For the next four hours, Helen recounted every detail of my end-of-life, final resting place search. Gwen asked as many questions as Helen had hairs on her head. Helen answered every one of them in minute detail. They were in their own separate worlds and as far as I can recall, never once did either of them ask for my opinion, or even look in my direction.

George had fallen asleep on the couch an hour into the "hash/rehash" diatribe, and I literally forced toothpicks into my eyelids to prop them open. My mind felt like cotton candy. Practically speaking, I had no idea of the actual words the women were saying since I continued to consume more and more Scotch. All I knew was that both Helen and Gwen's lips never once stopped moving. I was in an alcohol-induced trance.

Then, in the sixteenth inning of overtime, out of left field, Helen said, "Don't you agree, Mike?"

"About what? I missed that point."

"You weren't even paying attention. Were you?"

"Truth be told, no! I've been an observer for the past four hours. You hadn't even once asked me to comment on anything. I lost interest. George at least had the good sense to go to sleep and avoid death by boredom."

"You had every opportunity to participate, but you chose not to."

"I couldn't get a word in edgewise. Between you describing the length of the curtains in the various models and Gwen asking about the patterns of the valances, my input about cost and taxes were meaningless. So, what's your question?"

"Well, it's really my question," Gwen said. "I'd like to know which community you liked best?"

"Be careful," my little shoulder buddy whispered in my ear. *"It's a trick question. Avoid commitment at all costs...It's a trap!"*

"I take the 'fifth'."

"You can't," Helen said.

"I can and I do."

"Mike, that's not right. I respect your opinion and so does Gwen. Now come on," Helen implored.

Helen got up from the couch where she had been sitting next to Gwen and deposited herself next to me. Latching hold of my arm and gently pressing her nails into my skin she whined, "Mike..."

"I haven't reached a decision. All the facts aren't in yet. Florida's multitude of want-to-be Italian Riviera Villages, haven't had their chances to depress me yet. Oops...I mean impress me yet. My answer could be forthcoming within the week. Stay tuned. You won't want to miss it."

"No sense whipping your mule, Helen; he won't budge. He's as stubborn as ever.

Anyway, it's getting close to 6:00. We might as well eat now if we want to be in bed by nine..."

"Oh George, rise and shine. It's time for dinner, my dear."

The majority of the conversation during the meal concerned making plans for the next day. George and I decided to play golf in the morning. The women shockingly opted to go shopping...What else is new?

We'd meet up at 1:30 at the Mexican restaurant a couple of miles down the road for a late lunch, and then go back to their clubhouse, and sit around the pool for a couple of hours.

Gwen told us she had arranged for a small cocktail party around four at their house, so we could meet some of their friends. Then, if we were sober, coherent and still standing, we could go to a deli, wait two hours to be seated, because EVERYONE over fifty-five years of age goes out to eat dinner...early...all the time. Once seated, we could then enjoy a light dinner of matzo ball soup, stuffed cabbage appetizer, one-pound corned beef sandwiches, topped off with cheesecake or apple pie, ice cream optional, washed down with Dr. Brown's Diet Cream Soda.

22

I SHOT AN EIGHT-ONE...PISSED the hell out of George since I hadn't played for three months and he was out there four times a week year-round!

"Guess drinks are on you pal," I said.

"I can't believe the way you played, sinking twenty-foot putts and chipping in twice from off the green. Who the hell are you?"

"You know, George, I've been thinking about going pro, but the thought of leaving Helen for long stretches while I'm on tour is holding me back."

"You're really delusional my friend, and a very unconvincing liar. Now what do you say we go back to the house...shower and then meet the ladies for some margaritas and tacos?"

"Good idea."

We got to Senor Padre's restaurant a little early. They seated us in a secluded booth away from the Mariachi Band. The furniture was made of dark wood, and the light fixtures must have had only forty-watt bulbs.

"It's so dark in here I can hardly see your face, George."

"That's probably because they don't want you seeing what you're eating."

"Good point. So let's trick them and drink instead. We might not be able to see, but we surely can taste our liquor."

The waiter came over to the table and asked if we wanted to order some drinks. We did, and quickly swigged down two Dos X's each. The waiter removed the bottles from the table before the "girls" arrived. Then, after downing another two Dos X's, with the meal, I was content, feeling no pain, and no apprehension about the impending ordeal of house hunting over the next few days. However, I did have to loosen my belt buckle a tad to prevent the gaseous build-up in my gut from seeking a means of escape.

"How was your golf game?" Helen asked no one in particular.

Being the modest, non-braggart I am, I casually offered, "George's one hundred-four must have been an aberration. I've haven't bested him by twenty-three shots in over three years. Well...come to think of it, we haven't played in nearly three years...have we George?"

"Remind me again why I call you my friend," George countered as he simultaneously handed me the check for lunch.

"Diplomacy still isn't your strong suit, darling," Helen laughed.

"Nothing funny about it. No sense hiding the facts or denying reality. George had, to put it mildly, an off round," I responded. "Maybe the roles will be reversed if he ever has the nerve to play with me again."

"To paraphrase a famous quote: 'That'll happen when hell freezes over the golf greens in Palm Beach'."

"Don't be a sore loser, George. I hit some lucky shots. There's no getting away from it...you didn't. Is it possible for us to put this tragedy behind us and move forward? Can you ever forgive me?" I said, with the sincerity of a clergyman comforting a bereaved spouse.

"Drinks are on me," I cheerfully proclaimed.

"Neither of you will have another drink. You've both had too many already," Gwen said half-seriously. "In fact, neither of you is in any condition to drive."

"Let's get the hell out of here. I'll go with Helen; you go with Gwen," George proposed. "And no hanky-panky is allowed."

"Speak for yourself, George. I make no commitments," I said with a deadpan face, taking Gwen's hand in mine.

Gwen did a double take, gently shook her hand free of mime, smiled, took the keys out of her purse and said, "Follow me, Mike," in a voice betraying a little apprehension about the seriousness of George's and my comments.

"We'll meet you by the pool in an hour or so," George responded.

"Make that an hour and a half," I said, still showing no outward sign I was joking.

"Helen, I'll save us some chairs on the shady side of the pool. George knows where. See you in ten minutes."

23

I T WAS AMAZING how many people George and Gwen knew. During the short two hours we spent at the pool, at least thirty men came over to say hello. How George was able to remember each of their names astounded me. I'm lucky I remember my own name, no less be expected to repeat the name of the fellow I said hello to thirty seconds before. They should all have those permanent name tags that say, "Hello my name is…"; that way I wouldn't embarrass myself day-in, day-out.

"Hey George, can you do me a favor and use name tags tonight for your guests so I can read their names and not be a social outcast for not remembering them, especially for anyone I just met this afternoon?"

"Come on, that won't be necessary. No one expects you to. We all have senior moments now and then."

"Ah, if only they were only moments instead of weeks. Then I wouldn't feel so bad," I said.

"Really, Mike; there's no need for badges tonight. We're only having four couples over. You can handle that, can't you?"

"It's questionable; very questionable."

What a shock. I made it through the party without much difficulty. Primarily because George tutored me, repeating the names countless times before anyone arrived. I wrote them down on a piece of paper, put it into my pants' back pocket, and only had to refer to it twice during the course of the party. For some reason, the names stuck with me. Miracles do happen, but unfortunately now they occur less and less often.

Typically, as is expected, the men and women separated into their respective corners. I was happy that ritual was still practiced in Florida. It spared me the agony of listening to monotonous repetitive chatter about NOTHING of importance other than the latest and greatest sale going on at the mall, everyone's grandchildren, or the dreadful dye job one of the other women at the pool had... No need to explain further...But I will. I love women...I really do. However, I maintain that when the female gender is together, their topics of conversation generally have limited interest to men. It's just the way it is. No harm...no foul.

Conversation among the men generally focused on when I'd be moving south and where to. Every one of the men insisted that Tuscany Villas was the perfect place for us. They promised I could join their golf group, tennis, and pickleball teams. But, if I wanted to play in their softball league, I would have to pass muster and go through two weeks of rigorous tryouts.

I couldn't let that topic go by without comment.

"Really? Tryouts? You guys take this way too seriously," I said.

"Yes, we do. You have to understand, there's a good reason for having someone try out," George said.

"Like what, for instance?" I asked.

"Too many men have incurred way too many injuries. They weren't in shape, and as a result a lot of them had significant knee, back, and head injuries."

"The way you're talking, it seems the ambulance corps could have established a permanent sub-station next to your baseball field," I half-heartedly joked.

"No kidding. We were really worried. Bottom line, the Homeowners Association (HOA) was concerned there might be a liability issue, and asked the attorney to recommend a solution. He researched what other communities like ours did and then suggested we develop a system of tryouts. As an extra precaution, he recommended we require each player sign an injury waiver protecting the HOA and the other players from liability," George explained.

"Well, now that you put it that way, it does make sense. I guess I'll forgo softball…Do you have a rugby team?"

They all laughed. One of the guys asked me if we'd made any decisions on where we were going to move to.

"Gentlemen," I said in a loud voice, "Helen and I have not finished looking yet. We still have to see what the other three hundred and fifty Florida communities have to offer."

"How many? Are you serious? No way you're going to see that many. There aren't that many," they chimed in.

"There are probably more than that, and I certainly will visit them…Right after my testicles are removed."

"Hey George, you were right about Mike: he's nuts. Is he ever serious?" one of the guys asked.

"The short answer is, no! He's always looking for the opening to cause trouble, to turn a phrase, to repeat a comment someone just said, giving the words a different inflection, thus having the listener question the intent of the speaker. Beware of him. The man's a menace."

"I resent that, George. I can be serious when the occasion calls for it. My physician told me humor, laughter, and smiling can add years to one's longevity."

"In that case, you should live forever my friend," George said smacking the back of my head with an open hand.

"Ouch! That hurt!"

"Bullshit."

"You're right."

The banter took a turn; the men now knew I was someone who left to his own druthers could endanger the fragile balance between males and females. But I could sense they liked me; they really liked me…so long as I was kept away from their wives.

"Fellows, would you mind if I imposed on your good graces and asked you why you moved here. Why do you think this place is better than, say, The Villages, or Casa Rio, or Venevito Bento? Aren't they really all the same?"

"I'd say the cost of the houses, the size of the community, and also their location are the primary factors we compared and evaluated."

"So for discussion purposes, this place has five hundred homes at an average price of two hundred and seventy-five thousand dollars, and is twenty minutes away from Palm Beach. Casa Rio is less than two miles away. Why not move there?"

"Too many old people at Rio."

"Come on! I want to know. Why did you buy here and not there?"

"We knew three couples who were already living here. It made the move down here less traumatic for us. It was bad enough leaving the grandkids. We knew we'd have to start a new life, make all new friends, and find things to do all day. This place just worked. The prices over at Casa Rio were comparable except for the common charges. There they have to support a golf course. We don't have one to worry about here. We drive ten minutes down the road and play on the town course. It's not as foo-foo, but it fills the bill. We're really happy here. Honestly, we couldn't ask for more," one of the men said.

Generally speaking, they basically all agreed. One of the fellows disagreed about the golf. He wanted the convenience of not traveling to play. But since his wife didn't play, he said he couldn't justify the added expense of living in a community that maintains its own golf course.

When the clock struck six, Gwen and George announced that we'd have to leave in order to make it to the restaurant in time to keep our dinner reservations.

At the risk of repeating myself again, I have to tell you the ritual of hugs and kisses did not disappoint. Everyone kissed and hugged everyone else goodbye, including us. Promises and hopes were exchanged to keep in touch, to see each other again and again during our stay with Gwen and George. Not only that, but each of the women eagerly volunteered to accompany Helen when she visited the other communities. They knew they'd have to forgo either a game of mahjong or canasta, but were willing to make the ultimate sacrifice by throwing caution to the wind and enduring the hardship of touring newly constructed houses with their showcase furnishings. Their unselfish commitment to their newfound friend reinforced my faith in the female addiction of snooping. On the other side of the spectrum, not one of the men showed the slightest interest in joining the search posse. Probably because it would interfere with their golf game, and no doubt because I told them I wasn't going to be accompanying Helen on her quest.

24

RIDING TO THE restaurant was most pleasant. Why? Because I sat in the front with George not saying a word, while Helen in the back seat was getting the nitty-gritty from Gwen on each of the women whom she had just met: who had a nose job, a chin implant and/or breast lift or augmentation; who was divorced, was screwing around, a lousy mahjong player. It didn't stop!

On reflection, I might have been better if I'd talked about houses rather than being forced to listen to such drivel.

Mercifully, the trip took only fifteen minutes. However, it took over an hour for us to be seated. God bless the women; they continued their sisterly dissection of Gwen's friends for the entire time we waited. They couldn't control themselves. I know it's genetic. It has to be. There's no other explanation.

George and I were spared the agony of listening to them since there were no seats available next to the women on the benches outside the restaurant. We were FORCED to sit far-far away... Damn! But we had an unobstructed view of their moving lips and flailing arms as that accentuated their points of view.

Once seated inside at our table, Helen drew her guns and leveled them in my direction. I couldn't duck or run; I was trapped.

"Mike, what time do you want to leave tomorrow morning? We have so many communities to see. For my part, I'm willing to leave early so we can visit as many as possible."

"Here's an idea. Why don't you go by yourself? I'd only be a hindrance. You'll be able to accomplish so much more without me. Then, if you really like something, I'll go back to see it with you the next day. You already know what I like and what I don't like. There's no sense in me gumming up the works and having the sales force paint you with the same tarnished brush they'll likely color me with. I don't want them to be negative toward you because of me. You know these people always misinterpret my comments. They think I'm overly critical. For the life of me, I can't understand why."

Gwen and George could not contain their laughter.

"Who are you kidding Mike? You just want to play golf, lay around sunning yourself and drink yourself into oblivion," Helen said.

"I resent that. I don't want to sit in the sun. It's unhealthy. Remember what the doctor said about the thin ozone layer. The sun's rays will just permeate through the clouds and burn me to a crisp. Anyway, I've been on my best behavior. I've been a good boy," I said, patting myself on the head.

"Listen, honey. Take copious notes, and tomorrow night we'll review everything, especially those communities you truly would move into. And then once you've whittled the choice down to one or a maximum of two, I'll go back with you in a couple of days to see them. Cross my heart...hope to die."

In Montvale New Jersey.

"So be it. Gwen and George are witness to your commitment. No backing out now, Mike, unless you plan on sleeping in a car the rest of your life."

"Worse things could happen…My word is my bond."

"Can we please order now? My stomach is screaming for food. It's not fair to the waiter or the other people waiting to get into the restaurant."

"Not quite yet," Helen said. "I want us to plan out the balance of the week…Where we're going, when, and for how long?"

"A compromise is called for. I propose we first order and then, as we are waiting for the food, we can plan. How's that?" George proposed.

"A Solomonesque compromise," I responded. "No rational person can disagree with that proposal."

"Agreed," Helen cheerfully added.

I waved to the waiter that we were ready to order. He immediately acknowledged my request, nearly tripping over his feet as he rushed to our table. No doubt he wanted us finished with our meal as soon as possible so he could turn over the table and earn more tips. We obliged by making our selection in record time. The waiter was thrilled. Commenting how appreciative he was for the speed in which we chose what we wanted…So was I, since Helen normally debated her meal preference as if she had to choose which child's life were to be sacrificed. Then came her substitution requests: vegetables for potatoes, rolls instead of bread, broiled instead of baked. My discomfort level listening to her routine probably pales in comparison to what waiters feel having to smile.

Sorry for getting off track!

No sooner had the waiter left our table than Helen, totally disregarding her desire for us to plan for our visitation schedule, rose from her seat and announced, for all the world to hear, that she was going to the ladies' room to freshen-up. And in accordance with womanly tradition, Gwen felt the sudden urge to join Helen in the lavatory.

It's not possible for a woman to go unaccompanied to a restroom to apply a new coat of lipstick.

Within two or three minutes of the women leaving the table, the waiter brought us our soups. It was another several minutes before the wives returned. During that time, George and I planned our schedule for the following three days. We'd play golf each morning; then try to find some sleazy sports bar to have lunch at, and then lie around the pool until it was time for pre-dinner drinks. We accepted the inevitable that we'd be forced to take the women out to some restaurant for dinner since they'd feign exhaustion from such an arduous day of house hunting. Hope springs eternal that they'd opt to stay in for a home cooked meal or barbeque however unrealistic a possibility that might be.

As we were finishing the last remnants of our humongous matzo balls, they returned.

Helen sat. Then she began her fossil farm, home quest, "black site" torture routine on me.

"Since you unilaterally decided you're not coming with me, Mike, I asked Gwen if she would join me. I'm humiliated I had to impose upon our friendship for her to cancel her plans to play in a mahjong tournament, and in her regular weekly canasta game. Lucky for you, she's such a good friend she agreed."

Gwen tried hard, with limited success, to refrain from smiling. It didn't work! She was actually rejoicing at the prospect.

The women, I knew, would forgo most anything to have the opportunity of spending time looking at houses, whether they were models in a new community, or in a house where people were currently living. Think about all the fundraising house tours that are organized; they're always sold out. Don't think ill of me for saying...women clamor to snoop. Women pine to see the inside of a house that goes up for sale in their neighborhood, especially if, by some fluke of nature, they'd never been invited into it before. What's the allure? I don't get it; I really don't. Maybe it's chemical: you know, similar to the female gender's need for chocolate?

"So, here's what we're going to do. Gwen and I plan to visit at least four developments each day for the next three days. Should there be any I like, you and I will both go back to them and make a joint decision about whether we want to seriously make an offer."

"What about the other communities we already saw, like The Villages? Are you now saying you don't want to consider them?"

"I never said that."

"No, you implied it," I responded.

"I'm not ruling anything out right now," Helen said defensively.

"Fine, so long as we agree nothing will be decided until all options have been fully discussed," I said.

"Agreed."

"So gentlemen, now that you've eaten your soup, do you think we can ask the waiter to bring ours?" Gwen said.

"I told the waiter to cancel your order. We had no way of knowing how long you'd be in the power room hatching your plan."

"You did what?" Helen said, her voice rose with a distinct edge to it.

"Do you think we're total uncaring buffoons? We sent your food back to keep it warm, because we care...In fact, here comes the soup now," I said, pointing to the waiter heading toward our table.

25

THREE DAYS WENT by in a flash. I played great golf, even if I have to say so myself, and consumed more alcohol than I had in all the preceding twelve months. George was great company...So were his friends. I found myself continually laughing, sharing common experiences, and just having a good time. How I'd managed to occupy my free time the past three years without George and guys like the ones I've met was a miracle; I'd really missed out. I could see myself having no trouble spending the future with them.

The weather wasn't bad either, at least this time of year; nor was the comparative cost of eating out. A major drawback for me, however, was driving ten to twenty minutes each day to play golf. If the price were right, I would prefer to have a home in a golf community. It wouldn't matter if the house was not on the course, or even had a view of it; it was simply the convenience of not wasting precious time driving back and forth from the house to the course.

When I discussed my misgivings with George about spending so much time driving to play golf, he was miffed.

"Mike, are you telling me that if you found a house in this community, you wouldn't consider moving here?"

"Sure, I'd consider it, but it wouldn't be my first choice."

"You know you're hurting my feelings."

"It's not personal, George. I love you man...In a manly way," I said smirking. "What I'm saying is if Tuscany Villas had a golf course, it would be a no-brainer to move here. Chances are I...I mean Helen, can find us something nearby we like which does have golf. And I commit to you right here and now, that if you shave fifteen strokes off your handicap, I'll invite you to play as often as you'd like."

"Oh, I'm touched. Your generosity knows no bounds."

"Come on George, give me a break."

"Do you know how much more it's going to cost you to buy a home in one of those communities? To say nothing of the golf club member-ship fees and potential assessment contributions they might impose!"

"No. Do you?"

"Yes. As a matter of fact, I have some ideas. Remember Pete Stevens?"

"Sure I do. He lived down the street from you and had that knockout wife twenty years younger than himself. I'm shocked he didn't have a heart attack from keeping up with her...jogging."

"Yup. That's him. So anyway, he moved to the Venetia Grotto in West Palm Beach. His house is almost identical to mine. He paid seventy-five thousand dollars more for his, plus fifteen thousand for a golf membership bond. Yearly, it costs him three thousand dollars for green fees, and fifteen dollars each round for a cart. To make matters worse, this year they hit him up for an eight-thousand-dollar assessment to repair the damage caused by Hurricane Fred." He took a deep breath. "Quite the bargain, huh?"

"Holy shit! That's insane. Who can afford that? It would be cheaper to take an Uber every day back and forth to the airport and fly to Nassau to play golf."

"You can say that again," George agreed.

"Are all these golf communities the same?"

"Some are more expensive. The snobbier the community is, the larger the rip off. So, what do you say, my golf-pro buddy? Will it be lowering your standards and/or raising your handicap, or spending your grandkid's inheritance on golf?"

"Shall we just forget we ever had this conversation, George?"

"Fine by me."

Guess I resolved that issue.

As the sun set on day two of Helen's South Florida search for The Garden of Eden, she and Gwen arrived back at the house. Peering out the window of their living room, I saw Helen practically skipping, like a teenager who had been kissed for the first time, toward the front door.

This can't be good. To put off the discussion or not, that is the question? Is it nobler to engage the enemy on her turf or seek refuge in neutral territory?

Fool...The choice is obvious...Stall, deflect, and delay.

As she burst through the front door, Helen couldn't contain her excitement—yelling out, "Darling!"

Oh my God, I'm in trouble. Helen hasn't called me that since...actually she never has.

"Yes, my darling dearest," I responded with pure fright in my gut, and a sickening feeling coursing through my entire body that radiated up from my toes to the top of my head.

"I found it! It's perfect. It's everything I've ever wanted. The kitchen's enormous. You won't believe the appliances they're giving us. Granite countertops, and cabinets everywhere."

"Hold on, hold on a minute babe. What do you mean they're giving us? You didn't sign anything yet...did you?"

"Do you think I'd do something that important without first discussing it with you? I'm not a ditz, Mike."

Yeah, like the time you told the plumber to replace the entire septic system because the toilet backed up!

"That would be so alien to the way you do things, my dear."

"If only I could believe that."

Stall!

"So, what about you and Gwen first changing into something more comfortable? Then we can relax, have a few drinks, eat some munchies, and if we feel like it, we can talk about what we did today. I promise I won't bore you too much about how many strokes I beat George by today."

"If we feel like it? I most definitely feel like it!"

"Good. You girls go freshen-up. We'll be waiting for you with open arms."

And a closed mind!

"I'm excited to hear all about it," I said, summoning up all the enthusiasm I could muster.

The minutes felt like hours while I waited. I drank two shots of tequila on the rocks and was about to pour myself a third one when Helen and Gwen both simultaneously made their entrance onto the lanai.

Are they joined at the hip? Did they dress together? They surely must have arranged to come out to the lanai together. Helen must need Gwen's support for what she is about to tell me.

"Can I get you ladies something to drink?" George asked.

"I'll have a beer," Gwen replied.

"Nothing hard for me. Club soda will do fine," Helen said.

Oh boy, this can't be good. Helen refusing to drink is a bad sign.

"So, where did I leave off telling you about today's game?" I asked.

"Nowhere. Thank goodness you never began."

"Oh. I thought I did. So, we were on the first tee when George bent down to put his tee into the ground."

"Stop right there, Mike! I'm not about to listen to a play-by-play commentary of you demeaning George for each and every one of the eighteen holes you played. As far as I'm concerned, George shouldn't agree to play with you if you persist on making him the brunt of your humor," Helen lectured.

"No, no, no, I want Mike to tell me all about it," Gwen interrupted. "If George is as bad as Mike says, then I want him to give the game up and spend more time with me."

"Please Gwen, don't believe a word coming out of Mike's demented mind. He's a duffer himself. He couldn't hit a drive into the fairway if his life depended on it," George said in defense of himself.

This is good. Conversation has been diverted. How long I can keep it up without offending George is another matter.

"Okay, in the light of full disclosure, I will admit George has improved. Not much mind you, but enough not to embarrass me when I partner with him."

"You're way too kind, Mike. Your compliments are much too lavish...I'm blushing from the positive vibes I'm getting from you...I've got such a warm feeling."

"It's not running down your leg, is it?"

"Boys! Stop the bullshit," Helen said with no humor whatsoever. "I really don't care about your nonsensical game. I want to review with you NOW what we saw today, and get your input. You did promise me, Mike…I'm warning you: don't go back on your word."

Time to move on. She hasn't drunk; hasn't lost conscientiousness, and hasn't stormed out of the room. I'm dead.

26

"NO OFFENSE TO Gwen or George, but Ponte Vecchio North has the most gorgeous homes I've seen yet. It's in a league all of its own. Their clubhouse is truly indescribable. The place has everything you could ever think of, including two eighteen-hole golf courses, a three-star restaurant, three heated pools...I could go on and on and on. It's all in these brochures...They're so anxious to sell us a home, they'll even include an in-ground hot tub on the lanai."

"Helen, no one gives something away for nothing except maybe palmetto bugs," I said. "Are they having trouble selling their homes?"

"They said they're going like gangbusters."

"Sure they are, and I'm Santa Claus...So, how many homes are in the community?"

"Six hundred and forty," Helen responded.

"And how many have been sold?"

"Two hundred and seventy."

"When did they first start selling their properties?"

"Three years ago."

"George, when you were looking to move here, did you look at Ponte Vecchio North?"

"Sure did," he said.

"So why didn't you buy there?"

"Gwen and I thought it was too expensive and a little too far inland."

"When you were there, how many homes had been sold?" I asked.

"They had just started selling. There might have been ten or twenty lots under contract at the time," George replied.

"And now, if you were in my position and three years later they still hadn't sold two-thirds of their build-out, what would you think was going on, or more apropos, what's not happening?"

"Obviously, they're having a problem. It might be that they're just recovering from the down market, or potential buyers had the same misgivings as I did, or their homes are overpriced, or it might be something more serious."

"Like what?" Helen asked, now questioning her initial assessment.

"Could be the builders are having financial problems...There's no way for me to really know. In any case, Helen, at the risk of incurring your animosity for life, I must as a friend caution you against buying there."

"Helen, if George didn't volunteer his opinion, I would have nixed Ponte Vecchio North myself. Thanks George, you threw me a life raft to grab onto."

"And why are you so negative?" Helen asked me.

"I don't like the name. It's too bourgeois for my taste...It lacks a certain...panache. And equally as important, it's my understanding

Ponte Vecchio North doesn't even have an ambulance service on the property. What kind of place catering to old folks with one foot in the grave is so heartless?"

"You really are something. I shouldn't be surprised. How could I expect any more from you?"

"Now, now. Let's not go down that road. Do you honestly think those are my reasons for not pursuing Ponte North?"

"Yes. Based upon your history as a professional obstructionist, it is what I expected from you."

"Look...George hit the bull's eye right smack dab in the middle. Something's wrong there, and I don't want us to make a monumental mistake and end up holding the proverbial bag. Didn't it bother you in the least that so few homes had been sold?"

"No, not really. I thought nothing of it. But now that you've both pointed it out, I must admit something doesn't quite make sense."

"So moving on...There's a bright side to things. Tomorrow you're going to see a few more communities. One of them I have a feeling will tickle your fancy. All is not lost. Hope does spring eternal, my dear."

"Is the matter of Ponte Vecchio North put to rest now?" Gwen asked, hoping not to upset her friend.

Both Helen and I shook our heads indicating it was.

"So," Gwen continued. "Have you guys considered buying a resale? There are tons of them on the market. People are dying by the drove every day, and their kids can't wait to unload their parent's homes. You can probably negotiate a great deal."

"Dying everyday...How reassuring," I said.

Once again ignoring me completely, Helen said, "My heart was set on a new house with brand new appliances...everything new. No one else's headaches...Can you blame me? I'm no different than you, Gwen...You had this house built for you...It was right off the assembly line...spic and span...sparkling fresh. You know what I mean."

"I sure do. BUT," Gwen replied.

"But what?"

"But there's a house in this community which is going on the market next week. You can make a deal without a broker...I know the family.... I know the house... You'll just love it. We'll be neighbors...Won't that be just awesome?"

"Oh my God, Gwen, why did you wait so long to tell us about this?"

"I wanted to give you an opportunity to see the other communities so you could make a comparison. I didn't want you to feel any obligation or guilt if you wouldn't consider it."

"Nonsense, we're all adults. Correction...the three of us are," Helen responded smiling and pointing a finger in my direction.

This curve ball came out of nowhere. Why the hell didn't George warn me it was coming? Did he even know?

"Time out," I said, waving my arms like a referee. "Before we go down that road, I think that tomorrow you ladies should finish visiting the other communities you said you planned on seeing. Then in the evening we can all sit down again with a calming glass of libation and talk."

Surprise, surprise...they all agreed.

"Okay, since we won't be discussing the 'search' any further tonight, I vote we take the ladies out for a gourmet delight. All in favor?"

The vote was unanimous. After half an hour debating where to go, we settled on Chinese. The meal was acceptable...not on a par with New York or New Jersey, but acceptable nevertheless.

27

WHAT A REGRETFUL, inauspicious beginning to a day I had just experienced. Paraphrasing former President Franklin Delano Roosevelt, *this day will live in infamy.* I had just suffered my worst and only golfing defeat at the hands of George Gould in thirty years.

"My mind wasn't into the game," I muttered. "This is obviously a very bad omen of terrible things to come. I'm not a happy camper, George."

"Buddy boy, pal of mine, suck it up. Be a gracious loser and congratulate me for whipping your ass. It's been forever since I even came close to scoring better than you. Don't be a sore loser! Let me glow in the aura of my victory for...for forever! Can you find it in your heart to be complementary to me?"

"Sure I can, George...Nice game," I begrudgingly muttered.

"Oh, you're really something else. Here, sign my scorecard. I want proof should you ever deny me my glory."

"Give it to me, I'll sign it...You did great...never better. In the future, don't expect me to spot you so many strokes...Not going to happen... no way."

"Fine, I'll take what little scrap of recognition you've thrown my way. Will you at least buy me some rounds of cheer as a reward?"

"Of course, provided you limit your consumption to no more than three."

"Deal...Let's go back to that dark cave Mexican place...Senor Padre's you took me to a couple of days ago."

We sat at Padre's bar for close to three hours munching on tacos and salsa while we downed a full pitcher of margaritas. Both of us had a buzz on. Nevertheless, I drove back to George's house, thankfully undetected by the police, even though I was somewhat erratic in my ability to stay in my lane. I was very lucky, because had the Gendarmes stopped us and given me a Breathalyzer test, I would have failed with flying colors.

Once back at George's house, we showered, changed into fresh clothes and collapsed onto the lounge chairs on the lanai to await the women's return. The margaritas had taken their toll ...We both fell soundly asleep.

When the women finally got back, they had an enthusiastic, grand old time rousing us from dreamland.

"Get up," they said in sync. "Rise and shine. We have a lot to show you and talk about."

It wasn't easy shaking the cobwebs of tequila-induced sleep from my head...It hurt and was pounding, but no doubt it was about to get a lot worse.

Helen pulled up a chair next to where I was recovering on the lounge. I was thankful for that small favor. It allowed my body to remain prone and keep my head from moving. No telling what would have happened if I was forced to elevate my body.

"My search is complete," Helen announced, simultaneously withdrawing a ream of paper and brochures from her satchel, and placing them on a coffee table between our chairs.

"Let's see…Where do I start?…Okay, take a look at this," she said handing me a one-inch thick stack of glossy brochures, which must have cost a small fortune to produce.

In large gold lettering, the cover pamphlet read, "Verona by the Sea—Heaven on Earth," with a four-color illustration display of mountain villas on a cliff overlooking a gorgeous blue sea.

"Well," I said snickering, "in the first place Verona is not on the sea. It's in Northern Italy near Milan. The closest view of water is probably some fountain in some Piazza in Verona. And secondly, I must question the use of the phrase Heaven on Earth. I have a slightly different perspective of Heaven. More to the point, the map on the back of the brochure shows that Verona is a good fifteen miles from the ocean.

Then there's the matter of the mountains. The largest mountain in South Florida is a dumpsite off of the highway a few miles from here. So much for the sea and mountains…don't you agree?"

"Oh," Helen said irritably, blowing out a deep gust of air, as she spoke, "I don't have the patience for your games anymore, Mike. Are you starting up again with me?"

"Most certainly not. How can I believe anything the salespeople from Verona by the Sea say if their literature is so blatantly false and misleading? Don't you agree, George?"

I needed an ally. Hopefully he would rally to my cause.

"Sorry, pal, this is not a discussion I want to be a part of. You're not dragging me into the middle between the two of you. You'll have to make whatever case you want all by your lonesome self."

"So be it, traitor! Just wait until you need some support. Don't come looking for me to rescue you. I'll be out to lunch… permanently."

"Fine…We've settled that issue. So now are you ready to hear what I have to say?" Helen asked chomping at the bit to unleash the dogs guarding Verona's gates.

"Do I have a choice?"

"No, you don't…. So let me tell you all about Verona."

Helen described every detail of the community and the two models she had fallen in love with. There was no denying, she'd done her homework. Then, unexpectedly, she dropped another shoe.

"We finished earlier than we originally planned, so before we came back here, Gwen took me to see her neighbor's house. You know, the one she mentioned was going up for sale?"

"You've been a busy little girl, haven't you?"

"Someone has to take the bull by the horns. You certainly didn't and won't."

"You're right about that, babe; I don't want to get gored… Well, I suppose you also want to tell me about that?"

"I do."

"So let's hear it."

And I did…for the next thirty minutes.

"Any other surprises up your sleeve you want to spring on me?"

"That's it for now."

"At the risk of spoiling the moment, might I inquire what these slices of heaven will cost us?"

"I'd much prefer not to go into that now. I want you to wait until after you've seen the houses I like…I made an appointment for us tomorrow morning to meet the Sales Manager at Verona, and then at 3:00 in the afternoon, we have to be back here to go over to Gwen's neighbor's house."

"Does it matter to you that I have to disappoint George and cancel tomorrow's golf game? It would have been nice if you gave me a little advance notice first."

"Hold on there! We made no plans to play golf tomorrow. And if we had, I would be more than happy to let you out of your commitment, especially since I beat you today. You need a day to rest from the drubbing you received…at my hand…A day to sulk is what the doctor ordered…So go…go my friend with your wife and find your salvation."

"Bastard!" I said. And I meant it.

28

HELEN AND I spent a most pleasant morning at Verona. No fights; no mean-spirited comments from either of us, and as unbelievable as it might seem, I was a perfect example of manners and attentiveness, not once passing gas or interrupting her mid-sentence. I couldn't swear to it, but I do believe I even opened the car door for her once.

We had meticulously gone through the two models Helen liked most. We toured the community clubhouse and shared an omelet in the private restaurant restricted to residents, who were required to shell out a minimum monthly dining fee.

Within the property was an eighteen-hole golf course with its own clubhouse, twenty tennis courts, and of course a senior sized softball field. I understood why Helen liked the community and in particular the two model homes.

Verona was an upscale Villages with upscale costs. But something I couldn't quite put my finger on made me uncomfortable— a feeling I was not happy about. Then it clicked. The ambience, the atmosphere radiating from the few residents I talked with during our short visit: I sensed a formality, even in the casual clothes they wore. The deferential mannerisms of the employees and sales staff we came in contact with were off setting. They made me feel uncomfortable.

"Yes ma'am, yes sir, right away, sir."

Outsiders not welcome. When one of the women we were introduced to used the expression, "We summer on the Cape," I knew this place wasn't for me. Money and position were paramount to fitting in. I'm going to go out on a limb and say these people don't think their shit smells. Truth be told…mine smells like a fresh bouquet of roses, or so my mother told me!

Seriously, I couldn't see myself socializing with these people. I'm a down to earth guy with very few pretenses. As far as money and career are concerned, I'd probably fit right in…except for my wardrobe which I'd have to totally revamp, and my touchy-feely personality! Guaranteed, I'd be forced to buy an assortment of golf shorts and slacks with alligator and turtle designs, and purchase all new Ralph Lauren golf shirts and tops with Ralph's humongous logo dominating three-quarters of the available visual material.

No matter: a lot of these folks are probably beneath my very high, but warped social standards and intellectual acumen.

All in all, by no stretch of the imagination could I be happy living there. I suspect neither would Helen. She's too down to earth to want to, or have to put on any phony airs. Why waste our hard-earned assets on meaningless facades of success to be with people who feel the need to preen…to outwardly display the trinkets of superiority, which I suspect are really to cover-up an inferiority.

Remind you of anybody?

As we drove back to Tuscany Villas, I offered my opinions about Verona by the Sea…both the positives and negatives. Aside from some minor differences in perspective, Helen and I were on the same page. She realized she had been swayed by the houses and the ambience and had not taken into account the social aspects of living there. Verona was stricken from the list.

"I'm glad we both agreed we're not going to consider buying at Verona. That saves us from making a huge mistake for the sake of expediency."

"You see, Mike: we can agree without arguing."

"Of course, we can. We always have. Especially on the major issues like where we'll be buried."

"Funny boy."

"Now here comes the hard part. Do you really want to live in Tuscany Villas and have Gwen and George practically as your next-door neighbors?"

"What kind of question is that? They're our close friends and have been for thirty years. What am I missing here?"

"I don't want to jeopardize that relationship. Living so close, seeing each other day-in and day-out, can be very tricky. It could expose warts."

"Their warts? You're delusional? I thank my lucky stars they've ignored your short- comings and sterling personality."

"Me? I have shortcoming and you're impugning my personality? Now you're really hitting below the belt."

"My God, have you ever heard yourself…the way you talk to people? Even Don Rickles doesn't hold a candle to you."

"Okay, you've crossed the line. I've never knowingly insulted anyone. I joke around a lot. I see humor in almost everything. Can you give me one example of when I insulted someone?"

"Let's see…How can I count the ways?"

"Stop that. Just tell me once when you think I did that. No need for a litany of generalizations."

"Trust me; you do, all the time."

"No one's complained to me. Has anyone said anything to you?"

"Yes, many times. But I always have to explain away your quips as your weak attempt at comedy…Now can we get back to the real issue?"

"No. You're telling me our friends really have problems with me. That's important."

"It is, but don't make a major issue of it. Just filter your humor. Think about what and how you say things before actually saying them. Consider how the target of your pronouncements might perceive them…That's all."

"Wow, and here I thought I was bringing joy into people's lives."

"You do. BUT sometimes you go overboard."

"Do me a favor, Helen. The next time you think I say something I shouldn't have, pull me aside and tell me. That way I can learn. I'm never too old to learn."

Am I really that bad? Do I cross the line? I'm a pretty good judge of character. I've never verbally screwed around with anyone who gave me a negative vibe…Proof's in the pudding—I've never been hit, slapped, or had a physical altercation with one single individual. Helen's either being overly sensitive or deflecting. Either way the message has been received.

"Message received."

"Good. You asked me if I would move to Tuscany Villas…The short answer is yes, I would. Everything about the community is wonderful, including the people I've met. And having Gwen here is a major positive. It solves one of my biggest fears about moving."

"And what's that?"

"Us having to make a whole new set of friends. At least if we come here that won't be as big a problem. It doesn't mean we'll be attached at the hip to Gwen and George, but we won't have to try to be accepted into an already established social network of friends...It's never an easy thing to do."

"I know you've never had any problem making friends. If and when we move, it won't be any different then."

"IF?"

"Slip of the tongue...That's all...I promise."

"Mike, do you like it here?"

"Well, now that you asked, the biggest drawback to this place pertains to golf. They don't have their own golf course. I was hoping to be able to live in a community that had one. It's so much more convenient to be able to fall out of bed and land on the course instead of having to drive to one. I always thought these Florida communities were on golf courses; that's the impression I had."

"Is that a must for you?"

"No, but it sure would be great if we could live in a place that had one, and was not outrageously expensive."

"George and his friends don't have a problem driving to other places to play. Would it really be so bad if you had to drive two or three times a week to play?"

"Not if it's only two or three times. I was hoping to play more like four to five times a week."

"You're only deluding yourself into thinking you'll be able to play that frequently. Aren't you forgetting your chronic back and knee problems, my dear? How many times in the last five years have you missed work because of that damn back?"

"Fine. I guess it was wishful thinking on my part."

"I'm afraid it was."

"Aren't we getting a little ahead of ourselves? We're talking as if we already have a house we want to buy. Why don't we continue this after I've seen that house you want to show me? We're almost there."

Lou and Betty Frank were the owners of the house. They both greeted us at their front door and led us onto their lanai where Betty graciously offered us some ice tea and sliced fruit. She was extremely frail and looked her aged. Lou on the other hand was fit and trim. Gwen told us they were both in their nineties. We talked for a while, telling them about ourselves and our family. While Betty stayed seated on the lanai, Lou took us on a tour of his home. Aside from the dated furniture and a few structural issues, the house seemed to be in good condition. With some minor alterations, a fresh coat of paint, and new appliances I could see us living there.

As we were walking through the house, I asked Lou how long they had been living in Florida?"

"Twenty-eight years this coming May," he replied. "We moved down from Buffalo, NY. We first had a house in Fort Lauderdale; then moved here when Tuscany Villas was built."

"I suppose it wasn't too much of an adjustment for you considering the similarity in weather," I said, smiling.

"Oh yes, especially in January. Only difference is in Buffalo I used to swim in Lake Erie every morning for about an hour. Down here it's in and out quickly. You have to be careful of the alligators."

"Yeah, I know what you mean. Those gators can be dangerous."

Lou had a sense of humor.

"So Lou, can I ask you a personal question?"

"That depends on what the question is."

"Why are you selling?"

"Well I suppose you have the right to know...Betty isn't doing well and physically is having problems. I can't give her the support she needs. We'll be going back to Buffalo...to our kids. They want us with them. Doesn't make sense for them to keep flying down here every few weeks...You can understand that, can't you?"

"Without a doubt. Will you be living with one of them?"

"Most likely with my daughter and son-in-law. They have a large house with plenty of extra room for us...They insist."

"We understand completely. That's so wonderful you have that kind of relationship with your children," Helen said. "It's rare in this day and age where older parents or grandparents live together with their children. I'm envious."

"Thank you. We're very lucky."

"When are you planning on moving?"

"As soon as we can. If we can sell tomorrow, I'll call the movers and have them pack us up...Are you really interested?" Lou asked, his voice filled with hope.

"Honestly, we're still considering a few other options. If it's not too much of an imposition on you, can we get back to you tomorrow morning at the latest? We'll make a decision tonight... promise. Oh, what's your asking price?"

29

R ATHER THAN GOING back to Gwen's house we decided to go to
the Dunkin Donuts down the road for a cup of coffee and some
privacy. We needed to put things together, and tie up some loose
ends without feeling constrained in front of Gwen and George. Their
presence would have been an unneeded distraction and impediment,
especially Gwen who can have an undo influence on Helen.

"Well, I've made a decision. I want us to make an offer on the
Frank's house. We'll have such a great time here," Helen said.

She seems to want to buy in every community she's visited. Why is that?

"You will, that's for sure; because if we buy their house, you'll
be shopping for months buying new furniture, appliances, window
treatments, YADA, YADA, YADA. Need I go on?"

"I never even considered that...I was planning on bringing all
our stuff from Jersey."

"And hippos fly...Tell me another fable, Aesop."

"Let's not get sidetracked again. Do you want to buy the Frank's
house? Yes or no?"

"Before I answer that, does this mean you're ruling out The
Villages?"

"It does."

"What does Tuscany Villa have that The Villages doesn't?" I asked.

"Leaving out the shops, restaurants, and multiple town squares, it's practically the same, but on a much smaller scale."

"That's putting it mildly."

"Look, I admit the houses are not as architecturally diverse and there's less land between them. Aside from that..."

I asked her again, "What does Tuscany Villas have that The Villages doesn't?"

Without the slightest hesitation Helen said, "Gwen."

"Emphatic, are we? You're not giving me much of a choice, are you?"

"Not really, I guess. I'm sorry, Mike. Are you that opposed to this place not having a golf course, or is living in the same community as Gwen and George so bad?"

"I suppose I could survive...provided you don't give me grief about playing golf every day I'm physically able to, and you promise not to tie our social life to Gwen's."

"I agree on both counts."

Helen lunged at me from across the table, spilling her coffee and squashing my donut to smithereens. She was beyond happy.

"Hold on, tiger. I have some additional requirements. I want a new set of golf clubs, a new pair of golf shoes, and a new fifty-two-inch plasma screen TV with the super-duper sports package... Nothing more...nothing less. Do we have a deal?"

"Sold, American!" she screamed, causing every customer in the place to look in our direction.

Fool that I am, I could have asked for a full-time, live-in, thirty-year-old Swedish masseuse with intimacy privileges, and Helen would have agreed. I should have made that a provision of our agreement.

"I can't wait to tell the kids what we're going to do. They'll love it here. Can we call them now?" she pleaded.

"I'd rather not call them with so many people around. Let's go back to Gwen's; we'll call around dinnertime so we can also speak with the grandkids."

"Wonderful! I guess I can hold off till then."

30

HELEN WAS TRANSFORMED from a woman on a quest to purchase that perfect dress to wear to her daughter's wedding, into a teenager on her first date. She clung to me. I liked it: it felt good! I wondered though whether it was real affection for me, or total happiness for herself. I couldn't shake her loose if I wanted to. Her hands wrapped around mine, in what felt like a death-grip as we walked up the path to Gwen's house. Before we reached their front door, Gwen had thrown it open. She stood standing there with her hands on her hips, ready to say, "So?"

But instead she said, "Mike, why do you have lipstick all over your face?"

"I don't know! Linda Blair's taken over the body and mind of my poor timid frigid wife...Maybe we should go to an exorcist. Do you know of one nearby?"

"What in God's name is going on with you two?"

"Helen's pregnant...We're having another baby. We've been trying for so long—it's a miracle. Praise the lord!"

"I can't take it. What's going on, damn it? Tell me before I bust a gut?" Gwen said, not knowing whether to smile, scream, or cry.

Helen couldn't contain her joy. She pushed me away, grabbed Gwen by the arms, and twirled her around in a circle, jumping up and down and yelling, "We're going to be neighbors...We're going to be neighbors, Gwen!!"

The two of them looked like little girls on Quaaludes who had just heard they were going to camp together.

"Calm down, calm down, ladies. You're making a scene; it's embarrassing; the neighbors will complain to the HOA...and we haven't even moved in yet," I said with a slight twinkle in my eyes.

"Oh, I'm so happy, Helen. We'll have so much fun...It'll be like the old times."

The three of us came inside to find George leaning against a chair for support. The gleeful antics of the women were so loud, they had obviously woken George up from his mid-afternoon siesta.

"George, break out the good stuff—the single malt—we've got something big to celebrate," Gwen shrieked.

"Huh?" muttered George, who was barely able to decipher her demand through the haze of his alcohol-induced nap.

"I said...pour three of us a drink. Nada for you! Forget the Scotch; open up that bottle of Moet we've been saving for a special occasion. Helen and Mike are moving to Tuscany."

"They're going to Italy? How did that happen?"

"No...here," Gwen replied.

With us?...Permanently? Aren't we going to be a little bit cramped for space? I don't have enough space in my closet as it is," moaned George not fully comprehending what Gwen was saying.

"No, you idiot, they're buying the Frank's house. Now get that Moet!" Gwen demanded.

"Sit down everybody. I want to hear everything," insisted Gwen.

"George, hold up a minute on that Moet," I said, gently pulling George back onto the couch.

"What do you mean, hold up? I want to celebrate now," Gwen persisted.

"We will, but not just yet. No contract has been signed. We haven't even made an offer to the Franks yet. We're going to do that in the morning. So...until all the i's have been dotted and all the t's crossed, I refuse to toast...It's bad luck."

"Maybe we should wait," Helen agreed. "First, we're calling the kids to let them know...You understand, don't you?"

"Call them now," Gwen said in a beseeching tone.

"They're not home. They're still at work. We'll wait until 6:00; then we'll call."

"It's only 4:30 now. How can you expect me to wait another hour and a half? I can't wait...I won't!"

"You can...and you will wait, Gwen, because right now, Mike and I are going to take a shower...together."

Knock me over with a feather! I can't believe what I just heard.

Gwen was visibly crest-fallen at postponing her anticipated hours of hashing and rehashing the details of the possible purchase. But at the same time, she appeared dumb struck at the image of Helen and me showering together. I could tell by the loud intake of air emanating from her mouth that she was truly taken aback!

I was gob smacked again when Gwen loudly whispered to George, no doubt so we could hear, "You look like you could use a nice warm shower yourself…I'll even help you hold the soap. I don't want you falling on the hard tile floor; you still look a tiny bit tipsy."

A Senior Citizen's Love Fest at its best!

31

"**H**I SWEETIE PIE; it's Grandpa. I'm here with Grandma. We're calling from Florida. How's my little Roberta?"

"Where's Florida, Grandpa?"

"It's a long way away from where you live. You have to take a plane to get here," I said.

"I haven't seen you in so long. Are you sick? Why haven't you come to see me?"

This could turn out to be good in the long run, but it hurts me deep inside.

"We've been away for a long time, honey."

"I know, I know. Too long. You missed my school play," she exclaimed.

"Oh no, we didn't know. Mommy must have forgotten to tell us.

It's getting even better.

What kind of play was it?"

"It was Pocahontas and John Smith. I was one of the Indians."

"I bet you were the star."

"No, Suzie was. I was her sister."

"Oh, I see. But I'm sure everyone clapped hard for you. I know we would have."

"Why didn't you come even if you were in...? I forgot. Where are you?"

"We'll come to the next one. Cross our hearts."

"Can I speak to Grandma, please?"

"Of course, she's already on the extension so we both can talk to you at the same time."

"Hi, button face. I miss you," said Helen.

"Hi, Grandma. When are you coming home?"

"Very soon, sweetie. We're staying with some friends for only a few more days. Then we'll drive home."

"How long will that be?"

"Let's see...We'll leave here in two or three days and then it'll probably take us three more days of driving to get home to New Jersey."

"That's a very long time, Grandma. And then when am I going to see you and Grandpa?"

"The very first thing we'll do once we get back is to call Mommy and see when you can come over to our house. How does that sound?" Helen replied.

"Not good. I want to see you tomorrow."

Helen's facial expression went from a loving, joyful grand-mother to a visibly depressed one who had just gravely disappointed her grandchild.

"And we want to see you too, but we can't get there so quickly," Helen said.

"You could if you really wanted to."

Children have a way with words, don't they?

Helen's pleading eyes looked toward me for some help. I nodded.

I can, if I want to, make this situation worse for Helen by forcing more emotional tugs on her heartstrings, but there's no need. This conversation is a magical bullet. Roberta is doing what I couldn't do. Namely, wounding Helen in the most vulnerable area of her being: her emotional vortex—the grandmother's heart. And no doubt the other seven grandchildren will fling their arrows and hit the target with similar results. I'd better not be too obvious though. She'll see right through me.

"Sweetie, can you put Mommy on the phone?" I asked.

"Don't you want to speak with Billy?"

Billy is Roberta's ten-year-old brother.

"Absolutely, we do, just as soon as we finish talking to Mommy. Can you put her on the phone, sweetie?"

That had to earn me brownie points.

"But, Billy wants to talk with you now," Roberta insisted.

Helen shrugged her shoulders and pursed her lips as if to say, we have no choice—we have to talk with him now.

"Okay honey; we love you. Hugs and kisses. Please put Billy on the phone," I said.

"Billy, how are you doing my, little man? What's happening in school? Did you talk to your teacher about the girl who pulled your hair?"

"You mean that bad Sally O'Brien? The one with the red hair who invited me for a playdate and I said no?"

"That's the one."

"My teacher said Sally was just mad because I didn't want to play with her, that's all. Besides, she said, she thinks Sally likes me and was just 'acting out'. Do you think Sally likes me?"

"How could she not like you? You're cute, smart, and you're my grandson," Helen said.

"I agree," I added. "So did Sally apologize?"

"She said she would if I came over to her house to play doctor."

This kid's a chip off the old block. This happened to me all the time when I was his age. Hmm...Might have been as late as last year. Just kidding...in my dreams.

"Don't disappoint her, buddy boy. Say yes. You won't regret it."

Helen threw a pillow in my direction. She wasn't pleased with my male chauvinistic recommendation.

"I don't want to, Grandpa. The boys in the class will pick on me if I do."

One day, if he ever remembers this conversation, he'll kick himself for not listening to me.

"You do whatever you feel is right, okay. How'd you do in the tryouts for soccer travel team?" I asked.

"That's on Saturday. Can you and Grandma come and watch me?"

"We wish we could, but we'll still be in Florida on Saturday, sweetheart. If we weren't here, we'd be there, you know that."

"No I don't. You missed Roberta's play, and...and... and now you won't come to watch me play soccer. Did I do something bad? Are you mad at us?"

"Oh no, baby. We love you all so much. If we could be there, we would...cross our hearts. Promise."

"Then why are you away?"

"We're buying a house in Florida. You can come and visit us during the summer and on vacations, and go swimming all the time. Won't that be great fun?" Helen asked.

"No!"

The line went silent.

"Billy...Billy...what happened? Are you there?" I said into the phone.

"Mom... Dad...What the hell did you say to Billy? He just dropped the phone on the floor and ran up to his room hysterically crying. Now he just slammed his door. Oh no, Roberta is crying. What's going on? What did you say to the kids?" my daughter demanded to know in an uncharacteristically and distinctly unpleasant tone.

"Nothing; really nothing that the kids should be acting that way about," I said.

"So then why are they crying?

"Beats me," I replied.

"Mom, what the hell did you two say to the kids?"

"Um...Only that we were in Florida and missed them," Helen said.

"Bullshit. They wouldn't react that way if you said that. Now try again...this time for real."

"We might have told them we were moving here."

"You're what?"

"We're going to buy a house around the corner from Gwen and George. Can you imagine? We'll be neighbors again. It's amazing how things work out...Like it just fell out of the sky."

"You bet it did...Right out of the sky and onto your heads. It must have really hurt? What are you thinking? Are you both delusional? Have you ever even considered for a second what moving to Florida will mean to the kids, to my brothers, and to your other grandchildren and me? Don't you think we deserved the right to be consulted before you made such a monumental decision? Holy shit!...Mom ...Dad...I hope you didn't sign any papers yet? It can't be too late for all of us to get together as a family and talk about it. Please...say it's not final."

Throughout Cynthia's diatribe, Helen kept looking at me with a combination of expressions ranging from "what the hell's going on?" to "help me" and "what have I done?" I raised my hand and motioned with an up and down movement for her to calm down. I then went to Helen, took the phone from her with one hand and rested my other hand on her shoulder, gently stroking it.

Seems like I may have averted an Armageddon. Careful, you still have to appease Helen without showing how relieved you are. Yes, I was willing to move to Tuscany Villas, but that was NOT my first choice. The kids and the weather were still problematic for me.

But what a change of events! I couldn't have scripted the grandchildren's and Cynthia's reactions any better if I had hired a Hollywood drama writer to direct their responses.

Tread cautiously, old man, there are still mines under foot.

I put my hand over the phone's mouthpiece to prevent Cynthia from hearing me. And as an extra-added precaution I whispered in Helen's ear, "Looks like we stirred up a hornet's nest of emotions... Go with me on this, trust me."

Then, talking directly into the phone, I said, "Honey, we haven't signed any contracts. Things are still in the exploratory stage. We're only doing our due diligence now. I promise, once we get all the facts and figures together, we'll talk...All of us."

"You better...and you can bet your grandparent visitation rights, that as soon as I hang up, I'm going to call Paul and David and bring them up to date. I'm sure they'll be thrilled to hear their parents have gone rogue."

"Of course we'll talk with the family before we put our John Hancock's on the dotted line."

"Are we alright?" Helen practically whined.

"I will be in time. But now I need a while to digest what's happening. You really sent me for a loop...Now I've got to get off the phone so I can calm the kids down, and let them know you're not leaving them. You two upset them. If I were you, I'd buy them something pretty terrific and hope they're not scarred for life. We'll talk...luv ya."

We hung up the phone. Helen broke into tears. She ran to me and I put my arms around her and attempted to console her. I wasn't feeling so great either.

Looks as if I won the war...whoopee! So why am I not happy and gloating? The answer's simple: I can't stand the sight of my wife crying, nor the thought of my grandchildren feeling abandoned, or my daughter and sons being disappointed in me for not involving them in the Great Retirement Decision Process.

"Everything will be alright. You'll see. You know I'm a fatalist. Things usually work out for the best. The kids will be fine; no need to worry. Cynthia will explain things to them. They'll probably forget all about it in a day or two...you'll see. Can you imagine the horror show if we'd actually bought that house and then told everybody about it afterwards? It would have been hell. Luckily for us, we called Cynthia and the kids when we did."

"You promise me the kids will forgive us."

"They love us; they have no choice. We're a part of them. Anyway, they have to: we're their meal ticket to their retirement.

Just give it a while. This too will resolve itself without any bad feelings."

"Oh, I'm so sorry I rushed us into this," Helen mumbled into my ear as her tears ran down my cheeks.

"I guess there's no benefit for us to continue looking for a place down here until we settle matters with the kids...Don't you agree?"

"Of course I do."

"But, there's just one little thing I think we should do before completely discarding the idea of living down here."

"What's that?" she asked.

"I want to go back to see the Franks and explain what happened. You never can tell what might come out of our talks with the kids. It's possible that after the family talks are over, they might end up liking the idea of our moving down here. Hell, they might even encourage us to do it immediately. I doubt it, but who knows? No sense burning all bridges...In any case, I'd like to come to some agreement with Lou on a purchase price now, in the event Florida does become a reality."

"That's a good idea. Let's do it tomorrow morning. Why don't you call him now and find out what time we can see him," Helen suggested.

I did just that.

There was no popping of the Moet cork for the remainder of the evening. A dark cloud hung over the Gould household. Gwen was depressed...Helen was distraught...George was an enigma... and I was torn between gloating and indecision.

Dinner consisted of pretzels, white wine for the ladies and regular Scotch for the men. You can imagine what we talked about. Helen dominated most of the conversation bemoaning her insensitivity toward her children and grandchildren. Gwen tried unsuccessfully to convince her why she was wrong.

"Cynthia was overreacting. You caught her off guard, that's all. She only wants you two to be happy. She's not a selfish person. Give her time to take it all in," Gwen said.

"I don't know Gwen. She's never reacted to anything that way. Never in her life can I remember her saying things like she said to us. She was hurt. Mike and I went about this all wrong. We should have talked to the kids first...I hope they'll forgive us," Helen sobbed.

"You're the ones who are overreacting now, Helen. It's not as bad as you're making it out to be. Cynthia is a grown woman. She's not an infant who needs her mother to change her diaper," Gwen said, hoping to give her friend some backbone.

"Gwen's right, Helen. All's not as bad as you're making it out to be," I added.

"Yeah, so why do Billy and Roberta hate us?"

"They don't hate us. They're children—they cry when they break a glass or rip their clothes," I pointed out.

"We're breaking their hearts. I know it. I can feel it."

"Look, we caught them off guard. They're emotional and making a mountain out of a molehill. When they see us again, everything will be put into perspective. It'll be alright—I'm sure of it."

"Helen...I totally and fully agree with Mike. There's no need to continue this type of talk...So, what do you say we all go to the 50s dance at the clubhouse? It'll take our minds off the dark side of the moon. It'll be fun," said George, who hadn't uttered a word for over an hour.

"Excellent idea! I second the motion," I chimed in.

Begrudgingly, Helen acceded.

It wasn't American Bandstand by any stretch of the imagination, but it was a welcome escape from the torture of recriminations over the phone-call debacle. We stayed at the dance for two hours. When we got back to the house, the four of us planned what we'd do the next day. It was decided we'd all drive down to South Beach to see the sights, have lunch and watch the parade of skimpily clad bathers flaunt their stuff. Then in the afternoon, we'd tour the Vizcaya Mansion in Coral Gables, and then top it off by going for some authentic Cuban food in Little Havana. I insisted that before we head south to Miami Beach, Helen and I be allowed to visit Mr. and Mrs. Frank to let them know what was going on.

The next morning, right after breakfast, we met with Lou Frank. He was most understanding of our situation and tried to make us feel better by telling us how his kids pulled the same routine on him and his wife when they moved south. He said he'd give us another week to resolve the situation and make a decision. If we weren't ready to finalize a deal with him by that time, he'd hire a local broker and put the house on the market. I thanked him for giving us extra time and wished him well if things didn't work out between us.

The rest of the day was a total joy. Seventy-degree weather and refreshing sea breezes assaulted our bodies as we sat in an open-air restaurant on South Beach. George and I drank pina coladas and smoked some smuggled Cuban cigars. We ogled the hundreds of practically nude Gen X girls strutting their stuff on the street in front of our table. I even saw Helen smile as some men walked by in their thong bottoms. What a sight! We couldn't have asked for a better show. We had such a great time, we promised each other that if we did move to Tuscany Villas, we'd make it an annual ritual so long as we didn't have to go back to Vizcaya, a palatial estate in Coral Gables built by the industrialist, James Deering. This very large house situated on a piece of waterfront property has an awesome view of Biscayne Bay. It's now a museum and a very popular tourist attraction decorated to the nth degree—money was no object. Forget about going back though: traipsing through it once was enough…enough for a lifetime—no need to repeat the experience.

We weren't going to see Gwen and George before we left very early the next morning for our trip back to New Jersey, so we said our thanks and goodbyes that evening. I pleaded with Helen and Gwen to keep the crying and hysteria to a minimum before going to bed…A lot of good that did. No need to explain the scene that ensued. You've seen it in the movies or experienced it yourselves: a real Siskel and Ebert three-tissue tear jerker.

So, with red swollen eyes, mascara smeared cheeks, and wet tissues stuffed down the front of her blouse, Helen and I took a slow, labored retreat into our bedroom to pack our steamer trunks. Once they were filled to overflowing, I lugged them to the car. Miracle of miracles, I was able to fit all of them into the trunk and backseat, without having to tie any of them onto the roof of the car.

We woke at 5:00 in the morning, brushed our teeth and peed. I tried to dump, but had no success…Oh, I hate that feeling! There was no need to shower since we did it before we went to sleep.

On tippy toes we left the house, silently closed the front door behind us, got into our car and drove, leaving Tuscany Villas and Palm Beach's Italian Riviera in our rear-view mirror.

32

I'M HAPPY TO report the trip back to New Jersey was humdrum. During three days of driving, we had no arguments. In fact, we didn't have the slightest disagreement over anything, including decisions as to where to eat. I was free of tension headaches. As a matter of fact, the entire experience was quite pleasurable. The only downer was that we finished listening to "*Chaos*". If I must say so myself: what a book! What a story! A must read!...It was as if the author knew how the 2016 presidential primary would play out. Well, enough said on that subject. I don't want to be accused of hawking a book. You might think I'm getting paid to do it, which might be the case, but the author of this book will receive a royalty if you do buy *Chaos Reigns During the Presidential Election*, since he also wrote this novel.

In any case, back to my saga.

As soon as we walked through the front door of our home, Helen rushed past me, laser focused on reaching the kitchen phone. She immediately called each of our children to arrange a mutually convenient date they could all come to the house and talk through her master plan for our end-of-life years. She was not going to let the matter go unresolved another day. I also felt it was time to finally settle the question of our incarceration and again alert the cemetery workers to prepare our gravesites.

Saturday was a no-go since three of the grandkids had soccer games. A trifle disappointed in having to delay seeing them for an extra day until Sunday, Helen rationalized her frustration by realizing it would give her more time to cook the fifteen-course meal she was preparing to serve. Likewise, it gave me an extra twenty-four hours to ruminate about the least offensive, yet positive tactic I would take during the family discussion. Nevertheless, I went to each of the soccer games. I wasn't going to disappoint the grandkids. Helen chose not to accompany me for fear she would not be able to control her emotions and say something she'd later regret.

Everyone, and I mean everyone, was coming to Montvale on Sunday. Both sons, my daughter, each of their respective spouses, and all the grandchildren would be there. I could already picture the horde descending upon our home and turning a tranquil abode into a menagerie of screaming, ranting, and running lunatics, who, when were all finally called to the dinner, would eat as if they hadn't had a meal in weeks. Then, after they had departed and the dust had settled, the pillows, my shoes, and a basement full of toys would be returned to their rightful places. We could then run the dishwasher for four consecutive cycles. And once we'd accomplished all that, we could finally drag ourselves up the steps to our bedroom for a solid four hours sleep! Ah, blessed be the life of a senior citizen.

Why am I so negative? Look on the bright side of life: my granddaughters will spend at least an hour fussing over my hairdo, taking turns brushing and combing it into the most beautiful styles one can imagine...I just love it. Helen, on the other hand always looks a little envious when they do that, especially when they accessorize the do with pretzels.

I hate it if someone is late for an appointment. Especially if they don't have the common courtesy of calling to let you know they won't be on time. It took me quite a few years to change Helen's habit of being "fashionably late". Her family thought it was expected of people of their social strata not to be on time. To me, it's just rude. I'd rather be early and catch my hosts in their underwear than be late...Just saying! Luckily, at the stroke of one o'clock, the flock descended on us like a herd of wildebeests running from a pride of lions. Punctuality is one of the positive traits each of my kids inherited from me.

Well, all I can say is thank goodness I'm in good shape. For if I wasn't, I would have suffered some broken bones and possibly a concussion from the savage greeting I received from the grandkids. They assaulted me, throwing me to the ground and jumping up and down on my chest; and my face was drenched from their non-stop kisses. Only a grandparent can relate to the feeling I experienced...Nothing in the world compares. Finally, they retreated from their prey...me, and like little angels, ran to Helen, hugging and kissing her.

Greetings over, I corralled the grandkids and took them into the basement playroom safely away from the living room, so the din of their shrieks would be kept to an acceptable level. I then asked all the adults to join us in the living room.

Once everyone was comfortably seated, I began,

"First of all, for Mom and me, I want to apologize to each of you for going off and not explaining beforehand what we were considering and why we were contemplating such a drastic change in our life...Honestly, I didn't think we would have reached the point where we actually could make a decision about moving. At the risk of being severely punished by Mom, I have to admit to you and her that it was definitely not my intention, or desire to move...It was the farthest thing from my mind. I tried everything and every way I knew to sabotage Mom's plan...It didn't work...I ended up fooling myself. However, we both consider your opinions and feelings essential, and would never intentionally do anything to harm the family in any way. You know that."

"Mom...Dad...I understand what you're saying and know how you feel about us. But you guys have to realize when you told us last week, it came out of the blue. To say it was a surprise is putting it mildly; it threw me for a loop. I felt like a rug was pulled out from under me. I'm not exaggerating when I tell you the kids were...I don't know how can I say this without you thinking I'm exaggerating?...The kids felt like you didn't want to see them anymore. Can you understand that?" my daughter, Cynthia, said.

"Oh, Cynthia, we..." Helen started sobbing and couldn't continue talking.

Keep going, baby. Don't let up!

"What Mom wanted to say was...we made a terrible mistake by not taking you into our confidence and discussing what we were considering before we actually started to look for a new place to live."

"Don't get the wrong idea about our reaction. We want you guys to be happy and enjoy your lives to the fullest, but couldn't you be more empathetic to what the rest of us would go through? Full disclosure: after your call the other day, all of us spoke on the

MITCHELL G. KUHN

phone and are united in our opinions about the entire situation," Cynthia said.

"We don't think you've considered the unintended consequences of what moving to Florida would mean to all of us, including you two," Paul, our eldest son added.

"How so? I asked.

"What are you looking for, Dad? The fountain of youth?" Paul continued.

"That's not a bad idea. Unfortunately, that fountain is in Bimini, not in Palm Beach or St. Augustine Florida."

"Okay, I stand corrected. My mistake! Any who, what's the need? What's the attraction?" Paul said, still not satisfied.

Her crying bout now over, Helen offered in a weak voice, "The warm weather, for one reason."

"Oh yeah, Mom...ninety-five plus degrees during June, July and August is most appealing. Yup, that's my fondest wish: to sweat through my underwear at least twice a day. The only ones who benefit from that oppressive heat are Florida Power and Gas: they supply the air conditioning," Paul said.

"It's not as bad as you make it out to be, Paul. In fact, I hear it's quite pleasant most of the time," Helen countered.

"Who are you talking to? The Florida Board of Tourism? Take my word for it, Mom, you two will hate the heat during the summer; no question about it," David, my youngest, son piped in.

Helen challenged David's comment. "If it's so bad, why is it so many people our age are moving and living there?"

"Because the sun has dulled their ability to think clearly...and that's probably why Floridians have the highest rate of senility and Alzheimer's in the country," Cynthia added.

— 170 —

Enjoying the give and take, David joined in. "I thought that distinction belongs to Arizona."

Confident in his knowledge and unable to control a smirk, Paul continued, "Nope, Arizona gave up the title to Florida ten years ago. Don't you read the medical journals?"

"You boys are crazy. Can we stop talking about the weather... please!"

David again joined the fray, saying, "Only if you can tell us what's really behind all this...Not one of us believes for a second that this is Dad's idea. So, Mom?"

Ah, what a lucky man I am! They do know their father and mother, don't they!

The floodgates opened. Helen had no choice but to say it like she felt it.

"All my friends have moved from Montvale. Both my weekly mahjong and canasta games have ended. We have no social life as a couple, aside from seeing you guys. Also, I can't stand seeing your father spending day-in and day-out either playing on the computer or watching television. It's not right; it's not good for his health."

"Dad, any rebuttal?" Cynthia prompted.

"Thanks, babe, you really know how to put me on the spot! Why don't you just blindfold me and stand me in front of the firing squad? It's a better alternative than facing Mom's fury."

"No pardon is granted. So what do you say?" Cynthia persisted.

"Florida does offer some benefits," I said.

"Not good enough. Like what, Dad?" David asked.

"Hmmmm. Early bird specials, for one...and women with perky uplifted...you know...toenails," I responded.

"Will you please be serious, Daddy? This is not a time for jokes," Cynthia pleaded.

I gave a huge sigh. "So be it. Mom's not happy in this big house; she wants things to do and people to do them with. You know I can make do wherever I am. I'm easy...I'm being the good husband."

"Oh my God, Mike. Have you no shame blaming this all on me?"

"Sweetheart, it was your idea at first—and then I came to accept that there were some positives in moving to an active adult senior community. But, and a big but (butt)...not necessarily yours, I never said we had to move to Florida, and I repeatedly reminded you about how far away we'd be from the family."

Helen silently absorbed what I said. I could smell the wood burning and the wheels turning. She waited for what seemed like a full minute before responding. Actually, it was more like five seconds.

"Dad's right. He did say those things. I was so excited by the houses, the communities, and the people I met, that I never put two and two together. I was in a trance. I was blinded. I wanted to buy a three-bedroom house so we could have all of you sleep under one roof when you visited. Dad tried as best he could to get through to me the reality of your busy lives and the difficulty of your visiting us on a frequent basis. He knew that the kids' school schedules and your own vacation plans would not necessarily coincide with my expectations... and as much as I want to accuse Dad of being a naysayer...and an obstructionist...I have to admit, he was only trying to help me to make the right decision and understand the consequences of that decision."

"Hold the presses!" I declared. "We have a new banner head-line: **Dad is Exonerated!** Thank you, darling. I can't tell you how much I appreciate you saying that."

"We understand; we really do. It's not an ideal situation for you living in Montvale at this stage of your lives, isolated from your friends and peers. So having said that, where does it leave us?" David wanted to know.

"Up in the air a bit, I guess," I said. "Look, this house really is too large for only two of us. We could stay here, I assume, if some of you would move in with us." Silence. "What, no volunteers?"

"No Dad, do you think any of us have lost our minds?" Cynthia jokingly responded.

"Never can tell! That type of illness does run in the family you know," I responded.

"Back to the subject at hand," said Paul. "Obviously something has to happen. You want to move out of this house; that much we know...and understand your reasons for wanting to, but where to and when are the questions. Am I right?"

"Hit it on the nose my boy!" I said pointing to my big nose to make the point. "You're as sharp as a marble."

"From our perspective," said Paul, "your living in Florida is not an acceptable option for several reasons. Namely, we're up here in New Jersey and New York worrying about what's going on fifteen hundred miles away. Neither of you are spring chickens. What happens if either of you, or both of you become ill; need assisted living or nursing home care? What then? We'll feel an obligation to fly down to Florida frequently to make sure everything is okay, even if you say you don't want us to. It's only natural for you to want us with you and for us to want to be of help. But if circumstances are such that we couldn't come down for numerous reasons, the guilt that'll befall us won't be pretty. And you won't be happy either.

Did you seriously consider all the schedules we all have to juggle and the cost of flying down to Florida with our families? How many times do you think we can possibly see each other in the course of one year? Think about it, Mom—seeing us once or twice a year at the most; that's not an option if we can help it."

Then Cynthia added, "Practically speaking, Mom, if you were living in Florida, you'd miss all the grandkids' activities. Even Grandparents' Day at school would be a bust if you weren't there with the kids, especially if their other grandparents came and you didn't."

That was an arrow right to the heart!

Helen took a tissue from her pocket and dabbed her eyes now welling up with tears.

Cynthia waited while her mother composed herself. "Do you get the point? How about all the birthday parties, Thanksgiving dinners and all the other holidays? We could understand it if you had to move that far away for health reasons, or if we didn't function so well as a family…but we do…and both of you are healthy. There has to be a better way for this thing to work without causing such a traumatic disruption in our family."

"We're not being selfish," David said. "If you moved, we don't view it as losing our babysitters or chauffeurs or the countless free meals we mooch off you…Well, maybe the meals are a deal breaker."

"Funny…You sound just like your father," said Helen.

"Strong dominant genes, my dear," I proudly added.

"Then what happens when one of you...God forbid...passes? Do you expect us to leave either of you alone in Florida? No way in hell would we allow that to happen! We'd force you to move back up here to live with us," David said.

"I'm not moving in with any of my children. I can take care of myself," I declared.

"Who said we wanted you to? We're referring to Mom, big shot, not you."

"I also wouldn't move in with any of my children. That would be too much of a burden on your families," Helen said.

"Let us be the judge of that. At the very least, if something occurred where either of you would need to move back up north, we'd get Mom an apartment and, if it was you, Dad...a small doghouse."

I involuntarily smiled. I knew my son. *What a wise ass. Like his old man.*

We'd have to work it out when and if that becomes necessary to do so. We get it; you'd still want your independence, and you'd have it, except for driving a car," Paul said.

"Can I assume from what you're all saying that you've had a meeting of the minds and are prepared to offer a solution that meets Mom's needs and overcomes your own objections to our moving south?"

"Not specifically, but generally speaking we'd like you to consider looking for an active adult community which offers the lifestyle you want and is within a reasonable distance from us," replied David.

"We've already looked in South Jersey. It's not for me, I wouldn't be happy there…Mom might be, but we agreed that if one of us objects, it's a no-go…Anyhow, if we moved to South Jersey, it would be more than two hours' driving time, without traffic, for most of us to visit one another…That's not something I would relish doing on a regular basis."

"That definitely is a factor we took into consideration when we talked. That's why we spoke with a lot of our friends whose parents have moved to active adult retirement communities. Most of them found something in Long Island or Connecticut…There aren't that many of them to see," said Cynthia.

"Seems to me that most of our friends have moved south to the Carolina's or Florida, rather than stayed up north," said Helen.

"I don't doubt that, Mom," said Paul, "but who knows the real reasons why they did. Not every family is as close as ours. How many of your friend's siblings see each other on a regular basis, or talk regularly to one another for that matter? How many of your girlfriends get along with their sons or daughters-in- law? You never know for sure what the dynamics of another family are."

"I can't argue with you about that. Dad and I are extremely fortunate for what we have…for each of you. No question about it. And we're thrilled that we all get along so well together. We know it's a rarity."

"Time for a group hug!" I said, rising from my chair.

"Not so fast, Dad. We haven't resolved anything yet," Paul said gesturing to me to sit back down.

"You're right, Paul. So tell me…since you and Sue live in Glastonbury, CT, Dave and Carol are in Ridgefield, CT, and

Cynthia and Lou are in Pine Brook, NJ, where the hell can we live that's convenient for all of us?"

"Cynthia, tell Mom and Dad about what you've come up with," Paul suggested.

"Sure thing. I found four communities I think might be just what you're looking for. Two are in Connecticut, one in Westchester, NY, and one on Long Island."

"Where on Long Island?" I asked.

"Out near Southampton."

"You're kidding me...right?"

"No, I'm not. I don't know what town it's actually in, but let's just say it's in Southampton...I always wanted to tell my friends I'd summered in the Hamptons!"

"Helen, we raised a snob!" I uttered.

"I'm joking... Really, I am," Paul said in defense of his comment.

"And what, pray tell, does it cost to buy a home in one of America's most overpriced communities? Forget it...don't even tell me...It doesn't matter...I wouldn't even consider moving there if I could afford to...My haberdasher is Costco, not Armani's. I food shop at Aldi's not Whole Foods or Trader Joe's...and I'm partial to Dollar Tree not Neiman Marcus. I don't buy jeans with holes in them and I wear socks with my shoes. I'm not a yuppie, and there's nobody I have to impress, but my mistress. Who cares?"

"I do!" Helen yelled, raising her hand in a mock threatening action as if she was going to slap my face.

"Dad! Nicely said. We get the point: scrap Long Island. Now are you ready to hear about the other communities?" Paul asked.

"I suppose I have no alternative but to hear from the prosecutors."

"So members of the jury, I propose we send Mom and Dad on a road trip to Westchester County and Connecticut to reconnoiter the active adult retirement communities they have to offer. All in favor, signify by saying 'aye'…Hearing no objections, the resolution passes unanimously!"

"Paul, who died and elected you Chairman," I asked.

"I was designated by affirmation. Besides, I'm the prettiest of the sibs."

"Excuse me for living. You sound just like the 'Young Pope' portrayed by Jude Law on the HBO mini-series," Cynthia responded.

"No, not really. I've modeled my delusional behavior on the egomaniacal psychopath currently occupying the White House, His Highness Donald the Red," Paul stated.

"How dare you sell yourself so short. I didn't raise you to be a fool," I said.

"No, you certainly didn't, Dad. Now that that's put to rest, we can get back to the reason we're all here? Last year my friend Glen's parents moved to Oxford Fields in Oxford, Connecticut."

"Where the hell is Oxford Connecticut? I never heard of the place."

Sounds to me like Bumble Fuck, USA.

"We never heard of the place either. We had to look it up on a map," David said.

"So, where is it?" asked Helen.

"A couple of miles off of US 84 near Southbury."

"Can you be more specific?" I asked.

"Did you ever hear of Seymour, Derby, Ansonia, or Naugatuck?" Cynthia asked.

"Those are real towns? Are they near this Oxford place? I asked.

"Bingo. You got it. You're so smart. You're as sharp as a marble, Dad."

"What'd I get? I still don't have the foggiest idea where this place is. The only towns I know of in Connecticut are Danbury, Stamford, Hartford, and of course Glastonbury and Ridgefield where you guys live. I've never even driven past any of those other places you mentioned."

"That's because you're only familiar with US 91 and US 95," David said.

"Not true. I know about 684 and the Saw Mill River Parkway and Route 35," I countered.

"Well now Dad, you can expand your horizons and venture out into the big wide wonderful world beyond your comfort zone. It's no more than an hour and fifteen minutes without traffic from the Tappan Zee Bridge. You take 287 to 684 to US 84 heading toward Hartford, and get off at exit 16. Then a short ten-minute drive to Oxford Fields," Paul said.

"Thanks for that MapQuest synopsis, my dear child. Now how about telling us what we might find when we arrive on our journey to the hinterlands…What did your friend tell you about this place, David?"

"His parents love it there."

"That's it? That's all you got?"

"What more do you need to know?"

"I guess there's nothing else. Where do I send my check and when can I call the moving van company?"

"Dad, Glen said his parents are very happy there, and that they would be pleased to have you and Mom come by for a visit. He said they'd love to show you around their community anytime it's convenient for you, so long as you give them a couple of days' advance notice."

"That's very nice of them," said Helen.

"There's no need for that now. I don't want to put them out; I'd rather just go up there on our own to look over the place. Then if we feel it would be helpful, we'll accept their invitation and go up another time," I said. "By the way, how long will it take us to drive from Oxford to get to each of you?"

"A lot shorter than it would have if you had moved to Florida," Cynthia quipped.

"Yeah, I get the point, but answer my question. How long?"

"With or without traffic?" Dave responded.

"With!"

"That depends," Dave continued.

"On what?"

"The weather conditions for one," Cynthia chimed in, no doubt enjoying the discomfort they were causing me.

"Alright I surrender! Can we cut the BS now?"

Without saying another word, Paul handed me a manila folder containing printed copies of MapQuest travel directions detailing routes and approximate travel times from either Oxford, CT, Somers, NY, Southbury, CT, or Southampton, LI, to and from each of their respective homes. And supplemented it with charts and graphs of demographic statistics about each of the townships these communities were a part of.

"Looks as if you've anticipated some of my questions."

"That we have, Papa," Cynthia said.

"Did you include the cattle and swine populations in your presentation?"

"Actually, we wanted to, but felt it might do you some good to research that on your own time. Use the internet for once for something constructive other than spending time on those porn sites," Paul said.

"I choose to ignore that uncalled for attack on my morals. So you guys are really serious about not wanting us to move south."

"Whatever gave you that impression?" Paul said.

"I don't know... Just a hunch on my part."

"Did you consider finding a community up here and only going down to Florida for a month or two during the winter? You could rent, stay with friends, or stay in a hotel. Why live there all the time? The vote was unanimous: seventeen to zip, forbidding you to move south."

"The grandkids also voted?" Helen asked.

"It was their idea. For our part," Cynthia said, "we couldn't care less if you moved to Siberia."

The sarcasm was lost on Helen. It has never been her strong suit. I was touched. They really did want us to stay close, especially the grandkids who have repeatedly voiced such sentiments in the past.

"So," I said, "just to spite you all I'm not going to buy down south, or in Siberia, even if your mother insists we do; and I'm cutting you all out of the Will."

"What are you talking about, Mike?" Helen asked.

"I'm only joking dear," I said.

And before I could continue, all six of our kids (son- and daughters-in-law included) surrounded us...hugging and kissing us. Helen again burst into tears. We all did.

I had achieved a victory of sorts. Meaning I won a battle, but in reality, I lost the war. I now had to commit to finding that active adult community Helen so desperately wanted to move to. Only now my options were limited to a specific confined geographic area well north of the Mason/Dixon Line.

One rarely attains everything one wants. In this case, I kept what is most important to me: my children and grandchildren, and a wife who, with all her other shortcomings, shares with me the emotional attachment of family above all else. Yes, I know we must lead our own lives and enjoy what years we have remaining. I'm certain we can do that and not be bound or dictated to by the needs of our children. It's not selfish or uncaring of me to believe that at this stage of our lives, our needs must take precedence over theirs. Without a doubt we can do that without jeopardizing anybody's happiness.

Helen untangled herself from the love fest scrum. Her face had turned beet red and glistened with a mixture of tears and wet black mascara. She radiated the joy and sorrow she was experiencing. Then in an instant, her face suddenly morphed into a tortured mask of horror.

"Oh no!" she screamed. "The roast, it's still in the oven. It's probably burned to a crisp already. Dinner's ruined! What are we going to eat?"

A few seconds before Helen's outburst, the grandchildren had returned from the basement where they had been playing.

"Pizza!" a chorus of voices yelled out.

"That's not a healthy meal for growing children," Helen replied.

"We don't care. We want pizza...we want pizza..." the chant echoed through the house.

You guessed it...no surprise. It didn't matter that Helen spent hours preparing a feast of roast beef, mashed potatoes, carrots, homemade apple pie, and ice cream. So much for our sacrifices, or our cravings...we gave into the grandkids. The kids got their pizza. I got some more hugs and a couple of pretzel crumbs in my hair.

33

FIRST THING THE next morning, I went directly to my safe haven—my den. The dark Sherwood Forest green paint, plaid rug, and comfy leather chair always made me feel secure and serene. I turned on the computer sitting on my beautiful roll top desk and Googled "active adult retirement communities in Somers, NY, Southbury CT, and Oxford, CT."

Just as an aside: in my former life, every time either I or someone else mentioned New Jersey, I'd get an instant case of acid reflux. Sorry...I'm a New Yorker by birth...I can't help it. So it came as no surprise to me that I was experiencing the same discomfort when I heard myself read the name Oxford, Connecticut. What the hell was I getting myself into?

I called out for Helen to join me in the den since I had some more information about the communities the kids wanted us to look at. She must have immediately dropped what she was doing, because no sooner had the words come out of my mouth, than Helen appeared over my shoulder.

"Yes Mike, what is it?"

"I've done some research on those three communities the kids suggested we look at."

"No, they said there were four of them."

"Right, but there's no way I'm going to consider the Hamptons even if we could afford to move there, which we can't. Neither of us will be happy. Think about the outrageous traffic from all the summer tourists and weekenders. Can you imagine us socializing with the celebrities and Park Avenue debutants? It would be a nightmare dealing with those pretentious ass holes."

"I agree. Tell me what you found out about the other retirement communities."

"Alright, here goes...The place in Somers, NY was built in late sixties. Just look at this picture. The houses look old and they're not even cheap. They want close to seven hundred thousand dollars for a two-bedroom attached house. They're crazy."

"What about the taxes? How do they compare to Jersey's?"

"It's Westchester County, what do you expect? They're insanely high because of the school systems. Maybe if we wanted to start a family and take advantage of the schools it would have some benefit, but since you refuse to even entertain the thought of conceiving again, it'd be a total waste of money we don't have, and bottom line we'd get very little benefit from it."

"Are the taxes more than we're paying now?"

"No, they're less."

"Even so, it doesn't make sense for us to spend that much and get nothing for it, considering we don't have kids in the school system."

"Financially, you're right. So...moving on to the one in Southbury. Look here: this one was built around the same time as the one in Somers, and by the same developer. The taxes are much lower, but the place is old, and so are the residents."

"You're not young either, my dear."

"Sure, pick on me, why don't you."

"You opened the door and I ran through it."

"Fine, I'm old. But I'd rather buy a relatively new house and live in a community that's not falling apart."

"You'll get no disagreement from me."

"That leaves us with…" The name got stuck in my throat! "Oxford."

"What about it? Tell me."

"I don't think words can adequately describe it."

"Try."

"I Google earthed the place, but couldn't find it."

"What couldn't you find?"

"Oxford!"

"What do you mean you couldn't find Oxford?"

"The town's listed on the map, but when I zoomed in to view it there was no town. I saw a small building I assumed to be a town hall, a tiny school with Quonset huts behind it, a fire station, and two churches. No stores…nothing. What the hell are we getting ourselves into? Seems to me, judging from what I saw and read about these communities, we're better off staying put in this house. We can have a carpenter come over and construct some ramps, widen the doors to accommodate wheelchairs, and install grab-bars in the tub and showers. Maybe we could put in an elevator?"

"Notice how I'm ignoring you, Mike?…How old is Oxford Fields?"

"What?"

She just stared at me.

"Oh, you mean, when was this fossil farm built?"

"Yeah. Whatever tickles your fancy, dear."

"Says the first house was built seven years ago."

"How many houses are there?"

"Supposedly three hundred and fifty have been built and another couple of hundred are planned."

"Fine. Do they have a clubhouse and a pool?"

"Yes, there's a clubhouse and both an indoor and outdoor pool."

"Anything else?"

"A gym, two tennis courts, and a bocce court."

"And...?"

"Some card rooms, and a pool table."

"And...?

"Oh yeah, I almost forgot.... There's a public golf course on the property, but it's not part of the community. They don't even have a shuffleboard court or a pickleball court."

"And...?

"That's all."

"Are you sure?"

"Well, I was saving the best for last as a surprise."

"Should I get a glass of wine?"

"That won't be necessary."

"So...out with it."

"Rich's Ice Cream Emporium."

"Come again?"

"The world-famous Rich's Homemade Ice Cream Emporium is in Oxford...Can you believe that? No joke, people come from as far away as Derby to savor the high fat content served in giant waffle cones."

"I'm at a loss for words," said Helen.

"You're at a loss; can you imagine how stunned I am? But they really do come from far and wide to enjoy the delights. Rumor has it that some folks from Bethel Connecticut have been spotted there as well."

"Miracles do happen, don't they!"

"In Oxford they do. That's for sure."

34

THAT SATURDAY, AROUND 10:30, we got into our car and drove north. Throwing caution to the wind, I took the New York State Thruway instead of going over the Tappan Zee Bridge into Westchester. I avoided a near catastrophe as we approached the tollbooth at Harriman, NY, because Helen spotted signs for Woodbury Commons.

For the uninformed, Woodbury Commons is the ultimate destination for busloads of Asian and European discount shoppers vacationing in NYC, and for the female gender residing in the tri-state area of New York, New Jersey, and Connecticut.

Faced with the opioid of bargain shopping taking control of my wife's very being, I drew upon my legendary powers of persuasion. I had to avoid the likelihood of expending our life's saving on must have shoes, black slacks, pocket books, shoes, black pants, jeans, shoes, jewelry, shoes, sweaters, and more shoes. To say nothing of wasting precious energy traipsing behind my wife lugging her newly acquired treasures.

"Mike" she purred. "Can we stop at the Commons for a few minutes? I have to pick up a few things I desperately need. We're so close. It would be a shame not to stop."

"What was it Adlai Stevenson said at the United Nations to the Russian Ambassador about 'not happening until hell freezes over'?"

"Just a few minutes…please. It won't take long; I promise."

"Tell you what: I'll give you a rain check. It'll be good for the next thirty days. But right now, I want to keep driving. We still have at least another hour drive ahead of us. Maybe on the way back we can stop. Let's just play it by ear. Okay?"

I knew I'd take a different route back after we finished scoping out our possible new home in the cemetery. Brain dead I'm not!

"Fine…I suppose I can wait."

I increased my speed so I would pass the exit before she changed her mind. We continued up the Thruway until the exit for US 84 at Newburgh, NY. We headed east toward Hartford, Connecticut. We stayed on US 84 until my GPS directed me to take exit 15 onto Connecticut State Route 67. I was a little confused since MapQuest wanted us to take exit 16. Nevertheless, I followed the melodic urgings of the woman hiding under my dashboard, even though she was most annoying, especially when constantly repeating herself as to where I had to make a turn. God forbid, I deviated from her instructions…I'd never hear the end of it…She'd go ballistic: "Make a U-turn…make a left…take a right"——it drove me nuts. Ah, but I digress again.

Without a doubt, Route 67 would never win a "Scenic Highway Award"; not even an honorable mention. We drove by an abundance of decaying homes, one or two horse farms, one well-kept community of attached homes, a cemetery, Oxford Town Hall, and several abandoned one-story commercial buildings. Oxford showed the scars of the Great Recession. It had——and looked as if it was still——suffering from the ravages of economic hardship, without even having any commercial industry to speak of. The entire area looked as depressed as I felt.

It seemed like an eternity until my little GPS genie told us to turn off of 67 onto Riggs Road. There was a sign at the intersection advertising Oxford Fields. Finally, we were on the home stretch...I hoped.

I couldn't wait. Well, I could, but I couldn't.

About a mile up the road, we passed three men in camouflage pants, jackets, and hats walking single file on the side of the road with rifles slung over their shoulders.

"Tell me I didn't just see three men with rifles walking on a public street," I said out loud.

No response. Helen's head was down; her chin resting on her chest.

"Helen, did you see them?"

"Yes, I did."

"How, your eyes were closed?"

"Not fully...I did see them! And I can't believe our kids want us to live where people carry guns in the open. Where are we, in the Old Wild-West? Is it legal for them to do that here? Mike, maybe we should call the police?"

"I don't know. I know I don't like it even if it's legal for them to walk around on public streets like that. Let's wait until we get to Oxford Fields. If we're lucky enough to see anyone alive, I'll ask them what the story is...Assuming they can hear or see me."

"Mike...I beg you; don't start with that crap again."

"I'll try. I'll be on my best behavior. You'll be so proud of me, wait and see."

"Do you really think people walk around with guns like that all the time?"

"Maybe it's hunting season? I don't know."

"I still don't like the idea of living in an area where people can carry guns. We have to check on that. And if they can, I don't want to live here. It's not safe."

"Agreed. We'll definitely check it out before we do anything. Hold on tight, I think we're there."

We had driven on Riggs Road for about three miles when we came to the entrance to Oxford Fields. There was no waterfall, no palm trees, no big iron gates, no security guard house, no plantings; just a small stone wall and a white aluminum hitching post fence on both sides of the road leading into the community.

Not bad...Understated...Encouraging so long as the homes are not dilapidated farmhouses.

Signs on the side of the road directed us to the sales office about a half-mile from the entrance. We passed several homes under construction, even though there were piles of snow on the ground and the temperature was in the low twenties.

How the hell can people work under these conditions? I wondered. *I really was spoiled working my entire career in an office. Lucky for me...I never could have done what they do.*

We parked our car in a small lot designated for visitors on the side of one of the models they converted into a business/sales office.

I expected to be greeted by a perky co-ed or accosted by a sales staffer similar to the ones who welcomed you into a Raymour & Flanigan Furniture Store, and then followed you around as if you were going to carry a sofa or a chair on your back and run out the door with it...That didn't happen. In fact, no one was at the reception desk or anywhere I could see. I called out.

"Anyone here?"

No answer...

"I guess there are no houses left to be sold."

Still no one replied.

"Why not see if someone is in one of those offices?" Helen said, pointing in the direction of what looked like three offices in the back of the building.

"Yes ma'am."

Rather than knocking on the closed doors, I called out again. "Anyone here? Hello...anyone here?"

A few seconds later, I heard a muffled voice responding from down a corridor behind us calling out, "I'll be with you in a moment...Please help yourself to some cookies and coffee. They're in the display room to the left of where you came in."

Here we go again.

I couldn't wait to see the requisite display of chocolate chip cookies and Keurig coffee pods.

What? No Keurig!

I was beyond myself with disappointment. They had an old-fashioned bourgeois Mr. Coffee and some stale vanilla wafers.

This is no way to treat a prospective buyer. I'm intrigued. Maybe it's just a ruse. Fake me out with some modest offerings and then lower the boom with some high-pressure sales tactics in an attempt to catch me off guard. I'm ready for them. Just let them try.

I poured myself a cup of decaf coffee, and while I was mid-process digesting a mouth full of cookie, the salesman joined us.

"Welcome to Oxford Fields," he said, extending his hand. "I'm Chad, and who do I have the pleasure of meeting?"

"I'm Helen Chandler and this is my husband, Mike. We're so glad to meet you."

"Did you by chance make an appointment for a tour?"

"No," I mumbled, still trying to rid my mouth of cookie. "Should we have? It doesn't look like you're being overrun by a crowd of house buyers."

"No, no, no, don't get me wrong; an appointment isn't necessary. I simply wanted to make sure you had ample time to see everything...How much time do you have?"

"For as long as it takes," I said.

This isn't me. I should tell him he has one hour to make his case, and if not we're outta here...Alas, that's the old me. The new me has emerged. I'm now understanding, patient, and accepting. I've opened my mind...a little bit.

The child within me must remain hidden so as not to lose the opportunity of permanently putting the nail in the coffin of "moving south". This is a sacrifice I can make...I hope.

Helen shit her pants. NO, not really, but her face betrayed the absolute astonishment she felt hearing those words come out of my mouth.

"So where are you folks from?"

"Northern New Jersey."

"So why Oxford Fields? Do you have family in Connecticut?"

Bam! All my good intentions went out the window. I definitely have Tourette's syndrome. The words came out of my mouth before I even knew I'd said them. I can't control my desire to make the witty comment when the opportunity is teed-up for me to hit.

I deflected answering the question directly like every good political talking head. Instead I replied, "Because I want to be the only man living in a community who still has his teeth, mind, and can control the flow of his pee. I'll be a rock star."

"Sorry to disappoint you Mike, but we already have a lot of rock stars here. You won't be the only one. The majority of men here are very active; even those men in their eighties and nineties. In any case, do you have family near here?"

Nosy son-of-a bitch.

We have a son living in Ridgefield, CT, another son in Glastonbury CT, and a daughter in Pine Brook, NJ," said Helen.

"Three children. That's great…And…any grandchildren?"

"So many I can't remember all their names," I piped in.

"We have nine wonderful grandchildren," said Helen, a little edge to her voice, her facial expression pleading with me to rein in my unwanted demons.

"Oh yeah, that's right: we have nine grandkids…I forgot about little Stevie. He's getting so old now I think of him as an adult…my bad. Look, we're interested in Oxford because it's both close enough to let us see everyone without much difficulty, and yet far enough away from them as to not let any of our kids feel we're encroaching on their lives. It's a good choice…At least as far as geographic distance is concerned. On the other hand, I've always been averse to living in a cultural wasteland," I said, turning my body around and making a two-armed gesture, palms up as if to say look for yourself.

"Mike, I guess I have to throw caution to the wind and risk losing a sale by disagreeing with a potential client, but I must take exception to your characterization of Oxford as a 'wasteland'. True, the village of Oxford leaves a lot to be desired…"

I interrupted Chad in mid-thought. "That's an understatement if I ever heard one. You don't even have a movie theater, or a supermarket. Where does a guy have to go to read a porno magazine?"

Chad wasn't taking any of my crap. I give him credit: he had the balls to say, "As I was trying to say Mike, though Oxford lacks the physical presence of many of the urban amenities you're accustomed to, like crowded streets and alternate side of the street parking, you can avail yourself of them by driving a very short distance to New Haven or Hartford."

"Hold on a second, pal. New York City has alternate side of the street parking not New Jersey. Don't confuse the two. It's very insulting to my wife's family."

"Oh, excuse me for that slip of the tongue. No insult intended I assure you."

"And by the way, in Jersey we don't have stop signs every ten feet. Why the hell do you?" I asked.

"The Homeowner's Association asked the town highway department to install them."

"Why would they do that? Are there that many accidents with wheelchair-bound residents crossing the street?"

"No, it's just a precautionary measure."

"Do they realize the wheel chairs can go faster than a car can with all those damn signs?"

"I'll relay your observations to the Homeowners Association… promise."

Helen lost it. "Boys, enough of this nonsense. Shake hands and make nice, please!"

"I'll be the bigger person," I said, extending my hand.

"No need. I'm sure Mike and I were just having some fun with one another."

THE SOUND OF SIRENS

"I know I was, but I'm not so sure about you Chad."

"So, where was I?" Chad said, ignoring my invitation to continue our childish repartee.

I really couldn't read Chad very well. His face was a mask and his body gave no hint as to his attitude— a real enigma, this guy. I did have more than a feeling though, based upon some of his responses, that he was onto my antics and had probably come across my likes during his long career. I'd see how he continued to react.

"You were telling us about the many positives Oxford has to offer," Helen said.

"Right. Living in Oxford is no different than living in any other suburban community where you have to drive or take a train to go to the theater, movies, or a museum. New York City is an hour and one half away. You can get to Hartford, New Haven, or Danbury in about thirty minutes. And if you want to shop in any one of four local supermarkets, you can drive to either of them in less than fifteen minutes. You're not isolated."

"How close is the nearest police department?" I wanted to know.

"They're just down the road from here," Chad responded. "Why would you want to know that?"

"Can they protect us from the gun toting gangs roaming the streets?" I asked.

"Honestly, in thirty-five years in this business, I've never been asked that question. What are you talking about? Are you being serious now?"

"Without a doubt I am. Tell him Helen about what we saw driving up…uh, Riggs Road."

"We saw three men carrying rifles," she said.

Chad tried to suppress a giggle. I didn't hear it, but I saw it—there was no mistaking his twinkling eyes.

"I'm betting they were guards hired by Oxford Fields patrolling the streets looking for owners trying to escape."

Chad actually laughed. "No," he said. "They had to be hunters. It's deer season now. Nothing to be concerned about."

"Can they really walk in the streets with guns?" Helen asked, not willing to let the subject end.

"Legally, it is permissible...but believe me, there's no cause to be worried...I've never seen or heard of anyone else witnessing what you saw. Look, to set your mind at ease, I'll talk to the State Troopers and get an explanation, and then I'll let you know what I was told. How's that?"

"Sounds like a plan...Okay, you do that, please. We're both anxious to hear what you find out," I said, keen to move on to another topic.

"I definitely will. So, let me get back to what I was trying to tell you as to why Oxford is an ideal location for you to live...And by the way, you've already agreed is the primary reason our community is best for you."

"I have?"

"Yes, most definitely you have. It's the most important reason why most of the folks who live here chose Oxford Fields: they're built in baby sitters and dog minders for their children," said Chad. "Some residents want that closeness because they're ailing and need their kids' help. Others want their grandchildren to visit them all the time. And in some cases, it's the kids who need help and our residents go to their aid."

"Let's put this topic to rest. As I've already said, it's not our intention, or at least it's not mine to be at my children's beck-and-call. If my kids really need us to pitch in, in an emergency, of course we'll be there to help, but I don't intend on becoming a full-time diaper changer or chauffeur, and truthfully I believe they feel the same about being close, and maintaining one's distance… and a modicum of privacy."

"So be it. Enough said on that matter. Now, how would you like us to proceed? Do you want me to give you my sales pitch or do you want me to answer your questions first…Or do you just want to see our models? The choice is yours. Name your poison; I'm at your disposal."

"Why don't you tell us about the community and then take us through the five models," Helen suggested.

"That works for me. How much time do you have?"

"I already told you—for as long as it takes. But if we can do everything in two hours, we'll still have time to get a small bite to eat and get back on the road and avoid getting caught up in traffic on the way home," I said.

"It might be a little tight, but I think we can do it," Chad said.

"A little tight," I repeated. "Then let's get on with it; times a fleeting."

It took Chad almost thirty minutes to tell us the history of the community, how many homes were planned, the number of homes already sold, the number of residents, and his guesstimate as to the average age of the residents. He explained the relation-ship of the community to the golf course, and what amenities and activities were offered to the residents. Chad astutely avoided any reference to costs; probably because he wanted us firmly hooked on the place before throwing cold water on the fire of Helen's desire.

"This might be a good time to show you the models and the clubhouse. Then we'll come back here and talk more."

"Seems like a plan," I said.

"Would you rather go through the models yourself or should I go with you?"

"You're more than welcome to come with us…that's if you're thick skinned and won't be offended by my off-color comments and criticisms."

"I'm a big boy. There's nothing you can say that I haven't heard before. Take your best shot, Mike."

Our tour lasted less than one hour and forty-five minutes. We walked through five well-designed models. Two of the models had a second floor, but all of them had a master bedroom on the first floor. In this instance, the builder took into consideration the deterioration of the senior citizen's knees and hips. And aside from the stupidity of including a Jacuzzi bathtub and installing a shower the size of a linen closet that no doubt causes full-sized residents claustrophobic anxiety, I really couldn't find too much to fault with the homes. They wouldn't have necessarily been my first choice of home design, but they were more than adequate for my needs. And surprisingly, there was significant land separating the houses, providing the residents with a decent amount of privacy. This was especially true for the homes on cul-de-sacs: much more space than we'd seen in the other senior communities.

Now, are you ready for this? As mystifying as it might be, Helen loved them, especially the one with two additional bedrooms on the second floor, and a huge unfinished basement occupying the entire footprint of the house. The total square footage, including the basement, was more than our five-bedroom home in Jersey. So much for downsizing! And lucky me, it was the one model I had the most objections to. I know you already assumed that was the case! For me, it had much too much space for our needs. Then there were these ludicrous pillars...

"Chad, did the designer of these homes come from Greece or maybe New Jersey?"

"I don't have the slightest idea. Why would it matter? Why would you want to know something like that?"

"Because he or she felt the need to incorporate an architectural motif using pillars obviously stolen or taken in a fire sale from some gambling casino in Jersey or Vegas after it went bankrupt...I can't conceive they were imported...Besides, I'm under the impression Oxford Field is in New England; not ancient Greece."

"They're not everyone's taste, I admit. However, they're structurally necessary and are an integral part of the support system."

"Did they have to put them in both the living room and dining rooms? Can they be removed?"

"I'll ask the construction site manager, but I doubt it."

"Fine. If we end up buying this model, I'd like them removed."

"But I like them," Helen interjected. "They work so well with the space."

"What do you think, Chad?" I asked.

"My opinion doesn't matter. Your opinions are the only ones that count."

I tried to get Chad involved, but he wisely didn't take the bait.

Then, pointing up to the recessed lighting fixtures some twenty-five feet above our heads, I asked Chad.

"Tell me, how am I going to change one of those recessed light bulbs when it burns out? No ladder I own can go that high. And even if it could, I wouldn't risk climbing up there to replace it. The same goes for those windows," I said, pointing to a set of windows located some twenty feet off the ground. "How can Helen clean them, or open them if she wants fresh air?"

"Are you insinuating I'm going to be the one to clean them? Have you lost your mind entirely, Mike?"

"Of course not. I wouldn't expect you to clean them every week," I said with as much sincerity I could put into my voice. "Obviously, I'll have to hire a contractor to put up scaffolding each time a light blows or the windows get dirty.

"And then there's the issue of a heating bill. I can only imagine how high it'll be because the heat has no place to go but up… and it'll certainly waft up to the wide-open space up there," I said, pointing above my head. Why would I bother putting on the heat? It'll serve no useful purpose whatsoever."

"As to the heating bills, I haven't heard anyone complain… because maybe they most likely use the ceiling fan to push the heat back down and/or turn on the gas fireplace with its blow-out fan."

"Well maybe that would help a little…but not much, I'm sure of that."

"The windows however are another issue. I suppose if you wanted them opened, you'd have to hire someone to do that, but you could clean them yourself if you used one of those extension poles. In fact, the same implement can be used to change a light bulb…You can buy one at either Lowes or Home Depot."

When we finished perusing every room in the model, and before Helen could embark upon her routine questioning of Chad, as she had done after seeing the other four models, Chad quickly suggested our next stop be a tour of the clubhouse. "It's only a short car ride from here."

"Sure, let's see it," I said. "We have a little more time to spare before I sign on the dotted line."

That stopped Helen in her tracks. Her head pivoted toward me so fast I thought it would fall off.

"Mike, are you joking?" Helen asked, not knowing if I was just trying to get a rise out of her and Chad.

"Not really, sweetheart, but I am interested in what the costs of buying and living here would be."

"Let's get a move on, Chad; you're not getting any younger."

35

I KNEW EVEN BEFORE we saw the clubhouse it wouldn't be anything like those Taj Mahal's so prevalent in the senior communities throughout New Jersey and Florida. On the other hand, I was hoping it didn't look more akin to a nursing home lobby, with their chairs and sofas covered in plastic, occupied by residents asleep and spittle drooling down the sides of their mouths.

Well, I was right, thank goodness. It was no Taj. There was no marble, no plastic, no restaurants, and no crystal chandelier. Just several rooms with card tables, a billiard room, a small gym, an indoor pool and Jacuzzi, an outdoor pool, and both a men's and women's locker room, each with their own shower.

No, I was not hoping for co-ed showers. I do realize how unattractive seventy and eighty-year-old men and women's physiques can look. No matter how horny I could be, why would I expose myself to that horror? Banish the thought.

"Is there a charge for using the towels?" I asked.

"You have to bring your own towels. The community doesn't provide them."

"What about," I began.

But didn't have a chance to finish my question before Chad jumped in and said, "No, they don't supply bathing suits either."

Am I that obvious? How did the son-of-a-bitch know what I was going to ask?

Feigning a false sense of hurt, I responded, "That was not what I was about to ask you, Chad. What I wanted to know was what temperature is the pool water kept at?"

I guess the smirk on my face betrayed me, because Helen jumped to Chad's defense by saying, "Score two points for Chad."

Then my feeble attempt at hoping to recover the high ground was diminished when I asked Chad where the tennis and bocce courts were. Embarrassing, I know. Like I would ever play bocce ball. At least Helen didn't call me out on that one.

All in all, Helen was quite pleased by the clubhouse; it had everything she wanted. From my point of view, it was no big deal. It was what it was—nothing more, nothing less. At least I didn't feel like it was one of those kitschy Roman marbled edifices so prevalent in the other places we had visited.

Hands down, what stood out to me, and was the highlight of the clubhouse tour, was my discovery of a FOB: modern technology at its best! What's a FOB you ask? It's a golden, (really gray) small teardrop shaped electronic key you just swipe across a small pad that unlocks the main doors to the clubhouse and pool.

When Chad uttered those words, "Without it, no entry!" I immediately pictured the "Soup Nazi" from Seinfeld banning Elaine from buying soup.

Seriously though, this prized possession, only given to owners of the units, is a good security measure. It prevents unwanted

guests from utilizing the facilities if unaccompanied by an owner...
That is so long as the owner doesn't give it away.

"Ready to call it a day?" Chad asked.

Not giving Helen a second to react, I said, "Absolutely. We'll
call you in a couple of days after we've had a chance to review
everything."

"Hold on a minute, Mike. We don't know any of the costs yet.
I thought we were going back to the sales office with Chad to learn
about the pricing, fees, and taxes. We don't even know how long it
would take them to build one of the houses."

"Shouldn't take us more than a half hour to answer all your
questions, Mike. Why not stay a little longer?"

"Okay, lead on McDuff," I said.

36

I WON'T BORE YOU with the details. Suffice it to say you never end up being able to buy a house for the advertised price. Be prepared to pay twenty to forty percent more. The add-ons can kill you. They up charge you for everything. Whether it's for doorknobs that actually turn; appliances (newer than those opened by Betty Furness); kitchen countertops (other than Formica circa 1960); and to put the icing on the cake, you pay an additional amount for the location of the building lot. If you want to see the golf course from your deck...add seventy thousand dollars. Be on a cul-de-sac...plunk down fifty thousand. You get the idea?

The models they took us through were equipped with premium appliances. The floors were top of the line Brazilian hardwood. The bathrooms had the upscale step-up Jacuzzi with tiled walls and floors. The kitchens had marble or granite counters and top of the line cabinets. It's all a showcase.

We were seated around a small, cozy five-foot conference table. Chad laid out architectural drawings for the floor plans of each of the home designs we'd seen. Helen immediately vetoed the two smaller models. No doubt they didn't have enough room for the multitudes of guests she intended on entertaining and inviting to sleep overnight.

Lucky me.

Chad had been responding to Helen's frivolous questions for what seemed like an eternity. Thankfully, he finally brought her cross-examination to an end when, with pleading eyes, he asked Helen if she had narrowed down her preference to a particular model.

No surprise to me, Helen chose the model with the pillars, loft, and those impossible high windows and overhead lights. When I attempted to voice my opinion, Helen held up her hand. She was in no mood to hear from me.

"Don't I get a say?" I asked.

"I've heard your opinion and have taken it under advisement."

"And?"

"No ifs, ands, or buts. I know what I want…so as long as we can get what we want for a reasonable price, I'm satisfied. Now, can we continue, Mike?"

"I'm still not one hundred percent sure yet. The cemetery is acceptable…The plot selection is yet to be determined…Likewise the casket."

"Wonderful! What's the next step, Chad?" Helen asked, unsure of my opinion.

"Well, since you've now narrowed your choice of home style, I can put together a more detailed prospectus for you. First, I need you to let me know about what upgrades you want and what lot you'd like," he said.

I had to stop the locomotive from running over me!

"Helen, why don't we take all this stuff home with us? It'll give us time to map everything out, and make some well thought out decisions. Otherwise, if we just jump into this right now, we might regret things later."

"Are you sure?" Helen asked.

"Without a doubt."

"Chad, there's one important thing you haven't told us yet. Namely, from the time we go to contract, how long does it take to build the house?"

"Four to six months," Chad responded.

"That sounds reasonable."

We shook hands with Chad and promised to get back to him within a week. He thanked us and gave us, you guessed it again, some vanilla wafers for the car ride back to Jersey.

"What, no chocolate chip cookies?"

37

As we drove on the local cow paths toward US 84, I wondered what possessed me to allow Helen to seriously consider moving to this wilderness. There's definitely nothing charming about this place. I'm surprised the good citizens of Oxford, England haven't sued the State of Connecticut for slander.

"I really like Oxford Fields, especially the Edinburgh model. Can you believe how much storage space there is in the basement? Like Chad said, we can put another bedroom and full bath down there, and still have plenty of room for a workshop for you and cedar closets for me," she said.

"Helen, in what kind of dream world are you living? I don't know where to begin."

"What do you mean?"

"I'm incredulous. Three bedrooms and two and one half bathrooms isn't enough space for you? For what possible reason would you want to add another bedroom and bath? And while I'm at it, why would I ever consider building a workshop, no less spending any time in it? In case you've been asleep, or in a coma for the past thirty-five years, let me enlighten you to a little reality. I've never held a hammer, screwed a screw, or sawed a piece of wood; I'm all-thumbs. If I needed anything repaired, made, or installed, I hired someone. Those days are gone when I'd even consider hanging a picture."

"I didn't say I wanted to add those things now. I just meant, in the future, we could do that or use the space for something else."

"Like what? A bowling alley, or an indoor lap pool?"

"Please give it a rest, Mike."

"Okay, I'll put it on my 'To Do' list just as soon as I can get to my computer, or better still I'll tell 'Alexa' to remind me, if I forget."

"No you won't!"

"You're right, I won't."

"Why are you being so negative?"

"I'm not. After all these years, can't you tell I'm just being my old charming self?"

"No, I think you're being selfish."

"Okay Hon, let's get down to brass tacks. Can you truthfully tell me you want to live...I mean suffer for the rest of our active lives in nowhere's ville?"

"Yes I do. We've exhausted every other possibility. That's where I want to live. I'm sure you'll also learn to love it there."

38

FOR THE NEXT day or two, our house was the Korean Demilitarized Zone along the 38th Parallel. We avoided talking to each other about the topic forefront in our minds as if it were the Black Plague. I'd leave the house early to play golf for five hours with the only two remaining friends I had within a twenty-mile radius of Montvale. Then spend another two hours over lunch boring them to tears, talking about what the future held for me and for them if they weren't careful, and didn't make some pre-emptive plans for what lay ahead of them. Helen shopped...and shopped... and then shopped some more. The trepidation I had in opening my next Am-Ex bill was akin to jumping into an ice-plunge after twenty minutes sweating in the sauna. My poor little testicles would shrivel up to nothing.

Finally, the moment of reckoning was at hand. I'd lost... I knew it...I had no choice...No realistic options...Hari-kari not-with-standing.

At breakfast three days after returning from our meeting with Chad, I said, "Helen, let's move."

There, I said it, literally struggling to get the words out of my mouth without the acidic taste of bile rising in my throat. Some people say they saw the "white light", I was seeing the fires of hell ravaging my body!

"You're not playing games with me, are you? No kidding?"

"Yes, yes, let's do it. Let's call Chad now."

We ended up buying the house with Roman pillars, the insanely high ceilings and un-washable windows, a loft with two extra bedrooms and full bath, and a basement, where if I were to succumb to forfeiting the last vestiges of my long held minimalistic principles, I could construct at minimum three additional bedrooms, two bathrooms, a workshop, and enough closet space for a family of ten.

Needless to say, every conceivable upgrade they offered, Helen wanted…and we bought. Including, but not limited to a glass-enclosed, rolled Italian-tile walk-in shower with polished brass hardware, jet water fixtures spewing high speed projectiles of stinging spray at my body from front and back, roll-out kitchen pantry drawers, a California style master bedroom closet befitting a Hollywood movie starlet, Brazilian hardwood floors in the bedroom instead of wall-to-wall carpets, glass and internal lighting kitchen cabinets, granite countertops, door knobs that warmed your hand (God forbid Helen would touch unheated metal), solid oak floors throughout the rest of the house instead of soft shiny laminate fake wood, an expanded deck off the kitchen, Viking, Thermador, Sub-Zero, and Wolf kitchen appliances, and to put the cherry on top of the cake, their premium outside planting package which included a twenty-five-year-old Split Leaf Japanese Maple tree (something on every retirees bucket list).

Only my superior willpower prevented me from also including my must haves, namely thermal heated tiles on the bathroom floors, heating coils under the driveway and entrance walkway, and the installation of handicapped seating systems for the two staircases in the eventuality one of us would require them for our degenerating knees and hips...For if I had, Helen would probably have said, "That's a great idea. Let's get them."

Yup, we're definitely downsizing, reducing our footprint, helping the environment, and conserving our assets. Looking at the glass half full I could conceivably save tons of money on vacations, unlikely as that might sound. Can you imagine wanting to leave the palace we were building and stay in a Red Roof Motel?...I know I would.

One item I did forgo in an effort to save money was choosing a plot with NO view of the golf course. I wanted to bank some money from the sale of our home in Jersey. True, the cost of construction in Oxford was appreciably less than what it would be in New Jersey, Westchester, or Long Island. Regardless, it was more than I wanted to, or needed to, spend.

The next day, we drove to Oxford Fields. Sitting across from Chad in the sales office to finalize our purchase, Helen was dictating to Chad her laundry list of upgrades. I could see the wheels in Chad's head spinning out of control as he planned his next vacation on the bonanza of money he personally would make from our purchase. His head looked as if it were in a brace preventing him from looking directly at me. No doubt fearing I would sabotage the deal and take away the pot of gold he saw at the end of Helen's rainbow. I disappointed him (not really) and myself. I had surrendered to the inevitable. I had eked out some minor victories along the way, but Helen had won. My Appomattox was happening in Bumble Fuck, Connecticut. We signed the papers and I was now officially, for all to see, a eunuch:

"Yes, dear; whatever you want, dear; is that all, dear? Can I have another assignment, dear?" It's as if I were a fraternity pledge for life asking a brother to paddle me again and again, over and over.

"Since you're asking that we include a contingency in the contract on the purchase to stipulate that closing can only be effectuated upon the successful sale of your Montvale, New Jersey home, we cannot begin construction until that provision has been achieved," Chad informed us.

"Yeah, I know...I'm hoping we can sell our home quickly," I said.

"That depends on quite a few factors. Like, is your home in good condition? How many other homes are on the market in your community...?"

"I know all that. No need to go over them now."

"Alright, but let me say just one thing more."

"What's that, Chad?"

"A good broker is very important. It can make a tremendous difference to how quickly the house sells, and the agreed upon sales price."

"I know. I'm not a babe in the woods."

"I hear you loud and clear, Mike. So if it will help...and you haven't contracted a real estate agent in Montvale, I can recommend someone I've known for years who's really good. I'll contact her if you want and get the ball rolling."

"That won't be necessary, Chad. We have someone in mind already," Helen said.

"Good. I was just trying to be helpful."

Sure you were. And splitting a brokerage commission never entered your mind. Yeah, I was born yesterday.

"And we appreciate that, and all the help you have given us so far. Stay by the phone. We'll call the second the house sells," I said.

Mark my words, after we move in, he'll forget our names, and if he passes us in the hallway of the clubhouse, he'll ignore us.

"Please do that. And when I hang up from that call, I'll process your papers and give the go ahead to break ground."

"Sounds good to me," Helen said bubbling with excitement at the prospect of moving.

"Once construction begins, I'll keep you abreast of the progress...and please feel free to call anytime you have a question," Chad said.

"I will. Just be sure to call us immediately in the eventuality a giant sinkhole swallows up the community and we have to get our deposit back," I said.

"Absolutely."

"Oh yeah, that reminds me, Chad: if for some unexplainable reason, such as death, one of us contracts Ebola, or we're unable to sell our home in Jersey, how long will it take for us to get our deposit returned?"

"You won't get anything back since you haven't given us a deposit. Nice try, Mike."

"You can't blame a guy for trying, can you?"

"Oh, by the way, Mike, before construction can begin, you'll have to send us a certified banker's check for ten percent of the contract amount. That's very important; without it..."

"I know, I know. I'm not brain dead...yet."

39

WE HIRED A real estate agent to sell our beautiful home. Shockingly, during our interview of her, she told us our home was perfect, in a premier school district, and in a much sought after neighborhood ...and that it should sell quickly and garner a high price. BUT, she said, we first had to declutter and limit the personalized touches that permeated every room, including the bathrooms. Family photos had to go. She was particularly specific about the guest bathroom where she indicated that the sculpture and reading material I had on the shelf above the commode might be offensive to some potential buyers.

I couldn't imagine why. The accouterments I had in the guest bathroom were only some books of interest I assumed everyone would love, such as, *What's Your Poop Telling You?* and *Why Do Men Have Nipples?* And there was even a metal sculpture of a person reading on the potty. How could anybody object to that? I was making—oops, wrong word—I was creating a comfortable and enjoyably restful sitting environment for those that had to utilize my powder room.

For two full weeks we methodically eliminated all visible traces of our family's existence from the house. Family photos were removed from all walls, door frames were repainted to erase the growth measurements of our children, and the refrigerator was stripped of our grandchildren's drawings and report cards. The place ended up looking as antiseptic as a hospital's operating room.

What do I know? They're supposed to be the experts—I hope they are.

Sylvia Barrett, licensed NJ real estate broker and the women we entrusted the sale of our home to, wasted no time in including the sale on the multiple listing services. An open house for other agents was held the next day. The following morning, we received a call from yet another agent asking if they could come by with a young couple interested in seeing our home. Helen and I quickly dressed and left the house. We drove our car down the block and parked it at such an angle that we had an unobstructed view of our house. We could clearly see whoever came.

"Helen, crouch down, they're coming. I don't want them seeing us."

"If I do, I won't be able to see them."

"Yes, you will. They're not going to look down the street. They'll be preoccupied looking at the house."

For the next three weeks we repeated the same scenario. We literally spent more time in the car hiding then we did in the house. Finally, the dam broke. Sylvia called to tell us a couple had made an offer significantly less than our asking price.

"What do you guys think?" She asked.

"No way," I said.

"Do you want to make a counter offer?"

"Absolutely not. Their offer's insulting. It's our asking price or nothing."

"I can see taking that position if you had some other offers, but that's not the case. In fact, no other potential buyer has even expressed an iota of interest. I don't want you, as the saying goes, 'to cut off your nose to spite your face'. Why not counter with a reduction of a thousand or two thousand dollars? Keep them in the hunt."

"I don't want them thinking I blinked. If I do, this game will continue with back and forth offers to no end. I want you to tell the buyer's agent that I will not give this house away. I'm treating this as a war. We're under no pressure to move. This is not 'Let's Make a Deal'. We'll wait until they or someone else comes forth with a serious offer."

"I know the other agent; I've worked with her many times. She would never have forwarded her clients offer if she felt they were being insulting. It's just an opening gambit. You really can't blame them for trying to spend as little money as they can."

"Tell her I want their highest offer. If it's reasonable, I'll accept it provided there are no other impracticable demands."

"Okay, I will."

"Also, find out if there are any contingencies like them having to sell another home or getting a mortgage approved. If that's the case, it's a non-starter—I won't take a deal if either of those items are involved. The buyer must be preapproved for a mortgage or pay cash. Either one is acceptable," I said.

"I understand. Their agent told me they already have a preapproved mortgage. So that won't be an issue."

"Wonderful. If we come to an agreement on price, I want to see the commitment letter from the mortgagor. Can you get me a copy at that time?

"At the appropriate time, I'll insist on it."

"Oh, and please ask their broker where they're currently living, and if they own the premises, are they selling?"

Throughout her fifteen-year career in real estate sales, Sylvia had experience with sellers the likes of me: filled with bluster, their feet firmly entrenched in cement unwilling to give an inch. The pressure of moving and the fear of not selling more often than not resulted in the seller retreating from his or her staunch positions. When "push came to shove" they usually budged. This time was different; Sylvia was sure of it. She knew my reputation as a take no prisoners businessman. I was serious and would not bend. She knew she would have to let her colleagues know this was not going to be the "run of the mill" buyer/seller negotiation dance.

"So, are you going to be home for the next hour?" Sylvia asked.

"Yes, we'll both be here."

"Good. Hopefully, I'll be able to get you some answers to your questions. If I do, I'll call you right back."

"Fine. I'm waiting on pins and needles," I said. "Now go earn your outrageous commission."

Well, the dance began. Sylvia immediately called the agent for the buyer and told her the "lay of the land". The response she received was not what she expected. She couldn't believe what she heard. She put the phone down, pulled out her calculator, made some entries; then she typed the details of the conversation she'd just had into her computer.

"Helen, this is Sylvia."

"I know: your name came up on the TV screen."

"Right. Can you put me on speaker? I want you and Mike to both hear what I have to report."

"Sure, hold on. Mike's outside; I'll go get him."

Helen put her hand over the phone's mouthpiece and called out to me; I had just flushed the toilet.

Etiquette dictated that little white lie.

"Sylvia? Are you still there?" Helen asked.

"I'm here."

"I've put you on speaker so Mike can hear."

"Good, saves me time repeating myself."

"Well, don't keep me in suspense, Sylvia. Let's hear what you have to say," urged Helen her stomach now in full blown turmoil.

"The buyers accepted your counter offer."

"Look, Sylvia, this is no time to be playing with Helen's emotions," I said, "Are you trying to get a rise out of us? Be serious please."

"I'm absolutely being serious...And I'm as shocked as you must be. I'm truly amazed."

"What aren't you telling us? I want the full story," I said, not fully believing what she had just told us.

"So now that you asked..." Sylvia paused for effect. "Are you ready for this?"

"I warned you, Sylvia...don't play games with our fragile feelings."

"Well you asked for it: the buyers have decided to pay cash and are imposing no contingency relative to the sale of their current home."

"Holy shit!" I blurted out. There is a Santa Claus."

40

"CHAD, IT'S A go. Start the construction. I'm putting the check in a FedEx envelope right now. You should get it by close of business tomorrow."

"Congratulations. I'm amazed that in this tight housing market you were able to sell your home so quickly."

"Thanks. I was also quite surprised."

"Mike, once I receive the check, I'll process the papers, send you a signed copy, and make the necessary phone calls to get construction started ASAP."

"Great. When will I hear from you about when construction is scheduled to be finished? I need to know so I can tell my attorney. We'll need it to determine what closing date I give my buyer."

"I understand. I'll get back to you in a day or two. How's that?"

"The sooner the better."

"Will do."

The next day Chad called to let me know that we'd most likely be able to move in the week before Christmas. I called my attorney with the updated information, allowing him to prepare the final closing documents for the sale. Then reality reared its ugly head.

There's no way we can take everything with us. Our new home's living space, not counting the full basement, is about two-thirds the size of the house we currently live in. What do we take with us? What do we give away? What do we donate to charity? What do we try to sell? What do we put in the trash?

Conflict ensued, both between Helen and me, and between me and me. I didn't know which was worse: losing a fight with myself, or one with Helen.

Memories! My God, I didn't expect to have to decide whether to keep my records and memorabilia from when I was a kid, or the awards I won from work. When was the last time I actually looked through that stuff? Truth be told—rarely, if ever. Face facts, Mike, they're sentimental, but not really something I'm going to use or need...or am I? After all, when we're gone, the kids are just going to dump them anyway. One person's treasure is another's junk. What about the furniture and pictures and all the other stuff?

"Helen, we've got a problem."

"Now what?"

"What are we going to pack up and take with us?"

"Now that you ask, I was hoping to buy all new furniture, dishes, and silverware and give the kids a choice of what they might want from the house to take for themselves."

"All new furniture? Are you nuts? We're not made of money. Besides mostly everything we have is practically brand new."

"Mike the last time we bought a new piece of furniture was fifteen years ago. In any case, I want to make a different statement of who we are. Not the same old American Colonial stuff we've had since we were married. I'm thinking of a more modern look. One that pops out at you and says, 'these people are with it'."

"With what? No money? No sense? Five years to live? Please, the old farts that might wheel themselves to our house, if we invite them, probably can't see and will forget what they saw ten minutes after leaving."

"You're pathetic."

"I'm just telling it like it is."

"When you calm down, we can discuss this. But until then, please clean your garbage out of the basement. You might want to start with your collection of baseball cards and golf balls."

"My baseball cards? Do you have any idea what those little pieces of cardboard are worth?"

"They're garbage…kids' play things. Throw them out."

"Helen, they're collector's items. Some of them could be worth a small fortune."

"Yeah…so sell them."

"No way. I was planning on passing them on to the children. Besides, they only take up very little space. I'll fit them all into three shoeboxes. No big deal."

"What about your golf balls? You have thousands of them. How could you possibly need that many?"

"I don't. I give them away to other players every time I go out on the course…And when we get to Oxford Fields, I can use them to bribe men to play with me and be my friend. That's the only way I'll make friends."

Helen realized it was a losing argument and dropped the subject.

On reflection, I got off easy. Donny, my former neighbor had to part with ten cartons of Playboy Magazines, his porn tapes, and a slew of World Federation of Wrestling posters and magazines. I remember helping him go through his stuff before he moved. He zeroed in on his favorite Playboy: Miss October 1965! What pleasure he derived from her and her beautiful complexion. Unfortunately, I had to endure listening to him graphically explain the satisfaction it brought him. I had to console him. He just couldn't snap out of his depression. Then, when he came across his VCR tape, *Behind Green Doors*, and his autographed posters of Argentina Rocca and Haystacks Calhoun—wrestlers extraordinaire—he lost it, mumbling how he wouldn't wish this fate on his worst enemy. Did cruelty know no bounds?

Helen and I reached our compromised decisions without actually using knives or swords or verbally assaulting one another. We were going to keep our bedroom furniture, but would replace the living room, dining room, and breakfast room stuff. This was agreed to under the proviso that I wouldn't be obligated to join her on her impending endless search for the perfect home furnishings, since I'd be occupied perusing my collection of trading cards and golf balls. This time-consuming project would take up months of my time! Culling those items and selecting those that must be disposed of prior to my relocation to the Netherworld would not be an easy task.

Helen for her part would be in ecstasy: shopping until she dropped. My poor daughter and daughters-in-law, on the other hand, would be roped into joining her on her shopping excursions and have to suffer Helen's inability to make on-the-spot decisions as to fabric, color, and style.

One of my major assignments was to select a mover. I did my due diligence, finding the perfect moving company... Are you hallucinating?—There's no such thing. I solicited multiple quotes from various, sometimes questionable, "relocation specialists". I couldn't believe how much money those people wanted as a base price; especially since they probably paid minimum wages to the former Rahway prison inmates they hired. Then these thieves had the unmitigated gall to want to charge an additional fifteen percent on top of the base price for them to pack up for us, and another up charge for cartons and miscellaneous packing materials.

How generous of them!

I don't know how I let it happen...I was so weak and stupid... Helen convinced me we could do the packing ourselves—a decision that proved to be one of the worst I'd ever made. Aside from countless visits to liquor and grocery stores begging for empty cardboard boxes, you can't even begin to imagine how many weeks we spent separately wrapping each dish, drinking glass, and small porcelain and glass figurines with tons of old newspapers. We also spent a bloody fortune on bolts of bubble wrap material to protect our pictures and other hanging artwork, which adorned every single wall of the house.

To sum up the experience: if you want to suffer excruciating back pain, sore knees, filthy hands, constant quarreling with your spouse, contemplating whether to murder your spouse or commit suicide, consuming large quantities of alcohol, and a short-fuse-over-the-top temper, then by all means I suggest you relocate... Make it an annual event! Otherwise, save yourself the aggravation and let someone else do the work for you...or don't move.

41

Moving day had finally arrived. It would be a day that the employees of "Heavens Around the Corner Moving Company" would rue the rest of their working days, for they had to deal with a woman possessed by Satan. I'm willing to bet they'd rarely, if ever, come into contact with person so overbearing. I'm sure of it. Not understanding English was their only hope for salvation. It would be the only weapon they could use to protect their wellbeing and sanity; that is at least if they were not already brain damaged.

Helen had finally reached boiling point. She was demonic, frenetic, and downright scary. We hadn't had a conversation in the past three weeks that didn't degenerate into an argument, even though I did my best not to say or do anything that would stimulate a disagreement. It was a no-win situation for me.

No kidding, I really was a good boy on my best behavior.

Six movers arrived at 7:00 in the morning with two large vans. It took them until just before 5:00 p.m. to complete loading our stuff onto their trucks. Forty years of accumulated crap does take up a lot of space. During the entire process, Helen watched them with hawk eyes, all six of them. I tried staying out of the way and not interfering or making suggestions. It didn't matter though, because Helen was on them like glue. She hovered; she lurked; and wouldn't leave them alone for one minute to do their work.

No exaggeration, Helen must have said to those poor souls over a hundred times, "Be careful with that, it's very delicate," or "That was my grandmothers—please double wrap it," or, to me the most absurd directive, was when she claimed the value of the lamp was priceless, when in fact it was purchased at Home Goods. In my opinion, it was pure unadulterated garbage, but my opinion didn't matter. Bottom line...when all is said and done, Helen is the arbiter of all things.

The plan was for the moving vans to meet us the next day in Oxford Fields. We'd spend the night in a Marriott Courtyard in Danbury, CT then drive up the next morning to our new home... but first things first. Before locking the door behind us, we still had one more major task to complete—'Broom Clean' the house.

"Helen, where did you put the brooms? We have to get this place into some degree of cleanliness before we leave."

"What do you mean? Didn't you hire those people I told you about to clean up?"

"What are you talking about? You never told me to hire anyone."

"I certainly did. I even left their phone number on your desk."

"Well, that supposed note of yours and my desk are on the way to Oxford as we speak. Nothing I can do about that now. Anyway, we don't have time to waste trying to hire someone else. It's already 5:00. It'll take us at least two hours to finish up here and another two hours to drive to Danbury. Then we still have to grab something to eat. We'll be starved and exhausted."

"I'm beyond tired now. You can't expect me to start cleaning this house after all I've been doing for the past eight hours. It's not possible. I just can't do it. And to top it all off, I'm at my wit's end thinking about the possible damage those movers could do to our things, especially the lamp."

"So am I. The thought of that irreplaceable precious lamp being broken is enough to send me over the edge."

"I love that lamp!"

"Yeah, I know what a tragedy it would be not have it illuminate the basement storage area."

"This is no time for you to start up with your cutting comments."

"You're right. Forget it...I'll call Cynthia and plead with her to come over tomorrow morning and clean up for us. What do you think?"

"Good suggestion, Mike. I'm sure she'll do it. Make sure she knows the buyer's walk-through inspection is scheduled for 2:00 p.m. tomorrow."

Belligerence creeping into my voice I said, "Anything else I need to do?"

"Did you...?"

"Enough already!"

God bless my daughter! She agreed to help without me even having to offer a bribe. She didn't even ask me to alter my "SKI" (SPEND KIDS INHERITANCE) plans. Love conquers all.

42

I T WAS NOW almost 9:00 a.m. and we were still waiting for the moving vans to arrive at our new home. We'd left Danbury at 6.00 a.m., ate breakfast at a diner just off US 84, and then drove to Oxford Fields arriving at 7:30. Helen was going ballistic, pacing back and forth like a caged animal, fearing the worst possible tragedy had befallen her highly valued possessions. The movers were over an hour late.

"They must have been hijacked by a gang of thieves no doubt hired by the for-profit GoodWill Industries," I said. "Obviously they'd been tipped off about the treasure trove of household goods we were shipping from Montvale to Bumblefuck."

For some reason my explanation didn't appease Helen. She became even more agitated.

Unbelievably within a few seconds of me uttering my enlightened pronouncement, the glorious sight of "Heavens Around the Corner Moving Company's" vans came into view.

"Oh, thank goodness," Helen screamed. "They're here!"

What happened next you just couldn't imagine really happening. It was a classic episode of the old movie comedy characters in *Our Gang*. Picture this: our house was at the end of a cul-de-sac...

"Are you being serious?"

"No."

I couldn't keep this up. I had to end this "meet and greet" before heaven forbid, I became obnoxious.

"How long have you been married?"

"Look Trudy, I don't want to be rude, but we're in the middle of moving in. Tell you what, I'll send you my resume just as soon as my computer is hooked up...will that work?"

"Oh, I'm so sorry, I didn't realize I was holding you back from doing something."

"You're kidding, right? The moving van is sitting in the street and the six laborers are carrying in our stuff and you didn't think I had something more important to do than stand here and recite to you item for item my biography?"

Dementia is the only explanation or excuse that can explain her timing, bizarre questions, and reactions.

"Thanks for stopping by, Trudy. I'll see you around campus."

What a piece of work that woman is! I turned away and walked as quickly as I could into the house. It might not be too far a stretch of the imagination to assume Trudy won't invite us over for dinner any time soon. Boy o' boy what a welcome to the community.

We sure made the right decision to move here.

I heard later from another neighbor how Trudy gets into everyone's business. What an irritant. Trudy had berated another neighbor for putting boxes on the street for garbage collection, rather than cutting them up and placing them into the recycle container.

How could anyone be so thoughtless?

43

4:30 P.M. AND all was in disarray in the Chandler household. The movers left, boxes were piled high everywhere, our clothes were scattered throughout the rooms, the refrigerator and cabinets were bare. No food or drink to be had. And of course, Helen was frantic...again.

"I can't find anything. I don't know where to start. Where did you put the list telling us what's in what box?"

"Relax, sweetheart, I have it; it's in my attaché case. I'll get it...On second thought, why don't we take a breather and go out and get something to eat and do a little food shopping? We have to unwind. We have the rest of our lives to unpack. We can start tomorrow if we're still breathing."

Maybe I'll die tonight and won't be saddled with the task of unpacking for the next several months. If only I'd be so lucky. Helen's going to insist that the house be in pristine condition within a week.

"Believe it or not, Mike, I like the idea of having a quiet, relaxing meal. We can start organizing when we get back."

"Let's first see how we're feeling after we eat and do a little food shopping. When we get back, we might just want to hit the sack and start unpacking in the morning."

Luckily, I remembered passing what looked like a German country restaurant when we were last in Oxford. It was three or four miles down the road on the main drag. From the outside it looked somewhat rustic, but when we went inside (how do I phrase this without offending the local residents?) it lacked the ambience of fine eateries we were accustomed to frequenting when we lived in a more urban setting.

Heidi's was a scene out of *Deliverance* circa 1940—Formica tables and old beat-up wooden chairs. The menus were placed in stained cracked plastic protectors, and the floors covered in worn-out linoleum. Most of the male patrons wore plaid hunting jackets and earlap hats. Not surprisingly, a disproportionate number of the diners were overweight and a significant number had missing teeth, which they made readily visible whenever they spoke or smiled. Yet even in that less than appealing environment...everyone was nice, the food was wholesome, and the prices very reasonable. Thankfully, the patrons left their rifles in their pickup trucks outside. I knew this because as we were walking into the restaurant, I saw several weapons displayed in the back windows of the pickup trucks that dominated the parking lot.

Helen and I each had a stack of blueberry pancakes stuffed with real blueberries topped off with fresh whipped cream. They were exceptional!

After our meal, we went down the road a piece to the local "Stop and Shop" supermarket to buy some essentials: milk, coffee, cheese, and eggs...Then we drove back to the Fields. We were both exhausted. Neither of us had any inclination to start unpacking. We fell into bed, without sheets, and didn't wake up until 9:00 the next morning as the sun came blazing through the shade-less windows. We didn't shower. We put on the same ratty clothes we had worn the previous day…If for some incomprehensible reason a neighbor decided to welcome us to the embalmer's waiting room community we'd just moved to, they'd be greeted by the true aroma of New Jersey!

After downing two cups of coffee each we went back into the master bedroom. Helen stood transfixed, staring at the boxes of clothes that occupied most of the floor space.

"Where do we start?…Well, the first thing we should do is put our clothes away."

I remained silent.

"It would be a great help if you could locate the cartons with the hangers in them," she suggested.

An hour later, I finished my assignment after I had lifted, moved, and literally opened a hundred cartons. My back was killing me…so I thought I'd lie down for a few moments on the bed and rest. That turned out to be impossible. Our king size bed was piled high with my clothes.

"Helen, I thought you were putting the clothes away in the master closet?"

"For the most part I did, but there's no room for the rest of my blouses, or any of my handbags, scarves, or shoes."

"Your stuff? What about my clothes?"

"There's no room for any of them."

"Come again? Did I hear you correctly? You didn't hang up any of my things, just your stuff?" I was incredulous.

"I couldn't. There's not enough space in the closet."

"If you ask me, owning forty pairs of black pants is unnecessary even for a princess. Maybe if you reduced the number of black pants you have on hangers, we could squeeze in a pair of my jeans."

"I only have the essentials. They're not all the same, Mike. Every one is different. Either it's a different style, or a different shade of black, or a different length."

"Who the hell is going to notice any differences in Oxford? All they'll see is black."

"The other women here will. Besides I need them."

"Don't get me started...You need? You need air and food."

"Yes, I do, but I also require the proper clothes for the proper event."

"You *want*...you don't need! Oxygen, food, shelter and liquids are all you require."

"I don't want to fight, Mike. Are you asking me to throw away perfectly good clothes?"

"Give them away or cull the herd. Put some in storage down in the basement."

"I guess I could put my summer stuff down there. That might help."

"And while you're at it, what about selling some of your shoes to Emelda Marcos?"

"My shoes?"

"Your collection of foot coverings dwarfs hers."

"Stop exaggerating. I wear every pair."

"There aren't enough days in the year for you to do that. If you wear a different pair every day, it would take you over a year to wear the same one twice."

"Please!"

"Helen!"

"*Mea culpa*! I admit it, I do have more shoes than most women…
But I wear each of them."

To bring the debate to a close, we counted how many pairs of shoes Helen actually had. She owned one hundred and fifteen, not including slippers or flip-flops.

"I was wrong…I exaggerated the number of pairs of shoes you have. However, you do realize you could open your own apparel store stocked solely with the excess amount of clothes and shoes you own. We'd be rich."

"Nonsense."

"Alright, can we get back to the real problem at hand?"

"What's that?"

"Where are we going to put my clothes? Or are you suggesting I prance around Oxford Fields *aux-natural*?"

"Perish the thought…Let me see what things I can put elsewhere."

"I would be eternally grateful if you would allot me even one-quarter of the closet to call my own. Can we agree to that compromise?"

Let this be a warning to all men who contemplate moving with the intention of downsizing. *You'll* be downsizing, but your wife won't!

A week later we'd basically finished unpacking. Storage solutions for the unneeded surplus junk and seasonal wear were put off for the time being. We packed them in boxes and lugged them down into the basement.

Helen declared the house acceptable. She could welcome neighbors into it without having to feel the necessity of asking them to "excuse the mess".

I didn't give a damn one way or the other.

We were now ready to leave the safety of our new home and explore the hinterland.

"Mike, I want to go up to the clubhouse and see what activities are available for us to participate in the next few weeks."

"Okay, I guess…I've got nothing better to do. Let's see what's up." I sighed audibly.

I was reluctant to go to any event or activity, especially since I didn't know anyone. I wasn't a joiner. Besides these people were old. I had nothing in common with them. Looking around the club-house and at the resident's playing cards and billiards, I felt out of place. They had their own cliques. I was self-conscious. They wouldn't invite me to join their group and I wasn't going to force my way in…I was a newbie.

The golf course would open in three months, and I had a lot I could do on the computer, or as an alternative I could spend several days a week visiting my grandchildren.

We walked around the clubhouse looking into each of the rooms, the indoor pool, and exercise gym to see what activity was taking place. The place was basically empty except for one card and one billiard room.

Gently placing her hand on my arm, Helen nudged me forward toward some men who were playing billiards.

"Mike, why not stay here and play some pool with those men. I'm sure they'll be happy to let you join them. Go introduce yourself."

"They already have their teams. I'd be the odd man out. Maybe next time…I'll see," I said, hoping to postpone the inevitable.

I wanted to leave the place right then and there before Helen took it upon herself to introduce me to complete strangers, similar to the way a mother would do to with her young child. Thankfully she didn't press the issue because her eyes and attention diverted toward a table of women playing mahjong.

"Looks like those girls over there are playing mahjong," she said, pointing in their direction. "I'm going over to them to see what it's all about. Maybe I can get into a game."

"What girls?" I snorted.

"Over there at the table next to the window."

"What are you talking about? Those aren't girls; they're old women."

"Stay here if you want. I'm going over to introduce myself."

"Leave me out of it. I'm going back to the gym to look more closely at their Nautilus machines. I'll be back in five minutes. I'll meet you here."

"Whatever," Helen grunted. She turned her back to me and purposefully walked toward the mahjong group.

Returning from my inspection tour of the gym, I saw Helen sitting at the mahjong table chatting up a storm and occasionally laughing with four complete strangers. Fearing I'd be dragged into an uncomfortable situation where those women would ask me to recite the history of my entire life starting from birth up until my last bowel movement, I took refuge behind a tall, high-back chair, which afforded me a modicum of cover while at the same time allowing me to observe Helen and overhear her conversation.

Almost half an hour went by. Apparently, Helen hadn't even noticed my absence, not once glancing over to look for me. Finally, the game ended. The women individually—you guessed it again— hugged Helen.

WHY?

I swear, if her smile were any larger her face would explode.

You just can't make this stuff up, and neither can I because I keep repeating myself.

Helen took a seat opposite me. "Mike these women are so nice."

"I'm sure they are," I said sarcastically.

"No, really, they are. They asked me to join their game as a substitute."

"Wonderful! That's just wonderful! I couldn't be happier for you. Now can we go home? I want to take a shower and have some lunch?"

How am I going to fit in?

I stepped sideways into the phone booth sized closet—oops, I mean the poor excuse for a shower—for what I hoped would be the last time. It's not that I won't be bathing again, but rather that I won't wedge my body into such a small, unwelcoming, claustrophobic space, nor be forced to scale a three-foot high Jacuzzi tub risking life and limb to get clean.

Remember when I carried on about the idiocy of putting a Jacuzzi in an old person's home? Well, the builder of this fine community would not accommodate me by not installing one... so I hired a home improvement contractor to take out that monstrosity of a bathtub and convert the area into a walk-in shower, and convert the three by three-foot shower stall into a linen closet. I truly felt sorry for those residents with oversized backsides who could not afford to renovate. They had to wedge their bodies into that poor excuse of a space...forced to contort them into awkward positions so they could raise their hands above their heads to wash their hair.

That challenging task would make for a very amusing YouTube video.

As I am sure you are aware, construction schedules are not always met on time. Our project was no different. Our contractor told us the tiles in the new walk-in shower needed another day or two to dry. Only then would we be able to enjoy our new modern Italian tiled spa. Once finished, they could begin the conversion of the old shower into a linen closet. Whoopie!

During dinner that evening, Helen was wound up—non-stop talking. She recounted for over an hour without, it appeared to me, to even take a breath, the personal history of all the women she had met that afternoon: how many marriages they had; how long they were married each time; the number of children and grandchildren each had; where they got their hair and nails done; and the location of the closest shopping mall.

At the first opportunity, some sixty minutes into her diatribe, I was able to interject with a question.

"Did you happen to ask for referrals to a geriatric physician, a cardiologist, a dermatologist, a gastroenterologist, a urologist, an ophthalmologist, a gynecologist, a podiatrist, an acupuncturist, a chiropractor, a dentist, a brain surgeon, or a psychiatrist?"

"No, I didn't get a chance."

"Well please do the next time you speak with them. I'm particularly focused on the neurosurgeon."

"Is something wrong with you?"

"I need my head examined for letting you talk me into coming here."

Helen gave me a half-smile. I didn't know whether she was enjoying the conversation or was exasperated by it. She stood up... walked around the dinette table to me...leaned over...put her face close to mine and said, "You can ask them yourself tomorrow night for those recommendations."

"What?!" my insides instantly rebelled. "Hold on. I know I didn't hear you right. What did you say about tomorrow night?"

"You heard me correctly. We've been invited by one of the women I met playing mahjong to a potluck dinner party at her home. There'll be a lot of men there for you to meet and a good number of them are also new to the community. You'll have a lot in common to talk about. You can ask to your heart's content all the questions you want answers to."

"Including what gynecologist they recommend for me?"

"Come again?"

"I can tell them I'm undergoing a gender change."

"Sadly, they'll probably believe you."

"Did you really accept the invitation?"

"Of course. Why wouldn't I?"

"Because you didn't ask me if I wanted to go."

"I said yes because I knew you'd say no. You always do."

"I do not!"

"Mike, when have you ever initiated a social get together? When have you ever initially said yes when I've made a date to see another couple?"

"Humm...let's see...Well, I have to admit, not very often. And that's because I don't want to share you with anyone. I'm selfish. Our time together is precious."

"No, you're full of it. You're the most social person I know. Once you're in a social gathering, you're a charmer. Your challenge is to reign in your sarcastic, hurtful comments."

"Me? Sarcastic? You're probably thinking of my twin brother. I'm the most lovable, placid, non-judgmental person I know," I said warmly.

"That being the case, you should have no problem meeting and making new friends."

I have to adjust to my new fate. I have to be more patient when dealing with my new neighbors and their medical problems and mental lapses.

44

TIME MANAGEMENT WAS my most immediate concern.

How am I going to spend my days when I can't play golf or go shopping at Costco with Helen? I surrender…I'll make friends, or at a minimum be overly nice. One thing is certain: to do that, I have to temper my inclination to always twist what others say into what I think will have a humorous meaning, otherwise I'll become persona non-grata *to the very people I'll be around for the remainder of my life.*

Come to think of it, I hadn't heard the ambulance sirens in the past three days. Either my hearing had gone or, by some lucky fluke of nature, no one had recently been called to account for their sins.

Helen met so many women within the first couple of weeks, my head spun. I couldn't keep up with her. She had joined three card groups, that mahjong gang, and a Wine and Dine Club…And if that wasn't enough, she became intimately involved with some other women who were desirous of forming a Women's Club and another group who wanted to create a New Neighbors Club. Then, since she felt she had some spare time, she volunteered a couple of days per week at a local food bank. Her days and most evenings were occupied; mine not so much. I was too tired just watching her to do anything myself.

"Fred invited you to play bridge tonight up at the clubhouse."

"Who's Fred?"

"Your neighbor. You met him last week."

"And you expect me to remember his name? In any case, why on earth would he do that? I never told him I played bridge."

"I did. I'm still worried about you."

"I'm a big boy. I'll take care of myself."

"While you're taking care of yourself, bone up on your cooking skills."

"So, while you're shuffling cards all day, you expect me to prepare dinner every night?"

"No that's not why I said that. You're an excellent cook. I want to show off your skills."

"By me slaving over a hot stove?"

"Betty, Ruth, and I think it would be a wonderful idea if our husbands, you included, each be responsible for preparing a gourmet dinner party once a month. We all agree you three guys would benefit greatly from doing this. At the very least, we'll all have some good meals."

These three women all moved into the community within a month of each other and became fast friends. I think originally it was a self-protective mechanism, but then blossomed into a true friendship. Every new resident was in the same boat, searching for acceptance by people who were in established social circles. The new kid on the block syndrome was real.

"Do I have a choice?"

"No, you don't. In fact, you have the honor of being the first host."

"The other men agreed?"

"They thought it was a good idea? How can I thank you enough for the honor?"

"By preparing your famous al dente pasta and clam sauce with jumbo shrimp. And for dessert you can make those Italian cannolis...I just love them."

"When is this shindig supposed to happen?"

"Next month, sweetheart."

"No way. I need more time to prepare," I said as I busied myself pretending to write something down on a notepad, which I just happened to have picked up from the kitchen counter.

"Next month...In four weeks. You've got plenty of time to prepare."

That night, I had an epiphany: Helen had fully immersed herself in the social fabric of Oxford Fields. It was now up to me to adjust or vanish into the black hole of boredom. The light switched on. I started playing bridge with complete strangers; joined a Camera Club even though I didn't own a camera; started exercising in the gym, and doing laps in the pool. I became a seventy-year-old jock, and a regular social butterfly. The only problem was, I couldn't remember the names of the people I met. When I saw the same guy the following day, I had to avoid the need to say his name.

How you doing, buddy? Embarrassing!

During card games, without fail the topic of conversation revolved around a recitation of upcoming medical appointments, the results of laboratory tests, spouses' impending operations, and personal bowel activities, or lack there-of. The latter topic was the only one I joined in on. It moved me, and the subject always afforded me an opening for a sharp comment or two.

It isn't even dessert talk. I'll never mature.

My limited appearances with these groups did yield some valuable information. For instance:

- I'd have to hire a Connecticut attorney to update our wills, because Connecticut's inheritance tax laws are not the same as New Jersey's. Neither are their probate regulations. If I didn't make the necessary changes reflecting Connecticut's laws, it would have a significant adverse effect on the net value of our estate.
- I could have avoided spending over three hours registering our cars in Danbury by going instead to a remote satellite office in Derby, CT, where the wait time was usually under an hour.

For too many days, I was occupied by notifying every credit-card company, insurance company, and organization we were a member of, of our new address and phone number. I also had to arrange for a new Internet provider and home security company for their respective installations. The days went by so fast I couldn't tell one day from the next. I relaxed during the week and rested on weekends.

So this is what I worked all those years for!

When a snowstorm dumped twenty inches of the white stuff over my driveway, I didn't have to lift a finger to clear it away. By the time I drove the car out of the garage, there was not a flake to be seen on my driveway or front walk leading to the front door. The Homeowners Association's hired snow removal employees had done all the work during the previous night. No worries, no back pain, no nagging.

All was right with the world except for a void in my head that had existed since I retired. I just couldn't shake the feeling that no matter how many activities I participated in, something was still missing. I felt as if I should be doing something more. Did I miss a deadline or a meeting? The essence of my being had transformed from achieving goal-oriented objectives, hard work, and decisive decision-making impacting my company's stock price, into a *laissez-faire* go with the flow survive until tomorrow existence.

Settling into a new community was not an easy task. Control over your life in some measure becomes subjugated to the rules, culture, and even State Laws governing active adult senior communities. Pre-approval from your HOA must be requested in writing if you want to enlarge your deck, re-landscape the side of your house, add a storm door, change the color of your house, change the windows, install an emergency generator, convert to solar energy, and most intrusive of all, they have to give their okay if you wanted to open a brothel in your basement!

Before submitting your request to the HOA, you must get written approval from your neighbors on both sides of your house, even if one or both of those neighbors is not impacted by the change you want to make. They don't even have to be able to see the end result. If through no fault of my own, I inadvertently offend a neighbor and then some time in the future have to ask that individual to okay a modification requiring their approval, I'd be shit out of luck.

Rules had to be obeyed under penalty of fine or threat of being ostracized from all activities. One weekend we had a couple of the grandkids over for a sleepover. We took them to the indoor pool for a swim between the hours of 1:00 and 3:00 in the afternoon.

Kids being kids, they jumped in the pool and had a grand old time splashing Helen and me until the Pool Nazi appeared.

"No jumping or splashing is allowed in the pool," this over-weight female Gestapo screamed.

I bit hard on my tongue to stop myself from verbally accosting the woman. It worked...Sort of.

"Who are you to tell us what can't be done in the pool? Anyway, are we bothering you or anyone else? There's no one in the pool but us...What's your problem, lady?"

"The rules say 'no jumping or splashing'."

"Don't you have something more important to do than ruining these children's fun?"

"You're new to the Fields; we have rules that must be obeyed."

"You weren't even in the pool area. I saw you just walking out of the gym. Do you have a badge, a stun gun, a baton, a hat, or a sash?"

"A sash?"

"Yeah. One that says 'Ms. Mind Your Own Business 2013'."

"What's your name?"

"What's my name? What's your name?" I responded with more than a trace of irritation in my voice.

The Gestapo was speechless. No response. She clicked the heels of her black calf length boots, spun around and stomped out of the pool area.

"Mike, you went a trifle overboard don't you think?"

"That bitch had it coming. Who the hell does she think she is?"

"We have to live in this community. We'll likely see her again."

"I'll be wearing clothes and my hair won't be wet. She won't recognize me."

"Seriously?"

"There's a more appropriate way she could have informed us of any rules. That nosy body's confrontational attitude was out of place. What business of hers is it anyway? The kids weren't bothering anyone, especially her. I only hope there aren't more like Eva Braun living here."

If the budinski had looked at the clock on the wall, she would have also cited us for a time violation. We had exceeded the permissible time limit by five minutes. If she'd known, she'd likely want to impose a penalty on us punishable by the loss of clubhouse bathroom flushing privileges

"Hey kids," I yelled to them so they could hear me over their shrieks of joy as they splashed one another. "Stop splashing and start swimming. It's almost time to leave."

As it turned out, I learned later there *are* rules prohibiting jumping and splashing in the pool, and specific times children under eighteen can use the pool... My bad! Won't happen again!... That is if anyone is around to see my grandkids having fun!

As much as I enjoy spending time with the grandchildren, I love the peace and quiet of not having them twenty-four seven. That same yearning to hold on to each of them...kiss them, and hug them is challenged by a desire for their departure. They're exhausting.

"I'm tired, Helen. Can we take the kids back to the house now?"

"Maybe we should. Their parents are coming to pick them up soon, and when they leave you can take a nap."

"Thank goodness. I'll have a bite to eat and then go to sleep."

"No. No. We're going to the Smiths' for dinner."

"Again? We were with them last night at the who-ja-ma-call-its' house. What am I going to talk about? You can't expect me to listen to uh…talk about Pete's highly successful career again. He drove me nuts. He's a narcissist! He could give Trump a run for his money. It's all about him. He thinks he's the calmest genius in the community."

"Then talk to someone else."

"Who am I going to talk to who can remember what day it is?"

"There're plenty of things you can discuss. Talk about football, for instance."

"Be serious. I haven't watched a football game since La Palazzo. I've given up on the game…It's brutal and almost as boring as baseball."

"I'm sure you'll find something to talk about to keep your interest."

"I know. We can again discuss the major topics on everyone's mind."

"Pray tell. What are they?"

"Doctor visits, undiagnosed diseases, and hip replacements. Then there's the animated discussion bemoaning knee replacements, deaths, ambulance trips, and hospital visits…Oh yeah, and the biggie: the guys' non-existent sexual activity."

"For my part, I try to direct the conversation to the more thought-provoking topic of cremation."

"You're crazy. You know that, don't you?"

"It's been suggested by more than one person. You're not the first and by no means will you be the last."

45

TWO WEEKS LATER, we received a certified letter from the HOA, putting us on probation...citing our infringement of HOA rules. They enumerated several violations of the HOA Rules. No fines were imposed for this first offense, but a repeat offense would result in a significant monetary fine.

"Helen, look at this bullshit letter the HOA Board sent us. That Nazi pool monitor actually reported us to the HOA. Can you believe it?"

"What does it say?"

"If our grandchildren commit the same heinous crimes again, we'll be punished to the fullest extent of the law. Their visiting privileges will be revoked."

"No...they didn't say that."

"Well, I might have exaggerated a tad. It was just a warning letter."

"Oh. I feel much better."

"Something else is bothering me about the letter."

"What?"

"How did they know who to send the letter to? How did they know our names? Did they analyze our fingerprints or test my urine for DNA?"

Helen blanched. She looked a little sheepish. "Believe it or not, it's my fault."

"What do you mean, it's your fault? Why's that?"

"Well, last week, I was playing canasta in the clubhouse when, by pure luck of the draw, my partner turned out to be the Pool Nazi. Everyone else knew each other. I had no option other than to introduce myself. And women being women, they wanted to know my complete history from birth to Oxford. I'm guilty."

"Did you perchance lay her out in clovers, or promise to deport her to Argentina to live with her fellow Reich members? Did you even tell the other women what that budinski did?"

"Of course not. It wasn't the right time or place. Two wrongs don't make a right, Mike."

"Will it ever be the right time?"

"Probably not."

"You're too nice, Helen. I guess we should be grateful owners here don't have assigned parking places like they have in many Florida Condos. Those old farts down there go ballistic if someone parks their car in the wrong space. We don't have assigned parking spaces, but we do have our own wackos."

"Humor me: what are you talking about now?"

"Aside from the pool monitors, we have self-assigned speeding traffic monitors who run into the street waving their arms at passing cars and yelling at the driver that he or she is exceeding the speed limit. How the hell they can make such an objective judgment is beyond me...unless of course they have surgically implanted internal radar guns?"

"That's ridiculous. I never heard anything like that. Who told you anyway?"

"No one. I had the pleasure of personally experiencing this lunatic jumping out from behind a bush, charging the car like a bull attacking a Matador who was holding out the red cape hiding his saber."

"You never told me anything about that."

"It only just happened."

"What did you do?"

"I opened the window and gave him the finger."

"You didn't!"

"No. But I did moon the man. With a chaser!"

46

ENDLESS DINNER AND cocktail parties were taking their toll on me in so many ways. The most obvious was their effect on my waistline, which expanded from a trim thirty-four inches to one approaching thirty-six inches in just over two months. I was not accustomed to having two or three drinks of alcohol a day. Even when I was working and entertaining clients, I rarely drank or ate in gluttonous quantities. Alcohol consumption combined with every conceivable variety of pasta dish, topped off with high calorie pastries caused havoc on my physique.

Self-preservation prevented me from pointing out to Helen that she was also putting on the pounds.

What drove me to drink and eat more than I should were the real culprits: aging and death! They're the ones that will continue to challenge me, I'm sure, for as long as we live in Oxford Fields.

Patience is not one of my strong suits, whether I'm driving behind a slow driver or asking somebody a direct question and getting either no answer, or a non-response response...Through no fault of their own, other than natural aging, half of the guys I meet wear hearing aids. A good number of others should, but are too vain to buy them. Regrettably though, a significant number of those things don't work. End result, I constantly repeat what I say over and over again to those who wear or don't wear those things.

If having to reiterate what I say time and time again isn't taxing enough, I have to endure hearing so many residents repeat the same story over and over again. Memory loss is an inescapable result of aging. I know it's hard to believe but shockingly even I occasionally experience recall lapses! As a matter of fact, every day I find myself going into a room with a definitive purpose in mind, but once there I don't remember why I'm there. I wander around for a few seconds until, from the depths of my inner mind…bingo— I know why I'm there. Without fail, the relief of that accomplishment is so gratifying. It serves to reinforce my sanity and put off my fear of descending into the depths of dementia.

A humorous posting on the Internet captures the essence of what I'm referring to:

I finally did it! Bought a new pair of shoes with memory
foam insoles. No more forgetting why I walked in a room.

Remembering names is another matter altogether. I've always had a problem with that. Aging, I maintain, has nothing to do with it. Thankfully, there's a helpful tool which can alleviate some of the distress and embarrassment that accompanies forgetting someone's name… name tags.

This recalling names thing plagues a lot of people. We went to a social event at the clubhouse where a hundred plus residents sat around tables of ten with their non-penetrable clique -no openings=stay out of our group attitude. We were new to the community and relegated to sit at a table off to the side away from the action. We knew practically nobody. I did recognize a few residents sitting at another table by name, but most others only by sight. A few couples we had never met before made an effort to meet us, but by and large it was a very cold and unwelcoming experience.

No one wore nametags. If they had, it would have helped jog my memory and I would have avoided the embarrassment of not being able to greet someone by name as I bluffed my way through a handshake.

Helen asked the organizer of that community-sponsored event (the infamous Trudy), if in the future name tags could be used to help interaction and socialization between residents. Her idea was rejected out of hand: "We don't do things like that here!"

The real downer was that the evening ended as EMS volunteers carried out a resident who had collapsed after dancing a slow waltz. No one knew the name of the victim except the woman with him. No one knew her name either...They weren't wearing name tags.

47

SPRING ARRIVED. GOLF was just over the horizon; I could taste it...sense it...feel it. My clubs were cleaned, my balls washed (for you foul-minded readers, I'm referring to my golf balls) and sorted by brand, and my outfits taken out of cold storage from the basement. I was ready to spend at least five days per week out on the links. Hopefully on the weekends I could spend time with my children and grandchildren—speaking of whom, they actually did want to visit us, be pampered by us, and of course, fed!

Wanting to be on the top of my golf game, which I hadn't played since my visit to George's house in Florida, I had to build up my stamina, lose weight, and increase my muscle mass. Hence my daily routine changed. I went to the gym early in the morning, spending two hours each day using the Nautilus machines and treadmill; then I swam laps in the pool. It worked. I lost the winter party two inches and firmed up my belly. I was ready, willing, and able to hit the links.

Our community monthly newsletter reported that a Wednesday morning eighteen-hole men's golf league was having an organizing meeting in a few weeks. I joined. I played every Wednesday in the league, and was invited to play with several of the men during the rest of the week. Had it not been for the league's existence, I would have had to play alone or take my chances and be paired with strangers or, heaven forbid...a woman!...Hmm, I take that back... what was I thinking?

Of all the men I'd met since we moved to Oxford Fields, relatively few played golf, and a significant number of those who did wouldn't play on our course since it's considered too challenging. Disappointingly, most of the other guys for a variety of health reasons, didn't even try.

Having to use canes and walkers is no excuse for not playing golf... Wusses!

Once the course opened and I was able to play, my new daily routine took shape. On Monday and Friday, I finished playing eighteen holes of golf by 11:30; then went back to the house to shower and grab a bite to eat. At one o'clock I went to the clubhouse for three hours of pinochle. Tuesday nights, I played bridge for two and one half hours. On Wednesday after golf, I played by myself...No, you evil-minded people, not sexually...On the computer!

I became fixated with KenKen, Sudoku, and Spider Solitaire, amusing myself with those games for countless hours on end. Helen didn't know. On Thursday afternoons, a friend and I teamed up to play contract bridge.

If I woke up late and missed my regularly scheduled golf game, Helen, if she were at home, would encourage me to still try to go to the course and join another group. How great is that?!

All this activity physically exhausted me. Every evening before dinner I'd take a nap...Doing nothing is exhausting! Those computer games knocked me out.

I didn't even have to be concerned or feel guilty about not spending time with Helen. She was too busy with her committees, clubs, and card games to give me a second thought.

On one particular afternoon, Helen came home and found me sitting on our deck staring out into space.

"Why aren't you taking a nap, Mike? What's wrong?"

"Do you remember me mentioning one of the guys named Ralph?"

"Sure. You play golf with him on Tuesdays...don't you?"

"No. It doesn't matter what day I play with him. What matters is that he suddenly keeled over in the clubhouse. We had to call for an ambulance. But before the EMS ambulance arrived, he died."

"Oh, that's horrible."

"I know. The point is...the thing that happened to Ralph is not uncommon here. We hear those damn ambulance sirens all the time. And we get all those emails from the Social Director that another homeowner passed away. This place is depressing. Everyone's old and getting older."

"We're all getting chronologically older."

"I'm not."

"Have you looked in the mirror lately?"

"I avoid doing that for obvious reasons."

"You don't want to see your hair is now gray?"

"No...I don't want you or anyone else accusing me of being vane—always looking at myself in the mirror."

"You are conceited...but for good reason. You're very good looking."

"I didn't think you noticed."

"I have," said Helen coyly.

I was confused and shocked by Helen's comment. What did she mean? Was the 'Ice Maiden' melting?

"Forget the mirror. My eyes see old. It's upsetting."

"It's not as bad as that."

"Oh, it is. There hasn't been a time when I've played bridge or pinochle that more than one person isn't discussing their health issues, when their next doctor's appointment is, or how uncomfortable their colonoscopy examination was. I tell you, Helen, it's God damn frightening."

"You of all people have nothing to be worried about. You're the healthiest person I know."

"So why is it I wake up every morning and something else hurts?"

"Remember what Dr. Silver said. If you wake up with no aches or pains, you haven't woken up—you're dead!"

"Very reassuring."

"Mike, you're still active, healthy, and mentally sharp. Your acidic tongue has lost none of its sting. Your childish bathroom humor knows no bounds. And aside from accidentally being hit by a stray golf ball, I'm the only thing that will kill you."

"You better believe that thought hasn't escaped me."

"I'm glad you opened up to me. I'm worried about you."

"I'm touched. Truly I am."

"Are you going to take a nap now, or should I start preparing dinner?"

48

WHILE I WAS playing pinochle the next day, one of the men was bemoaning his impending full knee replacement operation. Another guy chimed in that he was having a hip replacement. Not wanting to be left out of the conversation, I expressed my own anguish over a hangnail that had been bothering me for at least five minutes.

"I have a suggestion. Why don't we ask the Social Director to set aside a portion of the bulletin board in the lobby to display medical alerts? Everyone can list their upcoming doctor's appointments, their impending operations, and their new aches and pains. That way there'll be no need to talk about all of our respective ailments during our card games. What do you say?"

"If the director actually went along with your suggestion, you wouldn't be able to ridicule us anymore. We look forward to you abusing us, Mike...You're such a confidence builder," one of the men said with a straight face.

Most of the other men laughed. The ones that didn't, no doubt didn't hear what was said in the first place.

"Hold on. I have another equally brilliant idea."

"Should we brace ourselves?" one of the guys sitting at the table asked, gritting his teeth—making a show of it, holding both arms of his chair rigidly.

"That might be a good idea. Here it is...are you ready?"

"Yeah—shoot."

"Instead of the listing I suggested why don't I ask her to publish only the names of healthy residents? It won't make interesting reading, however, because it'll be disconcerting how few people are mentioned."

"You really are brutal," said another guy who couldn't contain his laughter.

"Tell me, Mike, do you stay up at night thinking of ways to ingratiate yourself to us?" one of the other men asked.

"It just comes so naturally to me. My calling is to spread joy to one and all."

Several days later, after one of our impromptu eating and drinking parties, our friend Barry called Helen to ask if I was feeling okay.

"Why are you asking?" she replied, somewhat mystified.

"Mike wasn't himself last night."

"I didn't notice anything. He didn't complain about being ill. Did he mention anything to you?"

"No, he didn't."

"Then what makes you think he wasn't well?"

"He didn't insult me last night...Not once...Not even an inkling of a criticism."

"This is serious. Was your hearing aid working Barry?"

"I think it was."

"Was he the same way with the other men?"

"Not once did I hear him proffer a witticism or an off-color joke. No double *entendre*...No sexual references. He didn't even show us on his phone one of those videos his friend in California forwards him. We were all taken aback...and concerned."

"I'd better get off the phone now and call the ambulance," Helen chuckled.

"Let me know the doctor's diagnosis," Barry said, choking out the words, unable to mask his amusement. Be sure they do a brain scan to rule out an alien takeover.

"Thanks, Barry. You'll be the first person I call as soon as we get back from the hospital."

"Don't take any offense Helen with what I'm about to say, but based upon the tenor of your answers, my worst fears are confirmed."

"And what is that?"

"Mike has finally co-opted your gentle manner."

"Goodbye, Barry. Don't call me...I'll call you."

Just as Helen was hanging up the phone, I came into the kitchen. Helen was at the kitchen table drinking a cup of coffee.

"Where were you?"

"I was taking a shower."

"You didn't tell me. If you did, I wouldn't have made an omelet for you...It's cold now. Do you want me to reheat it?"

"That won't be necessary. I'll eat it cold."

"What about some coffee?"

"That sounds good."

As she was pouring my coffee, I asked her who was on the phone.

"Barry called."

"That's peculiar; he never calls. What did he want?"

"He wanted to know if you were feeling better."

"Feeling better? Am I sick?"

"He thought so. He said you weren't yourself last night...You didn't insult him."

"Barry is nuts. I spent a good fifteen minutes last night ragging on him. I was in my glory. The guy couldn't have been wearing his hearing aids. Tony even commented that I was in rare form."

49

IF I'VE GIVEN you the impression I was the only one in my marriage who wasn't totally satisfied about our new life in Oxford Fields, guess again. Helen, the newly crowned unofficial Queen of Good Deeds and Social Gatherings, and the Pearl Mester of Oxford Fields did have a major bone to pick. She couldn't tolerate malicious people.

"Can you believe the crap we're going through for wanting to start a Women's Club? It's kicked-up a hornet's nest of opposition from those petty-minded women led by Trudy. They're bad mouthing us to anyone foolish enough to listen to them. It's character assassination. Maybe I can sue her for slander and libel?"

"Helen, I have no idea what you're talking about."

"You know we petitioned the HOA to create a social club just for women, right?"

"Yeah, I recall you mentioning it."

"Well those creeps who run the Organizing Committee say it's not needed. They say the dances and holiday party they sponsor for all residents is enough."

"Are they right?"

"Of course not. What's wrong with having as many clubs as people want, and as many activities involving more people? We have only seven sanctioned clubs here. It's ridiculous. These self-appointed guardians of our lives claim that's all we need. The Pulte community we saw in South Carolina has what, a hundred, two hundred clubs? And The Villages in Florida have four hundred.

"Can you think of any reasonable explanation for their closed-mindedness?"

"Nothing I can think of…besides I'm sure the men in this community would have no interest in going to a Women's Club fashion show, or a discussion on women's health, or…"

"I get it. I get the point. Did you explain the programs you hope to offer to the powers that be?"

"Of course we did."

"And after hearing what you planned, they still objected?"

"They did."

"You're engaged in a turf war, my dear, against an entrenched group of people who fear they'll lose power…influence…whatever. The reason doesn't matter; it's emotional not rational. If I were in your place, I'd prepare a one-page, easy to read, description of what the club's all about, including listing those programs you hope to offer. Give it out to the women you think would be interested in joining and have them sign a petition."

"What a good idea!"

"The more women who support a new club, the harder it'll be for the HOA to refuse your request."

"I just don't understand their objection."

"Some people cannot accept change. It's part of human nature, and probably the most difficult thing to accept. Couple that with their belief you're encroaching on their territory...You're in a turf war."

"So how do we overcome their irrational opposition?"

"It's not easy. You'll have to alleviate their fears. Demonstrate to them why you're different; that you're simply filling a void, and that it's not a negative reflection on what they've accomplished."

"What if it doesn't work?"

"In that event: you tried playing nice, but they were unreasonable. Screw them! Start a revolution."

"Will you help us?"

"Have you completely lost your mind? My involvement would ensure your demise. Consider the ramifications of Mike "The Wise Ass"—emphasis on wise—trying to be nice and not insult anyone."

"You make a very good point. However, you can still meet with the girls privately and impart your wisdom."

"I could do that if some drinks and sexual favors were provided."

"Deal...But forget the drinks," Helen said, expressing a humorous side heretofore lacking.

"You almost got me there!"

Active Adult Community War ensued for several months; finally ending in an unsteady peace with intermittent skirmishes continually cropping up. The Women's Club was given a charter with the proviso they submit their programs in advance for pre-approval. If the Women's Club's program had even a scintilla of similarity between an Organizing Committee event, the Women's Club had to postpone their event for three months. Ah, the joy of peace…the spirit of community and fellowship…and the feeling of wellbeing and friendship!

I experienced a somewhat similar situation: I was bored. There is nothing here for me to do aside from cards and golf. I needed some intellectual stimulation.

When I expressed a desire to the Social Director that I was hoping to form a Chapter of the Council on Foreign Relations, she responded, "That won't be possible."

"Why?" I asked.

"Our by-laws prohibit any group, or club affiliating itself with a National or International Organization."

"You're kidding me…right?"

"No, I'm sorry that's the way the HOA rules are written."

"And the reason for such an asinine ruling?"

"I don't know. I'm only following the guidelines given me."

"Does it make sense to you? Can you find out before I seek legal representation?"

"You'll sue the HOA? Over this?"

"I'll consider it, especially if there's no legal basis behind this so-called regulation."

"Mr. Chandler, there's no reason you should be so confrontational."

"Look, this isn't about you. You're just a pawn in this. If you think I'm being argumentative now, you haven't seen hostility rear its ugly head," I said, clenching my teeth.

"Mr. Chandler I'm only relating what the HOA regulations state. Can I have one of the board members call you?"

"When?"

"I'm sure within a day. What's the best number to reach you at?"

"You have my number; it's in the resident's directory."

"Please don't take this personally. I'm only following procedure."

"Tell me one reason why this prohibition exists."

"I can't. Maybe it has to do with some insurance issue."

"We'll see what they tell me. Until then, I'm putting them on notice. This thing isn't over yet."

I felt sorry for her. She was a bright, competent administrator trapped in a bureaucratic morass. She had to deal with OLD PEOPLE...NOT easy!

As I expected, this group of self-appointed guardians of our lives—dictators of our activities—could not justify their mandate. When faced by someone unwilling to be bullied, they caved like the paper tigers they were.

Yes, I do have a very high opinion of myself, for if I didn't, no one else would.

If I'd been unsuccessful in creating a new Chapter of the Council on Foreign Relations, I was going to form an unofficial current events discussion group. When I conferred with some of the residents, they warned me that given the very prevalent political tribal divide among the homeowners, discussion and debate would likely turn into screaming matches. Sadly, they were correct...I deep-sixed that idea.

50

GOLF ENDED PREMATURELY due to unexpected snowstorms and frigid temperatures. Oxford Fields lost about twenty-five percent of its population. No, they weren't buried under the snow...they were the snowbirds who took flight to Florida and Arizona unable to bear occasional frostbite. The remainder of us hearty souls winterized our wardrobes, got our flu, pneumonia, and shingles vaccinations, and stowed-up on our wine and liquor supplies. A few of the men who made brief forays out of their homes during the warmer months, were now content to remain in hibernation indoors tending to their model trains, wood working, and even knife-making hobbies.

No hyperbole: these guys spend months on end never seeing the light of day; never participating in club functions, cards games, or other community social gatherings. They're recluses.

One evening, an ambulance, with sirens blaring, pulled up in front of a neighbor's house, which coincidently we were at that very moment driving by. Helen insisted we stop the car. I knew the woman who lived there from seeing her occasionally walking her dog. It never once dawned on me to say hello, no less ask anything about her personal life.

The EMTs wheeled a man out of the house on a stretcher. In the three years we had been living in Oxford Fields, I'm certain I'd never laid eyes on the guy.

"Who is that?" I asked Helen.

I pulled the car to the curb. We both got out and stood on the street a few yards away from the ambulance, watching what was happening.

"He must be Carol Butler's husband."

"Who's Carol Butler?"

"A woman I play samba with."

"You play dancing? That doesn't make sense."

"Samba's a card game, you idiot."

"Oh."

"Have you ever met her husband?"

"No. Carol said he's obsessed with his trains. Supposedly, he converted the basement into one big miniature village, replete with mountains and running rivers. He spends his entire day and most nights dressed in an engineer's uniform playing with his trains."

"Do you know if he had a thorough psychological evaluation?"

"Carol said he was totally fine. Besides, that's a terrible thing to say at a time like this."

"Seems pretty obvious to me he isn't the picture of health. Why else would he now be in an ambulance on the way to the hospital? Oh, I know—he inhaled too many exhaust fumes from his trains, or possibly was a victim of a train crash."

"Be understanding, Mike. Show some sympathy."

"I'm only kidding. Maybe you should ask Carol if we could be of some help. We could follow the ambulance and drive her to the hospital."

"That's really sweet of you to offer. You know, Mike, under that thick skin of yours, deep down, you do have a good heart. You should let that kinder soul out more often...I'll go ask her. Why don't you wait here?"

51

As I was clearing the dinner plates from the table, Helen cooed, "Mike, sweetheart."

I put the plate I had just rinsed off on the counter fearing I'd drop it after hearing what words would follow Helen's "sweetheart".

I instinctively blurted out, "No!"

"I didn't even ask you anything yet," she protested.

"When you 'coo', what follows is never good for me."

"How can you say that?"

"Really? Out with it. Let's get it over with."

"Can I get you a drink?"

"Oh, this one must really be a doozy."

"Do you recall when you said you'd give serious consideration to finishing the basement?"

"Was I sober, under the influence of drugs, or asleep at the time? I had to have been to agree with such a ludicrous idea."

"You were wide awake and I have witnesses."

"Are they still alive?"

Helen encouraged me to take advantage of my free time by finishing the basement. She wanted me to install a bathroom, add another bedroom, a humongous cedar closet, hardwood flooring, and a card room.

You already knew the chances of me agreeing to that insanity were non-existent.

"Yes, they're still breathing."

"But are they, or were they in a deep coma on life support, at the supposed time I allegedly held out a hint of hope that I'd accept such an assignment?"

"You're not a prosecutor. Stop with the foolish questions."

"How can you say that?"

"You said you'd consider doing the basement, and now I want to know if and when you will."

"I would never intentionally mislead you," I innocently replied.

"So then you'll do it?"

"Only if I can include a sauna and hire a masseuse three days a week."

"You're not going to be serious, are you?"

"Helen, we don't need the extra living space. We don't use what we have now. You insisted on having the loft with the additional two bedrooms upstairs. Dare I ask how many times both rooms have been used simultaneously in the past three years? Don't guess, I'll tell you. Twice.

"It's not cost effective for us to do what you want. Besides, the space will never be used."

"We need storage space."

"For what? More shoes and black pants?"

"Maybe."

"Clear out the crap in the basement you brought with us that we don't use and never will. Donate it to some worthy cause or ask the kids again if they want any of it. Wait a minute...before the kids come over and go through it all, be sure to hide the handcuffs and whips, and that cute little black leather outfit I love you in so much."

"Really? You want me to get rid of your mother's wedding gift to us?"

"That was a low blow! Why would you insult my mother in such a demeaning fashion?"

"I loved her also, but she was a bit off-center and you know it."

"Okay, forget what I said. Let the kids share them. Maybe it will spice up their lives."

"Good try, Mike."

"What do you mean?"

"You tried to change the subject."

"How dare you accuse me of such a thing?!"

I was just going to say that after you dispose of the garbage in the basement, we'd go to IKEA and buy some shelving and free-standing closets. They'll do the trick."

A win for the good guy!

The next weekend, we purchased several put-it-together with pegs, screwdriver, and hammer closets from IKEA, and a slew of shelving from Lowes. Shockingly, I was able to follow directions and assemble the closets within an afternoon.

That never happened before.

There was a downside to not spending the winter months converting the basement into a second home: it meant I now had too much free time on my hands.

I could read, go to the gym and exercise, play more cards, or try something I'd always fantasized about—writing a book. Helen, on the other hand, had barely had a free moment to spare.

"So now that you won't be spending time down below, what are you going to do all day?"

"I'm considering writing one of those vanity books."

"Interesting…About what?"

"Oh, I don't know. Most likely an autobiography with primary emphasis on my sex life."

"That won't be a book. At best it'll be a short story or a one paragraph limerick."

"And whose fault is that, Helen?" I said curtly.

Silence…

I let the silence linger for several moments, never taking my eyes off her. I didn't want to let her off the hook just yet.

She tried to retain some semblance of self-esteem by saying, "Come on, thin skin. I refuse to share your sexual prowess with the rest of the world. What went on under our sheets, stays there."

"Three times does not make very interesting reading," I rejoined, staring at her with unforgiving eyes.

Nothing I could say would be gained by re-litigating the gorilla in the room, so I sidestepped the issue and said, "Maybe I could write about our experience finding this funeral home waiting room we're living in?"

Helen sighed deeply, grateful for the change in subject.

"You might have something there. But I'd suggest not dwelling on the 'death's waiting room stuff'," she said in a warm, non-confrontational voice, I assume fearing I'd want to revisit the sex thing.

"What about a handbook on how to find your dream fifty-five plus active lifestyle community?"

"I think you're getting warmer."

"I could devote a chapter to suggestions on socializing with seniors who've lost their hearing and/or minds. Another with hints on how to ignore the frequent booming sound emanating from ambulance sirens cruising the streets looking for their next hospital bound victim."

"Mike, do some research on improving one's ability to show empathy, patience, and understanding when interacting with others."

"Is that subtle comment meant for my benefit?"

"Heal thyself before educating others."

"I'll take that under consideration."

52

OTHER NATURE HAD been kind to us the past few months. There was very little snow, and the temperature, except for two or three days, stayed between thirty-five and forty-five degrees. It was actually quite pleasant. The snowbirds wasted their money going south or west this winter.

It took me a good deal of time to finalize an outline for the book I committed myself to write. When I felt I was ready to put pen to paper, or as the new generation says, fingers to keyboard, the dreaded "writer's block" took hold. For weeks on end I drew a blank until things finally clicked into place.

Once I started to write, memories of humorous incidents, which I could include in the book, kept popping into my head. Several of them challenge one's belief in acceptable norms of behavior.

• • •

The women's daily (sometimes repeated multiple times a day) ritual of hugging and kissing the same person was something I could not understand. Not only would they engage in that physical act with each other, they would attempt to bestow the affection upon the men too. Some of the more risqué females would offer their lips instead of the more accepted air cheek kiss. I feigned invisibility. When I sensed an assault, I turned my back or hurried past their outstretched arms as if I were late for a meeting. If trapped, I claimed I was coming down with a cold and didn't want to infect them.

This hug routine was perplexing to me. Then, out of nowhere, my eyes flew wide open, and my neck tingled with excitement. Everything fell into place. I knew why they did it! Or at least, I think I did.

These women were thankful their friends were still alive; that they had made it through the afternoon or night without suffering a fatal stroke, heart attack, falling victim to a car crash...or, the worst tragedy of all, chipping their nail polish! There can be no other explanation.

I suspect a lot of these women don't like each other, but fear retribution from others if they don't partake in the hug/kiss formality. Just saying!

• • •

Then there was the episode of neighbors, let's call them the Browns, who wanted to install an emergency generator outside their home. This was not uncommon. A significant number of homes have these generators because the community suffers frequent power outages, due to the fact that the power and cable lines are strung above ground, intertwined between tree limbs and overhanging the roads. Wind, ice or snowstorms cause havoc with these wires, often resulting in them cascading down to the street and shorting out power in the surrounding communities.

The Browns, as per HOA regulations, sought the written approval of their next-door neighbors and "best friends" to make the installation. Their friends would not agree to approve the request even though the unit would be located on the opposite side of the house from theirs; it would not be visible to the "best friends" nor would they be able to hear it when it was in operation.

Why then, did they refuse the request? Their explanation was simple: they believed the generator was too dangerous to the safety of their friends' wellbeing...Incredible, but it happened.

• • •

Oxford Field's only two tennis courts are rarely used by anyone other than visiting grandchildren. When it's warm enough to play, I estimate the usage, if I'm being generous, at ten percent of the available time the courts could be used, including during the summer when the Tennis Club has their preapproved reserved time slots. The Tennis Club's membership consists of about twenty residents able to maneuver themselves relatively well without walkers. The Tennis Club claims oversight management of the courts. And when the members do use the courts, most of the time they play doubles. Some of the members are really good, even if they can't move too fast.

Enter the new fad: pickleball—a game played on a miniature tennis court with a hard wood racket. Seniors are attracted to the game primarily because it doesn't require much running, skill, or stamina. The appeal of the game, I believe, is that it gives the participants the illusion they're exercising and as an extra-added bonus they're out in the fresh air.

No doubt, residents who had visited Florida or the Carolinas, and who were either unwilling or unable to endure the physical exertion of playing tennis, discovered the joys of pickleball, and wished to engage in that activity at Oxford Fields. Unfortunately for them, and eventually for the Tennis Club, there were no pickleball courts at Oxford Fields.

What to do? A group of the pickleball player wannabes petitioned the HOA for permission to superimpose the necessary lines demarcating the boundaries of their game over the embedded lines of the tennis court.

The Tennis Club would have nothing of this assault on their sacred territory. They objected to both the perceived damage to their court, and to ceding playing time to this upstart group. The great tennis/pickleball controversy immersed the entire community in debate for months. Friends and neighbors were forced to choose sides.

Building a new, stand-alone pickleball court was objected to by a large number of residents who maintained that the cost of construction and maintenance of a new court was not commensurate with the relatively small number of potential users. The proponents argued it would enhance the community's lifestyle and increase home values.

A stalemate ensued among the sides, reminiscent of the ill-conceived Trump-imposed government shutdown. Neither side would concede ground. The pickleball renegades took it upon themselves and drew their chalk lines on the courts so they could play. It was not a pleasant time!

Finally, the HOA Board made their decision. Pickleball lines on one of the tennis courts would be added using a different color paint, so one could differentiate pickleball from tennis. Both games could be played without confusing the boundaries of either sport. Furthermore, both the Tennis Club and Pickleball Group/Club were required to submit a schedule of their respective time needs to the Social Director, who would in turn establish the court usage allocation. The monetary cost to the community was negligible.

●　●　●

How I forgot this one baffles me because I have a daily reminder of it. All I have to do is look up.

Remember how I complained about the height of the family room ceiling when I met with Chad? Well, it turns out that one of the bulbs blew out. My options were limited in the ways I could take out and replace the bulb. Since there's no access to the light fixtures in the ceiling by way of an attic, I could either levitate up twenty-three feet; have four or five neighbors come in and form a human ladder by standing on each other's shoulders, allowing me to shimmy up their backs resulting in the death or crippling of all of us; buy a twenty-five-foot ladder and have Helen use it because I have vertigo and refuse to climb that high; or buy one of those extension poles with various suction head attachments. I chose the extension pole.

Equipment in hand, I attached the recommended implement and the end of the telescoping pole, extended the pole, and placed the spring-like grabber around the bulb. I rotated the pole counter-clockwise expecting the bulb to dislodge from its fixture. Well, it did. And as an extra-added bonus the fixture itself came with it. I was pissed.

Helen saw what I had done. At first she laughed. But laughter turned into semi-criticism.

"What did you do?"

"Beats the hell out of me."

"How are we going to replace the fixture?"

"Beats me."

"Seriously, Mike, what are you going to do?"

"Nothing. Nobody will ever notice it. It'll just be a little darker in the room. They'll think it's romantic."

"No, they won't…What can we do?"

"Call an electrician. Ask one of your hugging buddies for a recommendation."

Well, Helen did. She got the name of someone who scheduled us for a look-see a month later. I definitely had been in the wrong profession.

When the much-anticipated day arrived for our electrical con-sultation, we were a jitter with excitement.

"So glad you could fit us in to your busy schedule," Helen said with a little edge to her voice.

"No problem. You know how it is. Everyone has an emergency that must be fixed yesterday. I do appreciate your patience with me, Mr. and Mrs. Chandler. So, show me what's wrong."

We took him into the family room.

"Yeah. This happens here a lot. This is the builder's fault. He should have taken steps to allow easy access to those fixtures."

"Right. But he didn't," I said.

"I'm sure you realize this is not a simple job. I can do it one of two ways. Either I can construct some scaffolding, or bring in a small scissor lift."

"One like Con Ed or tree pruners use?" I prompted.

"Yup. That's the one."

"What's the damage?" I asked, fearing the answer.

"You mean what will it cost you?"

"Yes."

"Two hours' labor at eighty-five dollars per hour for the scaffolding, or two hundred fifty dollars for the scissor lift."

"That's a lot of money for changing a one hundred ten watt bulb."

"Sure is."

"Well, give us a day or two to think it over. I'll give you a call when we decide."

"I appreciate your consideration and look forward to your call."

He left...We talked.

We called him the next day and asked that he go the scaffolding route. He said he'd be back in a month to do the job. It's now a year later and he still hasn't come.

"Helen, I think we should just live with the lighting in the family room the way it is. No need to spend that much money. Anyway he's not coming back."

"I agree. But what happens if another bulb goes?"

"We'll live in darkness. Think of it as a blessing. We won't see ourselves getting older."

• • •

We attend many community or club sponsored events where dinner is served and non-reserved table seating is the norm. Typically we arrive at the appointed time only to find we are practically the very last people to arrive, resulting in either us standing, sitting at a table behind a pillar with people who hardly acknowledge our presence, or located so far away from the action that we need binoculars to see. Adding insult to injury, quite often we are left with only scraps of food to eat. The residents attack the food as if they haven't eaten in weeks. It's no wonder that cruising the high seas with twelve meals per day is the vacationing preference for residents of adult communities!

I'm exaggerating the food thing for comedic effect. Don't take offense!

However, I'm not puffing up the story when I say it's acknowledged that if you're planning on attending a food function where Len is expected to attend, come early if you want enough food left over for you to eat. The adage "the early bird catches the worm" definitely applies.

Len is always the first in line to eat; and eat he does—to excess. It doesn't matter that there's a limited amount of food available. He couldn't care less; he still piles his plate high, others be damned!

At a recent party, jumbo shrimp were being served by a roving waitress. A few of the men decided to take matters into their own hands and prevent Len's gluttonous behavior. Every time Len approached the server carrying the shrimp, these two guys physically blocked his path...No shrimp for Len!

•   •   •

I'd be remiss not to tell about two separate incidents that have a common thread. I don't know why women take such liberties with me, knowing I'm a married man, but they do.

Marilyn, a woman in her early eighties who skis, plays tennis, and participants in a range of other activities, was walking—for exercise—when a neighbor's dog attacked her, biting her on the thigh. Luckily for all concerned, particularly Marilyn, the bite did not break skin. No rabies shots were needed.

The episode was the talk of the community. When I saw Marilyn in the clubhouse a day or two later, I asked her about the attack and how she felt.

"Do you want to see it?" she asked.

"Sure, let me see the picture."

"I don't have a picture!"

With that, she lifted up her skirt to reveal her entire leg from her ankle to her undies. I couldn't believe it. I hardly knew the woman, other than to say hello. Not only that, but we were in a public area.

"Wow! That's one ugly bruise you've got there. Does it hurt?"

"No, not really."

"Thank goodness. You're very fortunate the dog's teeth didn't break skin. It could be a lot worse."

At this point Marilyn was still holding up her skirt, exposing, for all to see, this humongous black and blue bruise that covered the entire length of her leg.

"Marilyn, please put your skirt down, women will begin to talk about us. You know how they can be."

"Don't be embarrassed," she said as she acceded to my request.

I begged off further conversation with Marilyn and walked over to Helen who had been glaring at me from her mahjong table several yards away.

"What the hell was going on between you two?" she asked

"She was only showing me her new thongs. They're not only attractive, esthetically speaking, they're so soft to the touch."

Two of the other three women at the table blanched. The third woman covered her mouth with her hand, hoping to cover her laughter.

"You're so uncouth; I don't believe it," Helen said, quite annoyed. "How could she do that with me sitting just a few feet away?"

"It's a curse. I have that effect on women. The combination of my good looks and magnetic personality are impossible to resist. I'm relieved she stopped by only showing me her leg."

"I've got a good inclination to give her a piece of my mind, right here and now."

"Helen, it was nothing. She only showed me the discoloration and contusion from the bite."

"Seriously?"

"That's it."

• • •

Focus now on what happened at a party in another friend's home. Envisage this: several of us are standing around in the kitchen, talking. One of the women is eating a tortilla chip brimming over with a salsa dip. A good amount of the dip doesn't make it to her mouth, but ends up on her blouse above her waist, below her breasts. She doesn't see it. The hostess hands me a napkin, suggesting I use it to remove the unsightly mess.

"Maria, if you're not accessorizing with food you might want to use this to clean it up," I say pointing to the salsa continuing to drip down her blouse.

"Oh," she says smilingly and looking down. "It does complement the pattern, don't you think?"

"You have quite an eye for design," I respond.

"The color blends, but the minced onions are a distraction."

"So here," I offer her the napkin, "wipe it off...maybe some club soda would help?"

"Why don't you do it for me?"

"Are you sure? My hand might slip upwards."

"I trust you, Mike."

"If you insist."

"I do."

As I raise my hand to clean her blouse, she lifts it so that the stain is now directly over her breast.

"What are you doing, Maria? You're crazy. You know that."

"I'm not crazy; I'm horny! My husband's been deceased for too many years; my little ladies deserve a little tenderness now and then. It's nothing personal, Mike. View it as helping an older woman cope with being alone, and there's a chance you also might like it."

Mind you, there are three or four other women, including Helen, standing right next to us listening to this lurid conversation...All of them laughing.

I hesitate. Helen, with what I think is a slight nod of the head winks at me, which I take as a signal of her approval to commence the onerous task of cleaning. I begin...Boy am I wrong! The group laugh...Helen is livid!

Unpleasant as the task requested of me is, I grit my teeth and scrub. Unable to contain her pleasure at my acquiesce, Maria says in a loud, booming voice, grinning cheek to cheek, "Thank you, Mike; my ladies owe you Big Time."

Maria turns and walks to join another conversation...Helen does not. Daggers and bolts of fire and brimstone radiate from her eyes, which are boring into my soul. My goose is cooked. Obviously I got her signals crossed.

●   ●   ●

Hank is driving me and another male resident back from a restaurant where we had just eaten dinner. I'm seated in the back seat behind Hank. We're driving in the left lane on US 84. The exit we were to get off on is a half-mile away.

In a conversational voice, I say, "Hank, you might want to get over in the right lane. Our exit's coming up."

He shows no inclination to heed my suggestion.

"Hank," I say, raising my voice slightly, "we have to get off in a quarter of a mile."

Still no reaction.

"Hank! We have to get off here!" I scream at the top of my lungs. I lose my patience.

We pass the exit and Hank is still in the left lane, oblivious to my warnings. I grab his shoulders from behind a gently shake him.

"What the hell's wrong with you? Why didn't you slow down and get off at the exit? I've been yelling at the top of my lungs for you to get off."

In a muted voice, Hank says, "I didn't hear you."

"You didn't hear me? Are you stone deaf?"

"I didn't hear you. What else can I say?"

"Well, in the first instance you've been living in Oxford Fields for over two years. You should know where the exit is. And secondly, go to an Audiologist and get your hearing checked."

The other fellow who is sitting next to Hank was equally unaware. It turns out he's also stone deaf.

The lesson of that incident is...never let Hank drive you or Helen anywhere, and before letting anyone else drive you somewhere, check their hearing and knowledge of geography.

• • •

This event was told to me by Barry and later confirmed by Hank. Yup, the same Hank and the same Barry.

It seems Barry and Hank went to play golf together. Both of these gentlemen had never shot under one hundred for eighteen holes...far from it. On the first hole, both men had driven the ball on opposite sides of the fairway. They separated, each of them going to their respective ball. Hank took several shots to reach the green. He putted out and went to the second hole and teed off. Barry in the meantime was still playing the same hole. When he reached the green, Hank was nowhere to be seen. They were no longer a twosome.

Hank recalls it didn't faze him. He never put two and two together that he was playing alone. For his part, Barry was mystified by Hank's disappearance. He wasn't worried though because he had driven to the course in his car. Hank had better find a ride for himself.

• • •

Helen and I were at a neighbor's house for a large dinner party. There must have been fifteen or twenty couples there. Food was abundant, and no dearth of drinks. I was seated at a dining room table enjoying some dip and munchies when a woman sitting across from me took a piece of potpourri in the shape of a slice of orange from the centerpiece and ate it. My eyes must have popped out of my head. Here was this adult, who I knew was college educated, munching on plastic, swallowing it, and obviously enjoying it. I was flabbergasted! I laughed out loud. Tears literally flowed down my cheek.

Another guest sitting next to me couldn't help but ask, "What's so funny? Let me in on the joke."

The target of my enjoyment was too engrossed in her quest to down another morsel of plastic to notice my hysteria.

"Fran just ate a piece of potpourri," I whispered holding my hand in front of my face so Fran wouldn't hear me. "And now she's eating more."

"Tell her, she could get sick from eating that stuff."

The Good Samaritan in me took over. And so as not to embarrass her any more than she would be, I got up, walked around the table and leaned over her shoulder and whispered into her ear, "Fran, that stuff you're eating is poison. It's plastic."

She showed no outward sign of embarrassment. She simply got up from the table and went into the bathroom. She avoided me for the rest of the evening. Before she left, she thanked me for the gentlemanly way I handled the situation. I was so proud of myself. I imagine, however, if she ever reads this book, she won't think too kindly of me and might consider retracting her compliment.

I wasn't completely surprised later that evening when a neighbor of Fran's, who was at the party, called and told me an ambulance had just taken Fran to the hospital to get her stomach pumped.

• • •

Helen finally got her revenge…or she's joined the ranks of the other memory-challenged residents of Oxford Fields. Here's what happened; judge for yourself.

I'm sitting on my deck around 6:30 in the evening smoking a cigar and drinking some red wine while reading a book. Helen comes out on the deck to tell me she's leaving for a meeting and won't be back until around 10:30 that night.

Ah, I think, *peace and tranquility for a couple of hours. I could even smoke another cigar and have a second drink without her knowing. No way I'd be able to do that if she were home…that's for sure.*

Maybe a half an hour later, I finish my merlot (although I'm not really sure how long it was). Then Nature calls….I have to answer.

I get up, put the stub of my cigar in the ashtray and go to go inside the house. Helen has locked the door! I have no key and no phone to use to call her! I am stranded! Nature will have to take a back seat to my survival!

So you're thinking, why doesn't he just go down the staircase and get some help from a neighbor? Well, here's the reality: there is no staircase and the deck is some twenty odd feet above ground level. And if that isn't bad enough, the weather forecast is for thundershowers later that evening.

Mike, I say to myself, *what the hell are you going to do? ...What are my options? I could stay on the deck and wait for Helen to come home; try to get a neighbor's attention; break a window; or jump.*

I immediately rule out jumping off the deck for fear I'll kill myself, or break some bones. Then again, I could fall and hit my head, rendering me unconscious, and remain unseen, lying on the ground until God knows when. And when Helen finally does come home, she won't even consider looking for me on the deck...no less on the ground under it...No...jumping is definitely out!

Likewise, destroying a glass window makes no sense.

I opt for the least dangerous alternative: SCREAM FOR HELP!

Unfortunately, in this instance, since our house is at the end of a cul-de-sac, the land separating us from our neighbors on both sides is appreciable. Add to that, that because of privacy issues, the builder has appropriately included only one set of windows on that facing side of their homes—bathroom windows. So if they were to hear me yell, they'd have to be doing their business in that room at that time.

I yelled...I screamed...I became more nervous...No response.

Think, Mike; think.

Eureka! I have an idea. I will use the water hose I had attached on the outside of the railing to water our plants, to determine which part of the deck is closest to the ground. Then test if the hose can withstand the full bearing of my weight without damaging or pulling the water socket out from the wall…It just might.

I have a chance to escape, I reason. If I wrap the hose around the railing, I could go hand over hand and slide down to the ground without falling. Having more confidence in my physical ability than I justifiably should have, I throw caution to the wind, scale the railing, grab onto the hose, close my eyes, and leave my fate to chance.

I made it unharmed! Frightening.

My success in escaping from the heights of despair and avoiding hypothermia now put to rest, I set off in quest of a phone to call Helen and beg her to return home.

53

I'D SPENT A good amount of time on the computer making progress writing the book. New Year's Eve came. Helen had invited some friends over to celebrate ringing in the New Year. We ordered in Chinese food and pizza, had a few drinks, and then played some board games.

"Mike it's your turn. Spin the dice already," my friend Lou bristled.

I just stared into space.

Mike...are you alright?" he asked, now sounding concerned.

"I'm not sure," I said in a very low voice.

"What does that mean?" Helen asked, raising her voice to be heard above the racket being made by our other guests in the living room.

"I'm a little dizzy," I responded.

"Well, you had two big glasses of Scotch. What do you expect?" Lou added.

"It's not the drinks; it's...it's something else, I'm sure of it."

Helen had gotten up from her seat from the far end of the table and stood leaning over me, her hand touching my forehead.

"What are you doing?"

"Seeing if you have a fever."

"Well do I?"

"No. But you are sweating profusely. I think you should go into the bedroom and lie down...now!"

"Alright. Give me a hand, please. I'm not sure I can make it on my own."

Helen and Lou each took one of my arms, supporting me and keeping me balanced as they led me into my bedroom, and helped me onto my bed. I didn't know what was happening. I was frightened.

By this time all our other guests had seen and heard the commotion, but didn't really know what the problem was. They waited in the family room for either Lou or Helen to let them know what was going on.

Lou stayed with me. He was checking my pulse. Helen rejoined our friends, stress radiating from every muscle in her face. She was scared. She couldn't mask her emotions. It was right out front for everyone to see.

"Maybe we should leave?" one of the women suggested.

"Please stay...It's only twenty minutes till the ball comes down...Enjoy yourselves. Have another drink. Mike will be okay," she said unconvincingly.

A minute later, Helen and one of the other guys came into the bedroom to check on me.

"Are you feeling any better?" he asked.

"Not really. I think it's my heart; it's beating too fast."

"Let me take your pulse again," demanded Lou.

"You're not a physician, Lou. You're only an accountant."

"Smart guy. I know what I'm doing. I did have some basic medical training in the army. I was a medic. Now let me do what I have to do."

"Okay, okay, get it over with."

He took my pulse. My rate was close to one hundred and fifty beats per minute.

"Mike I think there might be a problem. We can't ignore it," he said.

"Are you suggesting that I entertain the neighborhood with the sound of sirens?"

"This is no joking matter. We don't have an alternative. Helen has to call for an ambulance now."

She did.

At 11:50, to the melodic refrains of the ambulance's sirens, the EMTs arrived. They immediately took my pulse, blood pressure, and listened to my heart. Their verdict was unanimous. Bundle him up; put a few blankets on him, and put him in the ambulance STAT.

The temperature was below freezing. The wind was blowing hard and there were several inches of snow on the ground.

"What hospital do you want to go to?" the EMT asked me.

"Yale," I emphatically demanded.

"Sorry sir, we can only take you to Danbury, Waterbury, or Griffin Hospital in Seymour."

"Which one has the lowest death rate?" I asked.

"They're all good hospitals, sir. Don't worry you'll be fine no matter which one we take you to. So which one? It's your choice?"

"Waterbury."

HELP!!!

Helen went in Lou's car to Waterbury Hospital, arriving seconds after the ambulance.

My heart was racing so fast the EMTs had to do something quickly. They gave me a choice between getting the paddles to shock my heart or an injection of this drug, which would stop the heart and then restart it so hopefully the rate would be reduced. They warned me it was likely I might feel as if someone had taken a sledgehammer to my chest. The thought of being electrocuted by the paddles scared the hell out of me, especially since I was still conscience. I'm surprised my heart didn't jump out of my chest after hearing what they were planning to do.

I opted for the injection, praying the impending trauma it might cause would be bearable compared to the alternative use of the paddles. Thankfully the medication worked.

Oh yeah, I forgot to tell you: I had switched my supplemental healthcare insurance during the open enrollment period from Blue Cross to United Health Care. The effective date of the change was to be January 1st of the New Year. The ambulance picked me up at 11:50 p.m., at which time I was covered by B/C. I arrived at the hospital's emergency room at 12:10 a.m. My new policy under United Health Care was due to be effective at that time.

Thinking about whether I had medical insurance or not was not helping to keep me calm. It was having the opposite effect. As it turned out, I had no cause to worry; both carriers paid without asking a question.

I was wheeled into the Emergency Room and immediately examined by the attending medical staff. They believed I'd had a mild heart attack, but was stable. Then, even though the doctors wanted me admitted for further testing and observation, it took the admitting office several hours to get me a room in the cardiac unit. In the meantime, I remained in the ER hooked up to every monitor you can conceivably think of.

Both Helen and Lou stayed with me until I was safely in my cardiac unit bed. Lou, bless his soul, drove an emotionally spent Helen home...Time—4:00 a.m.

Helen was given the name of a cardiologist who had previously treated one of her friend's husband. She arranged for him to see me later that morning.

"Mr. Chandler, I'm Dr. Manley, your wife asked me look in on you. How are you feeling? Did you get any sleep?"

"I'm apprehensive. And no, I didn't get any sleep. How could I with all these wires and tubes sticking out of me, and the nurses coming in every hour to take my blood pressure?"

Dr. Manley reviewed my medical chart, which had hung at the foot of the bed.

"Well, from your EKGs it's quite obvious you've experienced a P.S.V.T."

"English translation, please."

"Paroxysmal Supraventricular Tachycardia—a sudden onset of fast beating heart. A cardio infarction; a heart attack."

"What caused it? I've never been diagnosed with any heart problem."

"Either ingesting excessive amounts of stimulants, or I suspect you might have a heart anomaly."

"And that would be?"

"In layman's terms, you could have multiple electrical starters. Normal hearts only have one. You might have a few more."

"If I do, can that be corrected?"

"Yes, by ablation. We surgically burn them out."

"You burn them out? Not with a torch, I hope. Do they crack my chest?"

"No, they insert catheters into blood vessels on each side of your groin. They wind the wires up into your heart so they can do an electrical mapping. If they're able to locate the site, they destroy that tissue by ablating it. To do that, they must repeatedly stop and artificially start the heart to see if there're any superfluous starters."

"That doesn't sound too pleasant."

"You won't feel a thing. You'll be under anesthesia the whole time."

"Do you do that?"

"No, I'm a Cardiologist not a Cardiac Surgeon. A specialist does."

"What kind of specialist?"

"A Cardiac Electrophysiology Surgeon."

"If I have to have that done, I'm not having it performed in this hospital. My heart might be failing me, but my good senses aren't. I want to go to Yale or Columbia-Presbyterian. Can you refer me to someone who has privileges at one of those hospitals?"

"Absolutely. I'll set up an appointment for you with Dr. Terry Cohen, Yale's Clinical Director of Cardiac Electrophysiology. He's a great surgeon with a wonderful personality. You'll be in good hands with him."

"Fantastic!"

I like Manley's honesty and the competency he emotes. I hope this fellow at Yale is the same.

It took me several weeks to get an appointment with Dr. Cohen. When he finally did examine me, coupled with reviewing the results of the additional diagnostic testing he insisted on performing, Dr. Cohen concurred with Dr. Manley's initial diagnosis. He felt the cause of the P.S.V.T wasn't definitive and was reluctant to put me through an unnecessary surgery. He wanted to eliminate outside stimuli as the possible culprit, rather than a structural deformity.

"The best course of action for you Mr. Chandler is for us to defer surgery until and unless you suffer another episode."

"I'm in your hands, doctor. You're calling the shots."

Several months went by without incidence. Then it happened again while I was sitting on the couch in the family room watching television. I felt as if my heart would bust through my chest it was beating so hard. I was lighted-headed and nervous again…but not in pain. I yelled for Helen to call for an ambulance. She had been in the laundry room sorting a wash when she heard me scream. She came running, saw my facial expression and knew immediately I was experiencing the same heart issue. Not missing a step, she called 911.

The EMTs came with sirens blazing, put me on a stretcher and carried me into the ambulance where they administered the same drug to slow my heart rate. I did feel some discomfort as the drug radiated up my legs, but it was a much better alternative than the paddles…without a doubt.

They still wouldn't take me to Yale. I was taken instead to Danbury Hospital's Emergency Room. This time Helen drove herself.

Deja-vu all over again. A different hospital…same routine.

The next day, it was determined I was medically stable to be moved. They transported me by ambulance—no sirens needed—to Yale University Hospital.

Surgery was scheduled for the following morning. Six hours on the operating table…another three in recovery…and five excess electrical starters removed from my heart later, I was a new man; eager and ready to assume the mantle of an active, fun-filled life, even if I didn't know it at the time since I was still groggy from the lingering after effects of anesthesia.

54

CHANGES HAD TO be made to my lifestyle. The physicians dictated that I limit my daily consumption of alcohol too two drinks maximum, and basically eliminate all caffeine whether in soda or coffee. If that wasn't bad enough, the doctors said I had to reduce the frequency of sexual intercourse to no more than four times per week, and no less than three. I swear, by everything I don't hold sacred, Dr. Cohen told me that in his office and witnessed by his nurse. I asked him to write a prescription for it, since Helen would be reluctant to reduce the incidence of her insatiable sexual appetite. But most assuredly she would honor the doctor's order and let me rest for three days a week.

Lying in my hospital bed post-surgery was a lonely experience. I had a lot of time to think; to contemplate my mortality, my wife, my children, my grandchildren, my parents and my friends, the way I lived my life, what I would do differently or what I wouldn't do. Did I have any regrets? If I had died, would I be eulogized? Would someone speak at my funeral? What would they say about me? Had I hurt anyone? Could I have helped or been nicer to someone? Would I choose the same occupation? Would I live in the same places? It was both sobering and scary to consider those things, but I'm glad I did.

I came to some irrefutable conclusions. By any measure, I was a successful man in most all ways: a happy, healthy family, a beautiful house, and a wife who loved me. I had enough money to live comfortably the rest of my days. However, I was not entirely satisfied. I realized I didn't let anyone other than family members into my inner self. Throughout my life, I had pushed close relationships away. Other than one or two friends of long-time standing, I couldn't say I had a best friend. I didn't. But I did have good friends. I was afraid of being rejected and so I put up a protective emotional shield to ward off potential unpleasant feelings. I know I suffered as a result and in retrospect Helen probably also did.

My behavior and comments at times did not reflect who I really was, or what I truly felt. For instance, at least five "friends" I've made in Oxford, who don't drink Scotch, went out of their way to purchase bottles of very expensive Single Malt Scotch solely for my enjoyment, so they could offer it to me when I visited their homes.

I didn't really appreciate the magnitude of their gestures, and as a result might have offended them by my lack of a wholehearted thank you. Now that it's finally penetrated my thick skull what an exceptional token of friendship their generosity was, in that instance and countless other expressions of kinship by so many others, I can...should...and must unreservedly open myself up to accepting a new level of personal relationships. It doesn't matter that these good people never met my parents or knew my children from a very young age. Nor do religion, political persuasion, or how much money these people have matter. All I care about now is if they are honest, caring, and have a sense of humor.

Hopefully, it's not too late for me to embrace my new reality... No, it's never too late. I'll reach for the golden ring.

55

ARMED WITH MY repaired heart now beating to an accepted rhythm, and my commitment to be more open to friendship and what it entails, I strode into the clubhouse prepared to resume my place at the card table with the other physically and mentally challenged.

I didn't resolve to alter my caustic sarcastic humor, though. Some things are impossible.

A chorus of voices greeted me, "Welcome back, Mike. We saved you a seat."

Maybe I was still suffering the after effects of anesthesia.

Did they really say that, or did my hearing acumen go by way of my heart?

Handshakes and backslapping followed their tone-deaf chants. I was touched; sincerely taken aback by their show of affection. I didn't outwardly tear up, but internally I was bawling. It threw me for a loop.

Why would these people whom I have continually chastised, ridiculed, and belittled be so nice? They haven't even seen the change in me yet.

Unexpectantly, this guy Tommy came up to me, his nose almost touching mine.

"You look like shit, Mike. What happened to you?" he asked.

Tommy was a big strapping bear of a man who, up until that time had rarely spoken to me or to anyone else.

"You talkin' to me?" I shot back in the best Brooklyn accent I could muster.

"Yeah, you wimp," he said without a trace of animosity in his voice.

"So, I go into the hospital not knowing if I'm going to survive and you in my absence pull a coup and take my place as the Chief Insulter in Residence? Who cloned my tongue into your mouth?"

"No one can take your place, Mike. But what's good for the goose is good for the gander."

"And here I am—a man who chose to change his ways; to let slide every opportunity you bunch of decrepit old men give me, to get a laugh at your expense and lighten-up your life—you now pick on me, in my weakened state, the same way I treated you. Shame on you! What you're doing is wrong and unethical, and behavior not befitting men of your stature."

I walked into the middle of the room...stood at attention raised my right hand and shot them the bird.

"Gentlemen, and I use that term very loosely, I applaud and thank all of you for your most gracious welcoming. There!" I said flipping them the bird again. Then took my seat at the card table.

Unfazed by my soliloquy and expression of gratitude, Tommy continued his newfound voice, egged on by the support of that group of smiling men.

"Deal the cards already, Mike, before Bill keels over again. None of us have much time to live, so let's make the best of it, shall we?"

I loved it!

56

INCOMPREHENSIBLY, HELEN ALSO changed. Something came over her. She morphed into a touchy-feely, sexually crazed woman… WITH ME! Maybe the fear of losing me shocked her physiological and psychological systems into action. Her urge for intimacy became insatiable. Finally, after so many years I was truly satisfied…so much so, I begged her for relief.

Go figure: my negative attitude toward Oxford Fields also radically altered. I transformed from a protagonist into a proponent. I admit, and as you might have surmised by my less than enthusiastic behavior to date, that I've never expressed a positive approach, in word or deed, toward living in an active adult senior community.

I was wrong; so wrong.

Think back to your youth, to your summers when school was over, when you played with your friends all day and well into the night. No worries, no homework, no nagging from your parents to study. Life was grand. You swam, played baseball, basketball, and the well-healed played golf. You ogled the girls in their bathing suits, dreaming of…

Compare my life now to what it was then…except the bathing suit part. Believe me….it's the same! We're living in a three hundred sixty-five day per year camp. We play, eat, and sleep as much and for as long as we wish. No one, spouses aside, dictates what, where, or how we spend our time.

It used to be that weekends were reserved for movies, going out to restaurants, having parties or going to parties. Now there's no distinction between days. We eat out any day of the week, probably too often as witnessed by our expanding waistlines, we party continually, and go to the movies whenever the mood strikes us. If we had heard years ago that people were behaving in the manner we are now, we would be aghast.

Structurally and organizationally, these communities are a blessing. They're a place where seniors having similar needs and desires can find like-minded people all in the same, aging boat—some suffering the effects of diminishing health, others the loss of a mate—all needing companionship and friendship, and each resident, consciously or unconsciously trying to compensate for the loss of a social safety net they were part of before moving.

The first lesson I pass on to anyone who'll listen is not to fall into the, "I'm not ready to consider moving" trap. Don't procrastinate. Delaying the decision to move out of my comfort zone was one of the hardest decisions I ever had to make. In retrospect, I'm glad Helen was persistent and forced the issue.

Finally, I became a member in good standing of Oxford Fields. I needed hip surgery, rotator cuff repair, and meniscus surgery on one knee. Helen broke a fingernail—a tragedy beyond all others.

I was now a card-carrying member of the walking wounded!

Live life to the fullest. Spend money if you have it. Eat to your heart's content so long as you're healthy. Love without reservation. Enjoy your children and grandchildren, and if you're extremely fortunate, your great-grandchildren, knowing you loved, cared, and nurtured them to the best of your ability.

POSTSCRIPT

HELEN INADVERTENTLY MADE my task of writing more complicated because she mentioned to every one of her many friends that I was writing a book describing Oxford Fields and the people living there. The residents who knew me, knew the book would be unapologetically cynical, and downright critical of them and Oxford Fields. Most of these people literally dreaded what I would say about them. If someone belched or accidentally passed gas, they would immediately look in my direction, hoping I did not see, hear, or smell what they did or said. And if they sensed I had witnessed their *faux pas*, they'd say, "You're not going to put that in the book, are you? Please don't put that in the book."

As time went by, these very same people had a one hundred and eighty-degree change of attitude, approaching me at the most inopportune times to inquire, "Am I in the book?" I became convinced they wanted me to talk about them...to write about them. Truth be told, I didn't want to or intend to humiliate anyone. A few hearty souls even described awkward situations they were a part of, hoping I'd think they were worthy of some mention in the book. What some people will do for a little notoriety—a moment of fame!

I concluded that, from a marketing perspective, if I did include their real, actual names in the book and promised to autograph a copy of the book, they'd hopefully buy one…I'd make a small fortune on the sales. What an idea! So I've listed them in alphabetical order as an addendum to the book.

I hope it works and hope they enjoyed the book.

Then just days before I finalized the book for publication, a friend of Helens was visiting us at our home. She knew about the book and insisted I read her a few chapters. I didn't want to, but I acquiesced because I reasoned by doing so would allow me some basis to gage a potential reader's reaction and help me to see whether what I had written was as good as I thought it was. I was pleasantly surprised by her reaction. She loved it… At least, she said she did. She laughed out loud even at the lines I didn't think were humorous. When I finished reading the first three chapters, she stopped me and out of the blue, asked if I would write a three-act play based on the book. Why? I wanted to know. For what purpose? She said the Wine and Dine Club, of which she was President, would like to perform a play at an upcoming dinner social. She felt an adaptation of *Sirens* as a play would fit the bill. She also said it would be a good promotional opportunity for me to interest people in the book. I agreed. Four months, fifty rehearsals later, *Sound of Sirens the Play* was performed to rave reviews in front of one hundred inebriated deaf senior citizens…Next stop Broadway…NOT!

A CAUTIONARY WARNING

To Potential Active Adult Community Owners

H ERE'S A HEADS-UP for you. The purchase of a home in this type of community should not be considered an investment, because in all likelihood the home will not appreciate in value; more likely it will lose value, or at the very least remain unchanged. Two primary factors account for this: in the first instance, when the camp trumpeter blows taps a final time, heirs who inherit the homes want to sell quickly. They don't hold out for the highest price, they want their inheritance yesterday. A capital gain or loss doesn't enter their calculations. Similarly, if one chooses to relocate to another area and needs the proceeds of the sale to purchase another home, or is forced to relocate to an assisted living facility or a nursing home, they're also not going to hold out for a selling price assuring a profit on the original purchase. Time and dollars in hand are the priorities.

These "quick sales" exert downward pressure on the resale value of the homes throughout the entire community. So what? Who cares? Let the kids worry about it. We won't be around to pay inheritance taxes or lament at the loss of dollars.

ADDENDUM

T HE FOLLOWING IS a listing of some friends and neighbors who might have been spared being referenced in this book, even though there were instances deserving mention.

Tom Assheton	Gloria Brook
Donna Atkinson	Rich Brown
Frank and Sally Baer	Greg Bruno
Gail Banken	Maria Bunzl
Fran Barr	Vince Calio
Joanne Barry	Joe Cannizzaro
Don Barry	Audrey Cardinal
Charles Bartlett	George Carfi
Ralph Bauco	Don Casey
Bob Bellemare	Vic and Janice Catalano
Barbara Berg	James Chamberlain
Barbara Bigham	Ron Charles
Fay Billings	Barbara Chinitz
Vincent Blake	Pat Clark
Terry Boyd	Rina Cohn

Fran Collins

Mike Coville

Paul Coward

Ellen Cyr

Sal DeFini

Michael Depalma

Pat DiDomizio

Laura Diou

Bob DiMantova

Ted Dunton

Mitch and Betsy Epstein

Jim Eves

Peter Fasino

Arlene Fettmann

Jill Fischer

Peter Fitzpatrick

Jerry Fogel

David Forber

Ellen Fox

Judy Friedman

Bob Fritzche

Ed Gaal

Bob Gardner

Earl Gershenow

Liz Giancarli

Ken Gillespie

Dave Giovanetti

Dave Gliserman

Tom Hasemann

Bob Haverl

Bill Heller

Alan Hertzmark

Bea Heyde

Grace Hily

Scott and Beth Hudkins

Art Keating

Bob and Mary Ellen Klembara

George Knezek

Ann Krane

Dick and Debby Kreitner

Ed and Mo Largarto

Harry Larson

David and Alice Liang

Charles and Bev Levine

Mike Lyons

Wayne and Betty McCormack

Tony Miodonka

Alan and Naomi Mohr

Bill Morton

Kerry O'Donoghue

Frank Oliva

Mike O'Loughlin

Sal Petriello

Joe Pirri

Rich and Penny Phipps

Pete Polstein

Lisa Purdy
Rick Raskoph
Anne Rickards
Regina Roper
Don Rosenberg
Ken Sanford
Bill and Marion Schrade
Vicki Shapiro
David Shlian
Larry Sims
Pat Slonina
Bev Stebbins

Ellin Sunshine
Mike and Johanna Tangredi
Tom and Rosalie Timlin
Jodi Trzyna
Anthony Urso
Jake Vagnini
James Van Der Beek
Barbara Vogler
Chris Volo
Cal and Caroline Walker
Glades Weisman
Les Wheeler